Rosa
By Any Other Name

Rosa
By Any Other Name

HAILEY ALCARAZ

VIKING
An imprint of Penguin Random House LLC
1745 Broadway, New York, New York 10019

First published in the United States of America by Viking,
an imprint of Penguin Random House LLC, 2025

Copyright © 2025 by Hailey Alcaraz

Penguin Random House values and supports copyright. Copyright fuels creativity, encourages diverse voices, promotes free speech, and creates a vibrant culture. Thank you for buying an authorized edition of this book and for complying with copyright laws by not reproducing, scanning, or distributing any part of it in any form without permission. You are supporting writers and allowing Penguin Random House to continue to publish books for every reader. Please note that no part of this book may be used or reproduced in any manner for the purpose of training artificial intelligence technologies or systems.

Viking & colophon are registered trademarks of Penguin Random House LLC.
The Penguin colophon is a registered trademark of Penguin Books Limited.

Visit us online at PenguinRandomHouse.com.

Library of Congress Cataloging-in-Publication Data is available.

ISBN 9780593525579

1 3 5 7 9 10 8 6 4 2

Manufactured in the United States of America

BVG

Edited by Jenny Bak

Design by Jim Hoover   Text set in Palatino

This is a work of historical fiction. Apart from the well-known actual people, events, and locales that figure in the narrative, all names, characters, places, and incidents are the products of the author's imagination or are used fictitiously. Any resemblance to current events or locales, or to living persons, is entirely coincidental.

The publisher does not have any control over and does not assume any responsibility for author or third-party websites or their content.

The authorized representative in the EU for product safety and compliance is Penguin Random House Ireland, Morrison Chambers, 32 Nassau Street, Dublin D02 YH68, Ireland, https://eu-contact.penguin.ie.

To my dad—
Everything I've achieved is because you told me I could.

This novel contains depictions of racism, homophobia, and police violence. These themes are explored within the historical context to highlight the struggles faced by marginalized communities, but some readers may find them distressing. Please proceed with care and prioritize your well-being.

Some shall be pardoned and some punished.
For never was a story of more woe
Than this of Juliet and her Romeo.

—**William Shakespeare**, ***Romeo and Juliet***

Our stories are important.
They give us strength; they give us power.

—**Sandra Cisneros**

Prologue

The world had a murky, melted look, like I was peering at it all through the bottom of a Coke bottle. *It's raining*, I told myself. *That's it.*

But my hands, my dress, the ground, were all dry.

And then I realized—it wasn't raining at all.

I was crying. That was why everything was a blur.

I swiped at my eyes, sniffling and gasping for choked breaths, trying to regain control of myself. Trying to calm down enough to understand what was happening.

What *was* happening?

There was that smell. Smoky and bitter. Was something burning?

The crinoline of this beautiful dress chafed at me. All these layers were unbearable. They made it so hard to focus. I pulled at the neckline, desperate for air.

My heart raced, hammering inside my chest. It was so loud it almost sounded like . . .

My vision whirled for a harrowing instant as the realization ripped through me.

It sounded like gunshots.

One

Thursday, August 18, 1955

I woke before the sun, in near silence. Such a rare thing in our barrio. No rumble of overworked pickup trucks chugging between fields of crops on dirt roads. No neighbors calling across fences to borrow a few eggs or a cup of milk. No scampering of feet or slamming of doors or music or . . . anything, really. Nada. Just the rustle of leaves in a gentle breeze, the faint cooing of a mourning dove, and my own pulse. Fast but steady.

It's the first day of school, I thought, scarcely a heartbeat before the rhythm and ruckus of our morning routine came roaring to life with my mother's approaching footsteps.

"Rosa, hija, ¿estás despierta?" Mamá's voice called out onto the sleeping porch from the kitchen. She didn't wait for me to answer before busying herself with her next task. I could hear her set a pan on the stovetop, could hear the rhythmic ticking of the gas burner trying to catch.

"Sí, Mamá," I responded, swinging my legs out of bed at the same time she repeated her question with a hitch of impatience. Mornings were not a time for idleness. I shrugged my robe on, tying the belt in a loose knot over my white nightgown as I made my way inside.

Mamá was already dressed, setting a plate of fresh tortillas on the table. She wore her usual long-sleeved cotton dress and headscarf to protect her from the sun on the long days spent in the fruit fields. The radio, a big old Westinghouse that sat on its own table in the living room, exuded a steady stream of music, the melodic thrum of the guitar and accordion competing with the noises of my mother's rapid movements. She wasn't one to indulge in many frivolous activities; we didn't own a television, and I'd scarcely seen her sit down to read anything longer than a recipe—but morning radio was her one vice. There weren't a lot of Spanish language options—even in Phoenix, where there were so many of us who spoke Spanish—but early in the morning, there was *En este momento*, a Spanish show targeted at all the farm laborers and workers who rose before the sun.

It was much warmer in the kitchen than it was on the sleeping porch, and already I missed the cool solitude of the cot I slept on in the summer months.

"Buenos días," Mamá said with a quick smile, though she did not stop moving, did not even slow down—gliding back and forth between the stove, table, and counter. "¿Qué estabas haciendo?" Her brows pinched together as her eyes darted up at me over the eggs sizzling in her pan.

Even though it was early, I knew what she meant; she wasn't really asking what I had been doing. She was worried, and what better way to show it than by prodding with questions she already knew the answer to. "Just waking up," I told her, forcing a smile to assure her that I hadn't been lying in bed for hours, contemplating what lay ahead, like she feared. The metal kitchen chair screeched against our floor as I pulled it out and sank into it.

She made a quick humming sound. "Mi querida, are you excited for school?" she prompted, switching to English and adding a cheerier lilt. Though her English was heavily accented and often interrupted by bits of Spanish, she tried to use it with me as often as she could so we could both work on smoothing out the edges of our accents. Mine was almost nonexistent at this point, but it would pop up on the most unexpected words, especially when I was nervous or distracted. Mamá had always thought it was important to speak in clear American English, no long vowels or rolling *r*'s. Even though I understood why she felt so strongly about it, it still made me a little sad to listen to her squash out her native tongue with the kind of unyielding force I'd seen Papi use to crush scorpions underneath the heels of his work boots.

"I ironed your skirt for you," she said before I could respond. "And your lunch is just over there." She tipped her chin at a paper sack to her right.

"Gracias, Mamá."

She shot me a look over her shoulder. "Oye, you need to eat something. You can't go to school on an empty stomach."

"Yes, Mamá," I murmured, setting a small scoop of frijoles onto my plate obediently. I could feel the genuine concern underneath her busy fussing. Even after a year of going to school on the north side, deep down I still felt a lot of the same anxiety my mother did about our situation.

And with good reason, of course.

What we were doing—what I was doing—was dangerous. Integration was happening, sure. The courts told us that it had to, but it wasn't nearly as quick or easy as those folks in Washington seemed to think it was. Race mixing was messy business, no matter how you looked at it.

Just because I was allowed to go to school at North Phoenix High didn't mean I was welcome.

"And your bus money?" Mamá continued, reaching over to smooth my hair. "You'll remember to comb your hair back, yes? It's gotten so long. Maybe I should've cut—"

"*Mamá.*"

She swept one last lock away from my forehead and sighed, turning back to the sink.

A few minutes later, Papi joined me at the table, his movements purposeful and urgent—as always—as he dug into the huevos and papas Mamá had placed in front of him. He began talking about the workday ahead of them at the citrus farm with barely a pause after he wished us a buenos días. He worried about the heat, about one of his friends who hurt his back the day before, about the foreman who always popped up at the wrong time.

"Oye, Maria, pack some extra napkins in my lunch box, will

you? My hands were so sticky yesterday"—he paused suddenly to shoot me a scowl, his cheeks full of food. "Why do you look so . . . ?" He gestured his fork at my face obscurely.

Mamá glanced at us, nodding in agreement as she placed an empty coffee mug in front of my father. "Sí, sí. I thought so too."

I struggled to soften my expression into something more pleasing for my parents. "I don't know what you mean," I mumbled feebly.

Mamá reached toward me, placing a warm calloused hand on my forehead. "No está enferma."

Papi snorted in relief, busying himself with pouring a splash of steaming hot water into his cup from the kettle Mamá handed him. *"Good.* What a day to be sick that would be, eh?" He wrenched open the lid to the Taster's Choice, scooping a generous spoonful of instant coffee into his mug. His dark eyes flitted up to meet mine every few words, watchful and concerned. "You're not too tired, are you? I told you it wasn't a good night to meet up with Ramón, didn't I? The night before your first day of school, Rosa?" His spoon *ping-ping*ed in his mug as he stirred. The bitter, acidic scent of the coffee wafted between us.

"I'm not tired. I was home before supper."

Another grunt from Papi's end of the table. "You can't be exhausted if you're going to school with the gringos, hija. You have to be at your best all the time."

"I know that."

"You know how important this opportunity is," he said,

his volume growing louder as he navigated toward a conversation we'd had countless times. A familiar lecture since I switched schools last year. "You must take it seriously, Rosa. You can't spend all your time and energy playing with the chico down the street like you used to when you were a child, eh? You're a young woman now. Almost an adult."

With a sigh, I gave him a slow nod. "Yes, Papi."

"And you must be aware!" Mamá chimed in, her pans clattering into the sink. "You must always be thinking a step ahead. If you are *tired*, you put yourself at risk, ¿verdad?"

She waited for one more dutiful nod from me before she continued scrubbing the pan in her hands. I turned my gaze down to my plate as I moved my now-cold egg around with the tip of my fork. I thought about the day that lay ahead of us. Me, across town at North Phoenix High School pretending I was just like all the white kids, with their new books and excited whispers about graduation and college and summers spent at the Valley Ho or whatever hotel they'd whiled away their days at sitting by the pool. *Passing*. Using my fairer skin to slip in undetected, despite the prejudices that led to de facto segregation. Segregation, not because anyone said we had to but because white folks wanted it.

And then I thought of my parents, plucking bushels of oranges on the south side as the scorching sun coasted across the sky. My heart began to quicken, competing with the blare of trumpets on the radio, and I worried my face had worked itself into whatever expression had put my parents on edge.

I took a breath, searching for that tranquil silence I'd been able to summon in bed.

Instead, my thoughts shifted to last night.

I thought of sitting in the shade of the Montoyas' mulberry tree, Ramón strumming his guitar as he made up joking songs about how he and the rest of the kids in our barrio didn't have to go back to school until Monday, how he still had four more days of jumping into the canals and sneaking into the dance halls and catching double bills at the drive-in.

"Aren't you supposed to be cheering me up?" I'd said, giving his high-top a kick.

He grinned. "Says who?"

I made a face. "Isn't that what friends are for?"

"You know you can't wait to get back to that place, Rosita," he half sang. "You love school. You've been bored for weeks, monkeying around Golden Gate with the rest of us."

I considered this and the easy way he said it. Like it was obvious. Like it was something everyone knew.

His fingers danced across the guitar strings, playing a familiar rhythm, a little number he'd written about me when we were little. "Rosita, Rosita, Rosita," he'd croon. "Una chica astutita."

I could hear the words in my head without him singing it. Only, I didn't feel like a clever girl. Not at all.

"I suppose" was all I could manage in response. "But it's still..."

He stopped strumming as I searched for the right word,

the melody fading as he waited. When it became clear I didn't know what I was trying to say about my life at the white high school, he just nodded, understanding anyway. Always understanding, even when I wasn't sure I did. Perhaps especially when I didn't.

"It's one more year, huh?" he said at last. "What's one more year of passing, when it's all said and done, hmm? You know you can do it. You can do anything. You're Rosa Capistrano." There was a teasing note to his voice, but his smile—that full-lipped smile that had broken the hearts of dozens of girls from here to the Rio Salado—was as sincere as they came. "Or . . . should I call you Ro*sie* Capistrano?"

I rolled my eyes, kicking his shoe again. "Please don't," I'd begged as he laughed.

Even in the kitchen, amid the flurry of my parents' fears and my own racing heart, I felt a wave of peace—of belonging—inside me at the memory. The evening sun on my face, Ramón's joking and singing and laughing. The easiness of being with my closest friend, someone who knew me like he did. Ramón was perhaps the only person who truly knew me back then.

Mamá took my face in her hands one more time, jolting me from my thoughts, her palms warm and slightly damp. I felt her thumb brush at something on my cheek as she held me. "Be careful, ¿eh?" There was a tightness in her voice that I could tell she was trying to hide.

I nodded as Papi rose and made his way to the front door. I saw a trace of the same unease in his eyes as he watched us.

"I will. I can do this. It's just one more year, right?" They didn't know I was just repeating Ramón's words.

"One more year," Papi reiterated from across the room, his voice firm and resounding.

One more year—of passing, of lying, of this dangerous deceit.

I knew I was *lucky* to have access to the same education all the white kids had, just because my skin happened to be a few shades lighter than the rest of my family's. It was my duty to use that privilege to do *something* with my life.

This was what Papi and I had discussed from the very beginning, when we decided I wouldn't enroll in the new school that had opened for south side kids—for Mexican and colored kids—like I was supposed to. It's what had been on his mind ever since he returned from the Second World War, and it's what led to this decision—this deception. It was our reason for . . . everything, really.

"Te quiero, mija," Mamá said softly. "We'll see you this evening. Be safe." She kissed my cheek, and with a quick wave, both my parents disappeared through the front door.

"That was 'Los caballeros alegres,'" the familiar deep voice on the radio told me as the upbeat tempo of the previous song faded out at the same moment our door clicked shut. "And as always, I am your friend Victor, here to bring you your daily dose of Mexican culture, art and social issues, *En este momento*."

Alone at last, I took a deep breath.

Two

Thursday, August 18, 1955

I always sat in the middle row of every single classroom. Up front drew too much attention, but the back was where the cool kids sat. The ones who exchanged phone numbers and had sleepovers at each other's houses. In the middle, though, I was practically invisible. Just the way I liked it.

Mrs. Folger, our matronly homeroom teacher, didn't even look up from her copy of *Life* magazine as I wound my way through the neat rows of desks. "Early, hmm?"

I gave a noncommittal gesture, half nod, half shrug, and smiled anyway. "Yes, ma'am. It's awfully warm outside."

Through the window I could see the crowded front courtyard swarming with people hugging and laughing, the noise muted by the crystal clear windowpanes of the liberal arts building. Inside, Mrs. Folger's magazine crinkled quietly as she flipped the page.

The classroom door opened again, letting a burst of excited hallway noise into the room as I set about adjusting my pencils on the desk. I focused on lining them up evenly along the right edge.

"Good morning, Mrs. Folger." As she slid past my desk, I recognized Connie Peterson, a red-haired girl I'd had typing class with the year before. Mrs. Folger grunted, but neither Connie nor I said a word to each other. I was reaching into my bookbag for my composition book when I noticed Mrs. Folger suddenly straighten as the door opened again, her dull expression brightening in a blink of an eye.

I followed her curious gaze to find Julianne Callihan standing in the center of the classroom.

Of course.

"Miss Callihan, so nice to see you!" Mrs. Folger greeted her.

Julianne tucked a strand of her golden hair behind her ear as she smiled back. "Good morning, Mrs. Folger. Hi, Connie. Hi, Rosie."

Connie's round cheeks flushed pink as she mumbled a greeting and sank into her chair.

"Hey there," I said quietly, distinctly aware of Connie's and Mrs. Folger's eyes still on Julianne.

After all, this was always how it was with Julianne.

"I'm so pleased to see you. How was your summer?" Julianne said, smoothing the folds of her skirt as she settled into the chair next to me.

"Oh . . . it was fine," I said.

She smiled encouragingly, but I didn't elaborate. I didn't

know what else to say about the months since we'd last seen each other. I spent my summer helping my sister take care of her newborn baby, working part-time at a cotton farm, and daydreaming with Ramón about our futures and how they'd be filled with music and adventure and opportunities. None of these were the kinds of things Julianne—or anyone here—would understand. They were parts of me I had to keep to myself if I wanted to keep going to school here. If I wanted to go to college next year. If I wanted more than what my life was now. "How was Washington, DC?" I asked instead, as a distraction.

Julianne blushed. I caught the way her eyes darted over to Mrs. Folger, who still held her magazine but no longer appeared to be reading it, and I knew I'd said something I shouldn't have.

It was hardly a secret that Julianne's father was the county sheriff and, judging by the sharp gazes of both Mrs. Folger and Connie, I wasn't the only one who had followed the Callihans' trip to the capital in the papers with avid interest.

"Oh, it was fine," she echoed with the exact same lack of enthusiasm I'd answered with. She leaned closer to me and lowered her voice. "I'm so tired of feeling like everyone's watching me, you know? It was like that all summer, at all these mixers and tours and fundraisers. I feel like . . . like a monkey at the zoo."

I nodded. I had seen a picture of her at the National Zoo a week ago, in fact, walking a step behind her father as he spoke with the zoo's new veterinarian. Though she was slightly out of focus in the background, I had recognized the pensive look on her face as she studied the hippo peering back at her from behind the bars of its cage.

"Well, for what it's worth, if you were a zoo animal, I hardly think you'd be a monkey. A swan, maybe?" She rolled her eyes, her lips quirked into a subtle smirk. "Or a flamingo at the very least."

"Hardy har har," she quipped good-naturedly. "Something pretty and graceful, yes, I know. You sound just like my father."

"Sorry," I told her, meaning it, despite the mild envy underscoring my sympathy. Of course I didn't want the kind of attention and scrutiny Julianne bore, but some part of me did wonder what it would be like to travel, to fly in an airplane, and to see the places she'd seen.

I'd cut out several articles about Julianne and her family over the summer. The zoo article, but also one of the sheriff shaking hands with Senator Goldwater, and another of her mother attending a tea hosted by Mamie Eisenhower. I realized I wasn't much different than everyone else who was utterly transfixed by the Callihans, but I couldn't help it.

Julianne's family had lived in Arizona since before it was even a state, and as both a veteran and a hotshot deputy, her dad and his meteoric rise to fame was inspiring. He was nothing short of an icon around here—the straight-shooting, honest sheriff of the Wild West. A real-life gunfighter, like Gregory Peck, but somehow *better*.

The door was thrown open once more as the first bell rang, and a cluster of girls traipsed in, chattering about last week's episode of *Father Knows Best*, until one called, "Hi there, Julianne. Swell skirt! You do a lot of shopping while you were back East?"

Julianne flushed again, her brows knitting together as she looked down at her skirt, a pleated plaid number with a thin belt. "Oh, jeez, this? No. Korricks, I think? Last season, I bet."

I knew from all the ads the department stores had been running in the paper that the chic two-piece set Julianne had on was, in fact, not last season. But I understood why she'd demur like that as these girls watched her with hawkeyed fascination. I couldn't help but let my eyes flit down to my own navy-blue broadcloth dress that was passed down to me from my older sister, like most of my school clothes.

Fortunately, the girls took no notice of me or my outdated outfit as they cackled in response to Julianne's claim, a sharp sound that certainly didn't seem friendly. Mrs. Folger shushed them as they claimed desks behind us.

"Ah, Winnie, give it a rest." Peter Duke appeared without warning, standing conspicuously close to Julianne's desk. He gave the curly-haired girl a devilish grin that sent her into another round of shrill giggles. Peter winked at Julianne, unbothered by the way she was leaning back in her chair to put an extra millimeter of space between the two of them, before he continued. "Julianne would look ginchy in just about anything. Just look at her! What does it matter where she got her skirt?"

She looked away, missing the lovesick way Winnie and her pack blushed and nodded at Peter. But I saw.

"I sure missed seeing you around the club while you were

away," Peter said, drawing closer still. He had a sun-kissed look about him. A sheen to his honey-colored hair, a bronze to his cheeks. Whether that was from days working on his family's cattle ranch—the biggest one in the state of Arizona, as I'd heard him mention many times—or from lounging by the pool, I wasn't sure.

Julianne nodded, eyes fixed on her desk.

"You know, I've been meaning to ask you, Jules—"

The final bell cut him off, an expression of rosy-cheeked relief falling over Julianne as Peter's face fell into a frown.

She shrugged as Mrs. Folger stood and cleared her throat pointedly. Peter shot our teacher a petulant look before sliding into the seat on the other side of Julianne. He stretched his long legs out toward her chair, almost like he was laying a claim to her with sheer proximity. She kept her head down, so her sleek blond hair fell as a curtain across her face.

"Betty Adams? Ah, yes, there you are. Rosie Capistrano?" Mrs. Folger barked, calling roll. I raised my hand silently, and she put a mark on her roster.

When I first transferred, it had been strange to hear my name changed like that—"Rosie" instead of "Rosa." And having just my father's last name, like the white folks did it, instead of using both my parents' last names. Not to mention the way they butchered it all. No rhythm or roll to it at all, saying "Capistr*ay*no" with a long *a* sound, when it was supposed to be more like when the doctor asks you to say "ahh."

But now, of course, it hardly fazed me at all.

Next year, things would be different. I would be somewhere

else, somewhere that not only had real opportunities but also other people just like me. That's what I told myself. Next year I'd be in college. Arizona State College, specifically.

I wouldn't be this two-faced imposter. I wouldn't be invisible. I wouldn't be skating by like this.

Next year, I'd be . . . *me*.

Three

Thursday, August 18, 1955

"Did you have a nice first day back at school, Miss Capistrano?" Miss Shaw asked as she began clearing the chalk from the blackboard after the final bell of the day.

The rest of our English class had vacated the room, eager for freedom after our first day back at our desks. But I was lingering, as I often did in Miss Shaw's room. She wasn't the only teacher I'd had before; both my math and home economics teachers taught juniors as well, but she was my favorite.

"I did," I told her. It had been a pleasant enough day, after all—not that I would have ever told a teacher any different. "How was your summer, miss?"

"It was quite nice, thank you for asking." She stood on her tiptoes to erase the date written in the top corner of the blackboard before turning to face me. "I visited my sister in Chicago in June. We saw that new Rodgers and Hammerstein play, *Me and Juliet*, and we ate way too much pizza. It's a lovely city. So much history and so much to do. Have you ever been?"

I shook my head.

She waited a beat to see if I was going to elaborate or offer any anecdotes of my own. When it became clear I had no charming summer tales of travel and adventure to share, she smiled politely. "Your senior year, can you believe it?" Her voice was warm even as she turned away from me to sweep the eraser back and forth across the board once more. "You must be thrilled."

"Yes, miss."

"Have you given any thought to what colleges you'll be applying to?" She glanced over her shoulder to arch an interested eyebrow in my direction.

I nodded in response. I often thought that kids liked Miss Shaw for the same reasons they liked Julianne: because she was young and pretty and dressed nice. It was odd how much stock we put into how appearances, wasn't it?

And sure, I liked the way Miss Shaw's dark hair was always so neatly coiffed and how the smart skirts she wore were always impeccably starched. Who wouldn't? But mostly, I liked the way she talked to us. The soft, melodic note to her voice when she read us Shakespeare or Brontë. And the way she genuinely seemed to be listening to us when she asked us questions. Like our answers mattered.

"You're going to the college fair next week, aren't you? They mentioned it on the morning announcements," she said sunnily. "A girl as bright as you, Miss Capistrano, why, you've got to keep your options open. Any school would be lucky to have you."

I fidgeted with my hair, even though it was still fixed in a bun with pomade and bobby pins. "Oh, gee—"

Miss Shaw pursed her lips good-naturedly, wagging a polished finger to cut me off. "Now, don't sell yourself short. You have a real gift! If you're serious about journalism, why—"

But she was the one who was cut off this time as her classroom door swung open. Julianne poked her head in with a shy smile. "Oh, sorry. I didn't mean to interrupt. I was just looking for Rosie. You ready to go?"

I nodded and finished collecting my books. "I'll see you tomorrow, Miss Shaw," I told her as she brushed the chalk dust from her hands and waved goodbye to both me and Julianne.

"You're so lucky you have her for English again," Julianne said as we left the classroom. "I've got crotchety Mr. Collins. I swear, even *he* fell asleep this morning when he was describing *The Scarlet Letter*." She rolled her eyes. "Are you going straight home?"

"No, I think I'll stop by the newspaper room before I leave."

Julianne shot me a look like I'd just announced I was going to strip down to my girdle right there in the main courtyard and sing that new Elvis Presley song that's been on the radio all summer at the top of my lungs. "*Why?* Our first meeting isn't until next week."

"I know," I admitted. "But the welcome back pep rally is tomorrow, and I know it's going to be on the front page of our first issue."

Julianne hummed understandingly. "And you want to make sure that weasel Simon doesn't give it to one of his bonehead friends, is that it?"

"Pretty much."

"That guy really bugs me. I don't know how we are going to stick out another whole year with him as the editor." She sighed, our pace slowing to a stop.

"So you don't want to come with me, then?" I said with a laugh.

She pursed her lips thoughtfully, shifting her bookbag on her shoulder as her gaze drifted around the quickly emptying courtyard. The sun and the excitement of the dismissal bell had driven most folks off campus at this point. Only a few lingered along the grassy areas. "I sure don't want to have to spend any more time around Simon Heathersby than I have to," she said. Though the way she hesitated made me wonder if something even less appealing than our bossy editor-in-chief was awaiting her outside our school walls. But I didn't pry; that wasn't the kind of friendship Julianne and I had.

I started to say goodbye, not wanting to miss my chance to catch Simon, when a shout from across the courtyard caught our attention. Caught everyone's attention, really. The last few stragglers peered in our direction as Peter Duke jogged toward us, grinning and shouting Julianne's name like it was his own personal rallying cry.

"Jules, I've been looking everywhere for you," he said. "The gang is heading to the Nifty Nook for some sodas and burgers. I'll give you a lift."

Julianne did not waver at all before shaking her head and linking her arm in mine. "That does sound like a gas, but Rosie and I have just got loads of work to do for the newspaper. Maybe next time!" She called the last bit over her shoulder, dragging me toward the nearest set of doors as I bit my lower lip to stifle my laughter.

Four

Thursday, August 18, 1955

"Those gringos kept you longer than I expected" was how Ramón greeted me when I appeared on his doorstep just after six o'clock holding two Pyrex dishes full of tamales to my chest. "What did Mamá Capistrano make us today?" He rubbed his hands together eagerly as he beckoned me inside with a bob of his head.

"Chicken tamales," I told him as he let out a happy whoop. "But half of these are for Blanca and Pablo, so don't get too excited. She barely let me inside the house before she packed me up and sent me out again." I set my dishes down on the Montoyas' kitchen table—a rickety little card table that wobbled under the weight of the food. His kitchen was narrow, barely big enough for three chairs and a refrigerator. To my right hung a crucifix and a picture of Ramón's father in his army uniform, much like one my father had of himself, though he stored his in a cigar box under his bed with a stash of other things I understood to be too painful to look at.

I kneaded my shoulder gingerly. My arms were a little sore from the hot walk over with the food, and I noticed for the first time that I still had my bookbag draped over my shoulder for extra weight. Mamá really had just spun me right back out the door. I eased the strap off and plopped the bulging bag down on the nearest chair for instant relief.

"Pobrecita Rosita," Ramón quipped, poking my cheek. I swatted his hand away, which only made his smile grow. "So how was your first day back at that bigwig school of yours?"

I shot him an unamused look. "You know how it is."

"Not really." He chuckled. "How was it?"

"Fine, I suppose."

"Just *fine*?" He gasped.

I nodded, ignoring the theatrical way his eyes widened at this.

"Couldn't you do 'fine' at South Mountain with me and the rest of the compas? Why do you have to go all the way to the north side to get 'fine'?" There was a taunting edge to his words, but there was also a curious gleam in the way he watched me.

"*Ramón*," I said, trying to tease back with a scolding of my own.

"De verdad," he pressed, unwilling to be cowed. "Haven't you heard? You'd think with all the newspapers you read, you of all people would know about all that *Brown* and education stuff." He waved his hand at my bookbag. "Separate but equal and all that? We're all the same now! Viva la integration!"

I frowned, not nearly as entertained by this display as he was. "You and I both know it's not all as simple as that."

"Why not?"

Part of me wished I had the answers to that question, and part of me was thankful that it didn't seem like anyone did.

Ramón had a point, I knew, but it was only a small piece of the bigger picture, as was often the case with my dear daydreaming best friend.

Yes, I was technically allowed to attend school at North Phoenix. Segregated high schools were never legally required in Arizona, even though Mexican kids often had to go to different schools. They said it was because these kids spoke Spanish, regardless of whether they also spoke English too, and it was always pretty clear there were a whole lot of other messy factors that were taken into account for those types of places. Regardless, the recent Supreme Court ruling said we all had to mix anyway.

But that still didn't mean we were welcomed with open arms.

There were unspoken rules to these kinds of things. I knew it. And even if Ramón refused to see it that way, well, it didn't make it untrue. That just wasn't how the world worked.

"You're a romantic, Ramón Montoya," I said, the best explanation I could muster.

"And you're too smart for your own good, Rosita," he fired back, humming the tune to "Rosita, Rosita, Rosita."

"Do you want to come to Blanca's with me?" I asked, changing the subject to something more familiar. More manageable. "You haven't seen the baby in a couple weeks. He's about to start crawling any day now."

"Would love to, but I'm afraid I'm all booked up." The teasing smile had turned into a mischievous one.

"A date, hmm? Who is it tonight?"

"Guadalupe Diaz," he said. "We're going cruising for a bit." He wiggled his eyebrows suggestively.

"No more Alma Mateo, then?"

His grin quirked up deviously. "Who said that?"

"Oh boy," I groaned. I picked up the top dish of tamales, ready to resume my food delivery errands.

Ramón reached around me for my bookbag, underestimating how full I'd stuffed it throughout the course of the day. The strap slipped out of his hands and a slew of yellow pencils, composition notebooks, and my coin purse spilled onto the kitchen floor. "Ay, hold on. I've got it!" he assured me as I stooped to help him, tamales balanced precariously on my hip.

A moment later, he'd swept up all my things with an apologetic smile, delicately placing the strap on my shoulder for me. "I'll catch you tomorrow night, though?" he asked.

I shook my head, following him to the front door. "I've got this pep rally at school."

Ramón snorted. "Don't tell me you're a pom-pom girl now."

"I'm covering it for the paper," I told him, leaving out the part that I never did track down Simon this afternoon and wasn't at all sure I'd get to write the article.

Ramón sighed, the playful exaggeration back in his voice as he held the front door open for me. "This is how it happens, you know. A tale as old as time. Two best friends growing apart. Who knows what'll happen next?"

I fixed him with a look as we approached the front gate, eyes narrowed in mock admonishment. "Especially if you keep giving me a hard time like this!"

I could hear him chuckling softly, singing my song to himself as I walked away.

Five

Friday, August 19, 1955

The annual welcome back rally always took place at the football field behind the school. I rarely ventured back there, except for the occasional gym class, but I joined the throng of students flowing through the courtyard that evening like it was nothing. Like it was something I always did.

I took a seat at the very top of the bleachers, painfully aware that I was the only person by myself—without a cluster of friends to link arms with or share a concession bag of popcorn. As I surveyed the growing crowd of students, I spotted Julianne standing along the football field in her ivory cheer skirt, navy-blue pom-poms dangling limply from her hands.

"Go, Mustangs, go! Fight, Mustangs, fight!" the cheerleaders chanted in rhythm with the blaring horns of the marching band.

Beside her, the squad captain, Frances, shot Julianne an

irritated glance, no doubt noting the listless way Julianne was bouncing. Distracted, a world away even under the bright stadium lights.

I remembered how last September, before we were really friends, when we were just two girls with neighboring lockers, she'd turned to me as she shoved her pom-poms inside her locker. "They bumped me up to *varsity*," she'd said in a low, scandalized whisper.

"Isn't that a good thing?"

She'd swatted at the stray tinsel peeking out of her open locker and shook her head. "They only want me because of my name."

I hadn't known her well enough back then to point out that they probably wanted her because she looked like the picture-perfect American cheerleader, straight out of the glossy pages of *Teen* magazine. Since then, we'd come to refer to her as the least peppy pep-squad girl in school.

I set my bookbag onto my lap to pull out my notebook. Maybe this year—with this article—I'd finally make it onto the front page. I wanted to capture every detail, every scrap of information, to better my chances of not being tucked away in the inner folds or beaten out by one of the more senior staff writers. I'd record every name I knew, every song and chant, *everything*. I could weed out the less important details later if I gave myself all the facts now.

As I dug around for my favorite pen, I noticed something missing. There was the notebook I used for my newspaper writing, a cheap composition book I'd gotten at the drugstore, but the leatherbound one I carried with me everywhere was nowhere to be found. I wouldn't need it tonight, surely. It wasn't one I wrote in. Its contents, instead, were a hodgepodge of newspaper clippings, pages from books, notes, and other collections of writing I'd accumulated over the years. An array of pieces I'd stowed away and pasted in to pore over later.

It's not something I need here, I told myself. I didn't know if I ever truly needed it, though I behaved like I did. It felt odd to be without it, all the same. When was the last time I'd had it? I wasn't sure I remembered seeing it at all today, though I didn't normally take it out at school. It was too . . . personal.

Had it fallen out at Ramón's? I desperately hoped I hadn't dropped it somewhere on campus.

The sudden boom of bass drums pushed my worries from my mind as the marching band began to take the field. With a sigh, I flipped open my composition book and began jotting down the names of each of the cheerleaders. As I scribbled away, Julianne caught my eye. She gave me a quick wave, an exasperated glimmer in her eyes as the rest of the squad erupted in a chorus of "Here we go, Mustangs, here we go!"

An hour later, I began collecting my things as soon as our class president thanked everyone and wished the class of 1956 a great school year. The band launched into one more round of the fight song, but no one was singing along this time. Everyone began to drift to the football field to mingle. I inched my way toward the exit, murmuring apologies for going in the opposite direction.

I squeezed past a cluster of sophomores who were bickering

about where to grab a bite after this. One girl mentioned a Mexican restaurant that had just opened up across from the Vista Theater. "Have you had their churros?" she squealed.

"I don't want *beaner* food, Sandy!" one of the boys scoffed as the rest of the group tittered. "Who wants a burger?"

I didn't look up until I was halfway across the courtyard, nearly to the front of the school.

I didn't look up until I heard Ramón calling my name.

Ramón.

I'd recognize his voice anywhere.

But what was he doing *here*?

"Rosita, I've been looking for you!" He stood near the front office. His voice was loud enough to carry above the noise of the crowd behind me but still light and cheerful.

I felt a surge of comfort and familiarity at seeing him—the feeling I always got when I locked eyes with my best friend—but my fear and confusion quickly smothered out the warmth in my chest. I drew closer to him with slow, nervous steps.

"W-what are you doing here, Ramón?" I stammered.

Grinning, he reached into his back pocket. He waved my leather notebook at me. "You forgot this at my house yesterday. I thought you might've needed it for this thing." He used it to gesture all around him, oblivious to the terror churning inside me. "Newspaper stuff, you know?"

"Oh, Ramón, thank you but—you didn't have to . . ." I nodded my head for him to follow me as I started walking toward the parking lot.

Ramón reluctantly trailed after me, but I noticed his gaze

was lost somewhere behind us. He was not moving as quickly as I'd like. *Probably trying to hear the marching band's music.*

"Is it over already? I thought for sure we'd catch you in time," Ramón said, brows pinched in confusion.

"Mm," I said, my pulse pounding so loudly I could scarcely hear myself. My eyes scanned the full parking lot until at last I saw his family's car. A rust-colored Chevy parked along the curb underneath a mesquite tree.

"Hey," Ramón said. "It looks like someone's following us." He stopped walking.

Stomach tight, I turned to follow his gaze. Trotting across the front lawn of North Phoenix High School was Julianne Callihan. Flouncing skirt and all.

"Rosie," she called breathily. "You left without saying goodbye!" Her eyes flitted over to Ramón briefly, though the warm smile on her face didn't falter.

"Jeez, Julianne, I'm awfully sorry," I sputtered, my grip iron-tight on the strap of my bookbag. "I've got to get home. I figured . . . we'll catch up on Monday, right?"

"Oh, sure." Julianne hugged her arms to her body, a flicker of something akin to disappointment dancing across her pretty face. Again, her round eyes drifted over to Ramón. A beat of silence passed between us all before she finally asked, "Who's your friend?"

"Um." I could barely get the word out. My throat was instantly desert dry, my tongue suddenly too big to cooperate.

Ramón stepped forward almost immediately. "Ramón. Rosa—Rosie and I, we grew up together." He wasn't trying to be unhelpful—wasn't trying to sabotage me. I knew that. I knew Ramón would never deliberately try to wreak disaster on my life.

But I also knew his heart often worked faster than his brain. Normally, I found this endearing. But now? Now it could unravel my whole world here, it could put both of us in jeopardy for this web of lies I'd woven, it could—

"Hi," Julianne said, that small word somehow coming out sounding like a melody all its own.

I did not like the effect it had on Ramón.

"This is Julianne," I said quietly, praying she wouldn't pick up on the note of alarm in my voice. Neither of them was even looking at me, though; I wasn't sure they heard me.

The horn sounded from the Chevy—saving us and startling us at the same time. I had assumed the car was empty, that Ramón had borrowed it from his brother like he always did, but now I realized there was someone sitting in the driver's seat. Someone watching us.

Not just someone. Marco Montoya.

"We'd better get going," I said, nudging Ramón's arm.

He nodded absently, rooted where he stood.

"It was nice to meet you, *Ramón*." Julianne spoke slowly, like she was savoring each syllable.

I *did not* like that at all.

The music from the pep rally was beginning to taper out, and I realized the sound of voices was growing louder. A quick glance behind Julianne, and I could see several groups of dark figures making their way toward us. At the forefront was a boy in a football uniform, helmet balanced on his hip, with a jaunty saunter that made my heart race in dread. Peter Duke, headed straight for Julianne. Straight for us.

"Come on, Ramón." I jerked my head toward the car. "I'll see you Monday," I called over my shoulder, hoping he would follow before Peter or anyone else got close enough to see us with this brown-skinned friend of mine.

I barely registered Ramón's voice as he murmured, "See you around."

Marco rolled down the window of the Chevy and watched us with narrowed eyes. One corner of his mouth was curled upward, not so much a smirk but a sneer. He didn't say anything as we approached.

"Will you take Ramón home, *please*?" I asked, my tone far more clipped than I intended. I flushed as soon as I heard it, as soon as I saw the way the muscles in Marco's jaw tightened.

Ramón glanced over his shoulder as he stumbled toward the car.

"That's it?" Marco looked at his brother, but Ramón said nothing. He then cocked an eyebrow at me.

I nodded hastily.

"Did you give her the damn notebook at least?" he snapped.

"What? Oh." Ramón clumsily thrust my notebook at me as he opened the passenger door.

I couldn't stop myself from looking back at Julianne—Julianne and Peter now—to see if they were still watching. The only thing that shone brighter than their curious eyes were the white numbers of Peter's football jersey. Forty-eight. I shoved the book in my bag. "Thank you."

Ramón didn't respond as he sank into his seat, staring over the dashboard at the darkened school. At the blond girl who stood in front of it.

Marco eyed both of us suspiciously. He was a year older than us, and he was like a more finely focused version of his brother. Where Ramón's features were soft and delicate and full, Marco was all angles and lines. Sharp cheekbones, blunt brow, and a wry mouth that was either in a fierce scowl or a twisted smile—nothing in between. It was the judicial glower that marked his face now. He tipped his chin at me. "Do you want a lift?"

"*No.*"

His brows rose. The complete lack of surprise in his expression made a fresh wave of humiliation crash over me.

"No, thank you," I amended, but it was too late.

I knew what he was thinking. I hated it, but I knew.

He thought I was ashamed of them, ashamed of where we came from.

It wasn't shame but fear that was driving me—though perhaps those two emotions weren't all that different.

I just needed them to go. I needed this to be over.

"*Bueno,*" Marco muttered with an unmistakable bitterness to his words that smarted inside of me until their sputtering tailpipe disappeared down Thomas Road.

I took a deep breath, my chest still heavy with dismay. Sometimes I felt like I knew Ramón better than I knew myself, and sometimes . . . Really, what could he have been thinking, turning up here like this?

I glanced back at Julianne one last time. Her confusion was clear, even from a distance, but she made no move toward me. She gave me a little wave before turning to Peter.

She would certainly have questions. I couldn't blame her for that, and though I had no idea how I'd deal with them on Monday, I was thankful that I wouldn't have to do it just now.

I'd find a way to explain Ramón—once I'd calmed down, once it was just the two of us. I had to.

I waved back, just a quick wiggle of my fingers, and walked away.

As soon as I got home, I pulled my dear leatherbound notebook out of my bag and sat with it for a moment in the front room. Running my fingers over the familiar, smooth cover. Thinking over the trouble it had caused me tonight.

I slowly opened it, thumbing through the crackling pages. My eyes coasted over the meticulous mix of newspaper clippings, photographs, and letters. I knew precisely what I was looking for.

It was one of my first entries.

I still remembered my father laying the paper flat on the kitchen table between us, his thick calloused fingers tapping the article.

"This," he said. "This is what matters. This is finally finding our place, ¿sabes? This is change, Rosa."

I had just nodded. At fourteen, my understanding of the world around me was narrow and flimsy, but I'd loved the way he was talking to me and I had promised myself I'd learn why it was so important. I'd become the sort of person who understood. He read it aloud at least three times, and when he'd left for work, I'd torn out the article and tucked it into the pocket of my dress.

I took a deep breath, feeling the turmoil in my stomach from the night beginning to settle—a little bit.

Ramón knew what was at stake, me passing as a white girl on the north side of town. He had to. He liked to play and pretend that none of this was a big deal, but he had to know the dangers involved. And he knew how important it was to me. Sure, he'd been trying to do something kind—something helpful—but I just couldn't fathom how he could've overlooked the risks.

Practically no one saw him, I tried to tell myself. *Except Julianne, but she's not a gossip. She's your friend.* Still, a pinch in my gut wouldn't let me forget that Julianne wasn't the only one. That Peter was there too.

It'll be fine. It was dark. It was just a few minutes. It'll all be fine.

TOLLESON SCHOOLS TO INTEGRATE

The Arizona Republic
Thursday, January 24, 1952

A federal court has ruled against the segregation of students of Mexican and Latin descent within schools in the Tolleson District No. 17.

The schools had previously contended that segregation for these students in separate schools was due to language deficiencies. However, families at the Mexican school argue that not only are the students' language capabilities not taken into account, but the school they are forced to attend has far less resources than the white school. For example, the Mexican school lacks a library, music and arts courses, and, in many cases, also lacks teaching staff with the appropriate instructional training.

Six

Monday, August 22, 1955

I took the bus to Blanca's house after school, one stop before my own house. Her new husband, Pablo, worked long hours at the warehouse where he packed produce, and baby Guillermo still didn't sleep much at night. By the end of the day, my poor sister usually looked like the Creature from the Black Lagoon, hair sticking up and spit-up crusted all over her.

Guillermo almost always cried the entire time I held him, but at least I could give my sister's arms a break—not that she rested when I came over. She immediately began fixing herself up and working on dinner, as Mamá had instructed her when we'd moved the three of them into this tiny casita two months ago.

As I clutched her wailing, wiggling infant to my chest, I watched Blanca race about her kitchen, clanging pots and smoothing her hair like a woman possessed. Though she certainly had my mother's speed, she hadn't yet acquired the grace and rhythm Mamá used to run our house.

I found myself wondering if this was what she wanted for herself. If anyone had ever asked.

Pablo was a nice man, and Guillermo was a beautiful baby. But when Blanca got pregnant at the beginning of her senior year of high school, it hardly felt like two sentences were exchanged before she was deposited at the altar in my mother's wedding dress, which Señora Montoya had helped us alter for her growing figure. There'd been absolutely no question that she'd be married.

Blanca hadn't been a particularly serious student, even though most of the classes she'd been funneled into were vocational or home economics courses, training the girls of the south side for keeping house—whether it was their own home or their employers'. But was *this* what she had envisioned for her life?

Our two paths seemed particularly different now that she had a family of her own and I was preparing to go to college. And I wasn't sure how I felt about that.

"Try swaying back and forth a bit," Blanca called over her shoulder, her brows pinched as Guillermo's wailing increased. "I think he's getting a tooth."

I did as instructed. "My poor baby," I cooed to him. "Don't tell me you had a bad day too?"

He gurgled as if in response, and though his crying was loud, Blanca didn't miss my question. She shot me a curious look as she poured a cup of arroz into her pot. "Bad day?"

I looked down at Guillermo, at the dark ringlets that covered the top of his head, and nodded. "I need to tell you about something."

"Me or Guillermo?" she teased.

"Blanca."

"Sorry. All right. What is it?"

"You have to promise not to say anything. Not even to Pablo. *Especially* not to Mamá and Papi."

She put her hand on her hip and gave me a knowing look.

I trusted Blanca. We were sisters; we'd always traded confidences with the utmost certainty. I'd spent so many nights as a young girl curled up in bed with her, fighting back tears as I told her the things other children would say to me, letting her hold me as she assured me that I'd feel like I fit in someday, that I'd have more friends who understood me, that someday I'd feel like a better version of myself. And I was the first person she'd told that she missed two of her monthly cycles a year ago, the one who'd held her hand as she'd explained to our parents that she and Pablo were expecting a baby. Though Ramón was my best friend, there was no one I trusted quite as much as I did my older sister.

And yet . . .

I thought of all the soda shops on my walk to school, with neat little signs that read WHITES ONLY or NO DOGS OR MEXICANS ALLOWED. I thought of how quiet Julianne was at lunch today, how she'd pulled out her drawing pad and doodled, leaving her Wonder bread sandwich untouched in her tin lunch box.

"Rosa?" Blanca prompted, dark eyes wide with growing concern.

Mouth dry, I forced myself to say it. I told her what Ramón had done on Friday night and that Julianne and Peter had seen him. And that I wasn't sure what they thought of it. Of him. Of me.

Blanca pursed her lips. "Those Montoya boys, Dios mío. Do they ever think?"

I sighed. "What should I do?"

"Well, first you need to talk to Ramón, and make sure he knows he can't pull a stunt like that again. I know he walks around with his head in the clouds all the time, but really, Rosa. Does he not pay attention at all? You remember what happened to Señora Velásquez's son last spring, don't you? With that white farmer and his daughter? That man just *suspected* that Ernesto was sweet on his daughter, and that was it." She grimaced, turning her gaze away from me and from her own son, peering into her pot of rice. She didn't have to say anything more, though. I remembered the bullet-ridden body that had been discovered a day after Ernesto Velásquez had gotten into a fight with that man. "How could Ramón put either of you in that kind of danger?" she added softly, almost to herself.

"I'll talk to him," I promised.

"And just keep your head down, Rosa, eh? Work hard. Stay out of trouble. Like you always do."

I left my sister's house and walked home just after dusk. The sun lingered so late in the summer; it was nearly eight o'clock, though it didn't feel like it. The sky was freshly melted, purple with streaks of orange sunlight not quite stirred in yet. A dim in-between, studded by only a handful of stars.

Like the Montoyas, Blanca and Pablo lived in the Marcos de Niza projects, the public housing built for Mexicans after the Depression. Though there were some efforts underway to desegregate public housing these days, when the projects first opened back in the forties, they were considered a sister neighborhood to the two other developments across town meant for Negroes and white folks.

I was too young to remember it, but Papi said there'd been tensions about the separate housing—especially when veterans came home from the Second Great War. The American Legion post on the south side, along with a few other community groups, got involved in trying to integrate the proposed new housing. The Montoyas were supposed to move to the new Harry Cordova projects, the ones for veterans. They were nicer than most of the homes in Golden Gate or even any of the other surrounding barrios. They were farther north, closer to downtown and the newer parts of the city. My memories of everything that was going on at that time were hazy, in the selfish, naive way all eight-year-olds' recollections were. But still, flashes of Señor Montoya ranting and raving at their dinner table were some of my last mental pictures of him. Señor Montoya had been ready for a change. After coming home from the war, he wanted . . . *more*.

Papi said a lot of veterans felt that way, that they expected better when they came back from overseas. But the Montoyas never ended up moving to the Cordova neighborhood or anywhere else, though the houses in Marcos de Niza weren't bad at all. Tiny little white brick houses, boxlike and neat in rows. Matching little patches of green grass. Small, but cozy. They were nestled tight against each other, and on warm evenings like this, neighbors often gathered in the shared front yards to visit or play games.

I waved to a few families we knew from church. The Gomezes surveyed a pack of children kicking a soccer ball between them and asked me to tell my parents they'd drop off fresh eggs from their chickens tomorrow. I thanked them as I walked by, nearing the end of the block and approaching the road that would lead me back to my own home, a warm but easy mile away. A walk I made nearly every day of my life. A walk I loved.

As I approached the Montoyas' house, the final one in the row, I could hear voices. Boyish, laughing and teasing, though I couldn't see anyone until I was just in front of their yard. Standing in the shadow of the house, a few steps from the side door that led to the kitchen, were five boys, not much more than silhouettes to me in the deepening dusk.

My gaze immediately sought out Ramón at the center of the semicircle, leisurely leaning against the side of his house, his hair tousled. He straightened as his amber eyes landed on me. "Rosa," he called. There was an odd tone of surprise to the way he said my name.

Almost in unison, each of the boys around him shifted to look at me. Farthest, almost on the outskirts of the circle, Marco fought with a temperamental lighter that he held to his cigarette.

"Um, hi, Ramón. Hi, everyone. How was your first day at school?"

They murmured disinterested responses as I realized that perhaps some of them weren't even in school. I knew Marco had dropped out the year before Blanca had. It wasn't terribly uncommon, and I could've kicked myself for speaking so carelessly. For further highlighting how out of touch I was.

A beat of uneasy silence passed between all of us, Marco's clicking lighter the only sound.

"How was your day, Rosita?" Ramón asked, either not noticing or not caring about the tension my presence had created. The boy next to him snorted at the pet name he used—the one he'd used since we were kids, when he'd tease me about how pink and rosy my cheeks got when I was embarrassed.

Thank goodness it was too dark for any of them to see how pink and rosy they were now.

"It was . . . it was fine." I took a deep breath, trying to ignore the way everyone was watching me, like they were just waiting to hear what sort of phony thing I'd say next. "I was hoping to talk to you, though."

Ramón's eyebrows rose in clear interest, but he didn't say anything.

"Alone, please, Ramón."

Another boy snickered as Ramón nodded, walking a few steps away with me toward the street.

"It was really sweet of you to bring me my notebook the

other night," I began slowly, the guilt already pinching at my throat. "But . . . um, you really . . . you really shouldn't have."

He cocked his head at me but still said nothing.

"It's dangerous, you know? People at school, they assume I'm white, and you being there . . ." I waited desperately for him to cut in, to show some sign of comprehension, but he remained silent. "You understand, don't you?"

He bit down on his lip thoughtfully. "Rosa, you're *allowed* to go to school at North—or wherever you want, for that matter. You know that. It's not illegal. You have as much right to be there as the rest of them."

I sighed. Not this again. "Yes, but Ramón, you have to understand. I'm the only Mexican one there, at least that I know of. And if they knew what I am—who I really am—things would just be . . ."

He nodded dismissively. "Yeah, yeah."

"I'm sorry," I said, though I didn't know what exactly I was apologizing for. I didn't make the rules we were forced to live by. I was just trying to make the best of the situation. Did that really make me so bad?

Marco's voice cut in before either of us could say anything else. "¿Todo está bien con la princesa?" Not his most creative jab, but it always stung when he called me a princess. He took a long drag of his cigarette, staring at me with a look of pure defiance.

Ramón rolled his eyes but didn't defend me.

"Well, have a good night," I said feebly, the feeling of being so frustratingly misunderstood thick and prickly in my throat.

Particularly painful since I wasn't used to feeling this way with Ramón of all people. I began walking away.

"Ah, Rosita, one more thing?"

I paused and looked back at him, at his brown skin and wild, inky jumble of curls.

"Did your friend . . . did Julianne say . . . anything? About me?" His words tottered out uncertainly, but the solemn way he peered at me in the darkness was far steadier.

I shook my head. "No, thankfully she didn't say a word about it."

Seven

Tuesday, August 23, 1955

Simon stood at the chalkboard in front of the newspaper room, inspecting the long list of stories we'd compiled for the upcoming issue. The pep rally was at the top of the list, right above the fall Girls' League charity event and a spotlight on the new civics teacher.

I tapped my pencil on my desk as I anxiously waited for him to begin assigning articles.

Everything I'd written last year had either been scrapped entirely or edited beyond recognition before being tucked away on the second or third page in whatever space was left after ads were placed. At first, I assumed it was because I was new and quiet, that it would take time to earn my spot. But by the end of the year, Simon's comments about my writing being too bland, about it lacking perspective, had grown from a frustrating hurdle to what felt like a personal attack.

I desperately wanted to prove him wrong. But perhaps more than that, I wanted to prove to myself that I could do this—that everything I was going through to be at school here was worth it.

"Don't be nervous," Julianne whispered to me, placing her hand on my arm to steady my furious tapping. "You'll get a story. This will be your year."

I tried to match her encouraging smile, but it withered away on my lips.

"I think this is a really solid list," Simon said finally. "We're going to have a really good first issue of *The Mustang Minute*."

Julianne's hand shot in the air. "What about the conflict in Vietnam?" she said without waiting for Simon to even look at her before speaking.

His expression was blank. "W-what about it?"

"We should cover it," she said. "People think—"

Simon silenced her with a flick of his hand. "I'm not really sure that's pertinent to our student body, Julianne. Let's keep it local. Focused on student interests, okay?"

Julianne sighed, slumping in her chair.

I didn't know why she always did this—why she was surprised when Simon refused to listen to her. She got so worked up, so heartbroken about it, every time. She'd sulked for weeks last year when he'd refused to let her write anything about the *Brown* case or school integration, calling it "too obvious" and "not newsworthy."

"But how come it didn't affect the Indian schools?" she'd said to no response. "Schools here have already begun integrating, and yet all the Indian kids still have to go to those *awful* boarding schools? What about the Phoenix Indian School three miles from here? Why doesn't integration affect them?"

But it had been to no avail then too.

Simon tapped his foot thoughtfully as he scrutinized the list once more. "All right, the feature on the civics teacher—Tommy, why don't you take a stab at it? And let's see, Henry, the op-ed about whether girls should be allowed to wear blue jeans to school—"

Julianne perked up again, throwing her hand in the air a bit more emphatically this time. "Shouldn't a *girl* write that?"

Henry and Simon exchanged puzzled looks. "Henry really has the voice I'd like for that kind of piece," he told her, not without a tone of impatience. "Actually, Julianne, I'd love for you to work on the article about the City of Phoenix's award for school safety. I know your dad was involved in that, and it would be swell if we could get a quote or two from the sheriff."

I knew precisely which award Simon was referring to. Papi had pointed to it with pride one morning over breakfast, commenting on how pleased he was with my school. I glanced at Julianne's disgruntled expression as she nodded begrudgingly.

"And the pep rally, I'd like that to be our front-page story, of course."

The metal chair of my desk squeaked as I leaned forward.

"Rosie took *great* notes! She should do it," Julianne chimed in once more.

My cheeks burned red hot as Simon's gaze flitted over to me with clear disinterest. "Ah, I'm actually going to have Walter write that one, but I'm sure he could make good use of those notes, Rosie. I'll have you working on the photo captions this month, all right?"

I nodded, unable to look at him. I kept my gaze trained on the desk in front of me as he rattled off the rest of the stories before closing out the meeting.

"He can be a real jerk," Julianne muttered to me as we began collecting our books. "Don't let him get to you. Don't be discouraged."

I wished it were that easy, but my disappointment was still lodged in my chest. The whole reason I went to this school was so I could be a writer one day—but I couldn't even do it now at our school newspaper. What did that say about me? What did that say about my whole purpose?

I turned to Julianne. "I guess I—"

But I stopped myself there because Julianne was no longer beside me. I barely looked up in time to see her disappearing out the classroom door, calling out a quick goodbye over her shoulder as she dashed off toward the exit.

Phoenix to Be Awarded "Safest City"

The Arizona Republic
August 1, 1955

Event details for next month's Safety Awards have been announced, with the luncheon set to take place on September 28 at the new high society hot spot, Hotel Valley Ho. This ceremony will celebrate Phoenix as the nation's safest city for 1954.

"In the wake of school integration especially, this is an impressive accomplishment," said Sheriff Callihan, who spearheaded student-led school safety patrols on many secondary campuses in the Phoenix metropolitan area. "There were a lot of very valid concerns about how bringing together students of different backgrounds would impact our schools and students' well-being, but I'm proud of the way colored children have assimilated and shown how beneficial integration is to their learning. Our teachers and school leaders are doing a commendable job and deserve to be recognized for the safe school communities they are supervising."

Eight

Thursday, August 25, 1955

"The first issue of *The Mustang Minute* should be coming out soon, isn't that right?" Miss Shaw asked me from behind her desk.

It was just the two of us yet again. I'd gotten in the habit of lingering in her classroom after the bell. I was still tinkering with the grammar exercise she'd given us, crossing out and rewriting the same sentence, unsatisfied. I glanced up at her. "Simon says the end of September is the goal. The first issue takes a while, training the new reporters and all."

"I look forward to reading some of your pieces this year," she said pleasantly.

I flushed, my gaze drifting to the classroom door as I avoided responding to that comment. Julianne usually met me here to say hi to Miss Shaw too. But she was nowhere to be found.

"If you'd ever like me to look over any of your articles before you take them to your editor, I'd be happy to," Miss Shaw continued. "I know it can sometimes be tough to break into those boys' clubs."

I smiled, not sure I wanted Miss Shaw to know how dismal I was already feeling about my spot at the paper. "Thank you. Yes, I'll—" I stopped as I saw a flash of golden hair pass by the window in a hurry. I scrambled to my feet, thanking Miss Shaw again, and bolted into the hallway.

"Julianne?" I called.

She skidded to a stop, whirling around so fast that the books she was clutching to her chest tumbled right out of her arms. "Oh, oh no. Darn." She laughed as we both dropped to pick them up. "So clumsy." Her movements were frantic as she reached for her books, her cheeks red and her eyes fixed downward.

"Is everything all right?" I asked, stacking a few sheets of paper that had fluttered loose.

"Hmm? Oh yes, of course—"

I wasn't sure if she'd stopped herself or if I'd just stopped listening because my attention caught on the piece of paper I was holding. A sketch from her drawing pad. A beautiful charcoal illustration. The outline of two figures embracing. Sweeping lines and deep romantic shading, it was an unquestionably intimate piece. Instantly, I was sure I was looking at something I wasn't supposed to see.

"Thanks," she whispered, tugging the papers out of my hands and tucking them in between her books. Out of sight. She rose, but it took me a beat longer to get to my feet.

"You were in quite a hurry."

She adjusted her books. She still wouldn't look at me.

"Julianne, is everything all right?" I repeated.

She scrunched her brows. "What do you mean?"

I tilted my head. Had she really not noticed how distant she'd been? Was she avoiding me, or was I imagining it?

"You'd tell me if something was bothering you, wouldn't you?" I leaned in, forcing her to meet my gaze. I searched her blue eyes for a hint of . . . anything.

"I can assure you, nothing is bothering me, Rosie," she said in a voice that was far too measured to be trusted.

I couldn't shake the feeling that there was still *something* going on with her. Something on her mind that she wasn't telling me. Which, I supposed, was her right. After all, I certainly had secrets I didn't share with her.

And yet . . .

I thought of that drawing as I watched her hand move to her smooth golden curls, tucking a strand behind her ear and revealing a red bruise on her neck.

A love bite, just at the base of her throat!

I couldn't help it. My eyes widened the second I spotted it. Julianne realized her mistake immediately. Hurriedly, she tried to sweep her hair back over her shoulder, but of course it was too late.

"I'll see you later, Rosie," she said hoarsely, her gaze dropping as she turned quickly and darted down the hall.

I stood there for a while longer, completely dumbfounded.

It wasn't until I heard the janitor's cart rolling behind me that I gained enough sense to get going myself.

A hickey. Was that what this was about?

A hickey from . . . well, it had to be Peter Duke, didn't it? It was hardly a secret, the way he'd been pursuing her. And the night of the pep rally, hadn't she gone out with him?

It all made sense, I told myself. The daydreams and the romantic doodles. That had to be it. She was embarrassed about the mark he'd left on her, which I understood. The way people watched her, she didn't want a reputation for being fast. I couldn't blame her.

And maybe she was hesitant to tell me about it after all the time we'd spent complaining about Peter. A change of heart like this . . . Well, it didn't make sense to me, but after watching Ramón bounce from sweetheart to sweetheart, I understood better than she'd imagine.

Not that she knew that, of course.

I breathed a sigh of relief as I left campus that afternoon. Julianne and Peter. It wasn't ideal, but it also wasn't unexpected.

It was a heck of a lot better than her or anyone else here discovering my secret, that was for certain. The thought of Peter's mouth anywhere near Julianne made me cringe, but if that was what it took to keep her too distracted to ask about Ramón—well, I could at least try to warm up to the idea of them going steady.

AMERICANIZATION FOR THE YOUNG LADY: ETIQUETTE FOR MEXICAN WOMEN FROM THE DEPARTMENT OF AMERICANIZATION AND HOMEMAKING

Published 1929

With large numbers of Mexicans entering our fine country, both legally and otherwise, it is our profound civic duty to properly assimilate them to this new land. This mission undoubtedly begins within the home. As girls are the future mothers and homemakers, their success in areas like hygiene, sanitation, and etiquette is essential to improving their families' conditions.

The fact of the matter is Mexicans are an economic necessity in the Southwest. However, they require our guidance to raise their standards of living.

For example, we must teach the importance of a daily bath, as Mexicans have earned the common term "dirty Mexican" due to their laxness in this regard. This practice is a safeguard to all.

Nine

Monday, August 29, 1955

As I walked to school Monday morning, my thoughts continued to bounce around like one of those paddleball toys from the five-and-dime. Pinging about incessantly, going nowhere. It'd been like that all weekend. The newspaper article. Julianne's drawing. The college fair this week. Ramón at school. Marco calling me princesa. The feeling that I'd never be worthy of Miss Shaw's praise or the opportunity of being at North at all.

Back and forth, back and forth. I couldn't focus long enough to work anything out.

I'd hoped to talk to Ramón about it, to puzzle over it all with him. Even his goofing around might've been a good distraction. But I hadn't seen him since last week, since that quick chat in front of his house. It was unusual for almost anyone in Golden Gate to go a whole week without seeing each other but especially for us.

Perhaps he was mad about what I'd said to him that night?

But it wasn't like him to keep his thoughts to himself. If I'd upset him, he would've said so. I felt a bead of sweat slide between my shoulder blades as I rounded the corner on Thomas Road, the red-roofed school and the cluster of golden school buses visible in the distance.

Something caught my eye as I took in that familiar sight something that was equally familiar but also startlingly out of place.

The Montoyas' rust-colored Chevy.

Parked along the side of the road, right under the bright green branches of a paloverde tree.

My heart lurched at seeing it again *here*.

But before my full dismay could take hold of me—before I could even begin to wonder why their car was here at all or what it could possibly mean—the passenger door swung open.

And whose slender, fair leg should swing out and onto the sunlit sidewalk but that of Julianne Callihan.

She was laughing, turning toward the front of the car as she bumped the door shut with her hip. Her back was toward me, blond locks spilling over her shoulders like a waterfall of pure sunlight. Ramón was now crossing in front of the car. He wore a smile that seemed to reach every single part of him, from the giddy flounce of his curls to the free, easy way he carried himself. I watched as he placed his hands on her waist, his skin a rich brown against her pink gingham dress. And then Julianne turned so I could see her profile, see the sparkling way she gazed right back at him. Her matching grin, every bit as radiant as she reached up and wrapped her arms around his neck and drew him close, her face angled up toward his.

And they kissed.

Ramón and Julianne kissed.

Right there on the street. In full daylight. In clear view of . . . well, anyone!

I was unable to look away as he pulled her close, as her fingers found their way to his dark hair. As they seemed to melt into one another.

It was the kind of full body embrace that transformed two people into one. The kind of kiss I'd never seen in real life, only on the big screens of the drive-in theater—her fingers were in his hair, lost in those unmanageable curls, and he stroked the small of her back with such intimacy and affection it was as if they'd been doing this all their lives.

The world went silent for just an instant. Birds chirping, car engines passing, chatter of passersby—all snuffed out into a noiselessness so complete it practically buzzed in my ears.

Ramón and Julianne?

Ramón and *Julianne*.

I'd thought . . .

It didn't matter what I thought.

At last, Julianne withdrew, still smiling adoringly. She leaned in through the open passenger window to grab her bookbag. And as she turned, her eyes landed on me.

The rest of the world came rushing back at me in a deafening wave.

Her mouth fell open, her perfect pink lips forming a perfect round O. She straightened, leaving her bag on the seat, and took a step toward me instead, her arm still extended as if ready to grasp something. Anything.

By now, Ramón had spotted me too.

Their expressions of surprise were hard for me to understand. It was all very hard to understand, of course. But the alarmed creases in their brows, the wordless ways their mouths hung slightly open—and the striking similarities of these expressions on these markedly different faces—stuck with me.

We were a block from school! *Anyone* could've seen them, after all. Who knew who else had? What did they expect?

"Rosie—" Julianne said at the same time Ramón said, "Rosa."

Both my names. My two worlds, colliding into one.

All I could do was shake my head rapidly.

Ramón started to say something else, but I cut him off before he even got a few syllables out.

"Don't" was all I said before I marched past them and hurried toward the school.

When I first transferred schools last year—before Julianne and I had exchanged more than a few cordial smiles as we rifled through our lockers—I used to spend my lunch period in the library, sneaking bites of my food from my bookbag whenever the librarian wasn't looking and paging through books I'd never heard of. I didn't have anyone to eat with in the cafeteria or the courtyard, and I didn't want to draw attention to myself as the strange, lonely new girl. The library was usually empty, and even when someone happened to stumble in, it looked like I was busy doing schoolwork.

Today, that was where I went as soon as I got to school. I knew Julianne was chasing after me, but she was careful not to make a scene, and I pretended like I didn't see her. She hovered in the library doorway contemplatively for a few seconds before disappearing down the hall with a thoughtful frown scrunching up her face.

I didn't have any words—for her or for anyone. Not yet.

I truly didn't know which of them was more thoughtless in this scenario. Julianne—who knew how this world worked. She knew there wasn't a single person who looked like Ramón at this school—or anywhere else in her circle. The country club. The Girls' League. All those fancy dinners she went to with her family. Besides the waiters and the drivers and the housekeepers, she knew as well as I did there wasn't a brown face to be found. She was aware her whole world was designed to keep people like Ramón out of it.

And Ramón. Dear God, Ramón.

How could he not understand what great danger he could cause by indulging in this whim? Dangers for both of us. How could he not see that?

It was all so recklessly, horribly, unbelievably *stupid*.

"Does his brother know?" Blanca asked me later that evening.

She stirred a pot of pozole with a troubled scowl, one hand

clutching a wooden spoon and the other resting on her hip. It was a very maternal pose, I thought, and again I was struck by how rapidly my big sister had made the transition into someone's mother.

Marco and Blanca had been in the same grade before they both dropped out. She rarely mentioned him growing up, but that may have been due to our father's general disapproval of the rebellious and headstrong oldest Montoya boy more than anything. Her husband, Pablo, worked with Marco at the Bashas' warehouse, storing farm goods for the grocery store—at least for now. Marco often bounced from job to job for reasons that were unclear to me and worrisome to his mother.

"Blanca, how would I know that?" I snapped, earning a reproachful glare from her. Jeez, more and more like Mamá by the moment. "Sorry." I sighed. "I have no idea what Marco Montoya knows." I considered this for a moment. "Does Pablo ever talk about him? About what's going on with their family?"

Blanca shook her head thoughtfully. "No, not really. I can ask him, though. He says Marco keeps to himself." She raised her eyebrows as if to say, *You know how he is*. She tapped her chin. "But didn't you say he was there that night? At the pep rally? That's when Ramón met this girl, yes?"

I nodded, hating how all of this sounded. How all the pieces came together in this huge mess.

"So he probably has some idea of what's going on," she mused.

"I suppose." The knowing smirk she shot me told me she could read the skepticism on my face.

After all, Marco might have been the man of the Montoya household, but he tended to show very little regard for any sort of rules. It was anyone's guess what he'd make of his younger brother's current romance.

Guillermo let out a squawk from where he was lying on a quilt in the living room. I moved to grab him, holding his little body to mine as I turned back to my sister.

"Ramón can have his pick of any girl, you know," I said, wincing as Guillermo seized a lock of my hair and gave it a sharp tug. "He can go steady with *any* girl in *any* barrio in the south side. Why does it have to be *Julianne Callihan*?"

Blanca looked at me meaningfully, lips pursed. "I do agree with you. That boy is being careless. But . . . well, I know you're not going to like this, but the heart wants what the heart wants, hermanita. It doesn't always play by the rules."

"You're right," I fired back, uncurling my dark hair from Guillermo's fingers. "I don't like that answer."

Ten

Thursday, September 1, 1955

"What are you doing here?" I called from my front step, scowling at the wild-eyed Ramón pacing in the front yard.

I'd heard Mamá talking with him nearly half an hour ago, asking him if everything was all right and pleading with him to come inside for some breakfast. He'd assured her he was fine, he was just waiting to walk me to my bus stop—which, of course, put Mamá even more on edge. She knew as well as me that Ramón was not an early riser.

"What's going on, mija?" she'd asked me as she set my breakfast plate in front of me.

"I'm sure it's nothing," I'd lied. "You know how Ramón is." But I was certain I hadn't convinced her. That woman could smell trouble a mile away.

"I need to talk to you," Ramón answered, his voice resolute, as soon as I shut the front door behind me. He was dressed in a cream-colored button-down shirt and jeans, his black curls combed back haphazardly, like he was headed to school, even though I knew he didn't have to be there for an hour. South Mountain was only a short walk from our houses.

"Well, I don't want to talk to *you*." I jammed my key into the lock, jerking it until I heard a click.

"Fine. I'll talk, you listen." When I turned to face him, he had his arms folded across his chest. "You can't avoid me forever."

I rolled my eyes. Blanca had said something very similar to me last night, accusing me of hiding at her place after she'd noted how much more time I was spending with her after school. And she didn't even know that I'd been walking the long way back and forth to steer clear of the Montoya house.

I did not like that Ramón had noticed this too. "Walk and talk," I grumbled finally, tipping my head toward the road, intentionally starting off at a much quicker pace than normal.

"Julianne says you've been avoiding her too." He was taller than me and, to my disappointment, had no trouble keeping up.

I scoffed. "Jeez, now you two are talking about me?"

"Rosita, we're worried—"

I stopped suddenly, kicking up a cloud of dust around my shoes. He was a half stride ahead of me before he stopped too, looking at me with brows furrowed. "You *should* be worried, Ramón."

He winced. "Come on. It's not what you think."

My eyes bulged. "Not what I think? Let me tell you about

what I think. *I think* you've let yourself get swept up by another beautiful girl—"

"Julianne is different," he cut in sharply, a shadow of warning in his brown eyes.

"No kidding she's different! She's the *white* daughter of one of the wealthiest, most powerful men in Phoenix."

"I thought you liked the sheriff," he said. "You're not making any sense."

"*I'm* not making any sense?" I couldn't keep the biting derision out of my voice. My grip on my books was white knuckled. "Ramón, it doesn't matter whether I like him or not. Yes, he seems like a good man. A leader. Progressive, fair. Sure. But that doesn't change who he is in the world. Or who you are." I added the last part a little more softly, instinctively trying to cushion the blow despite my anger.

I saw the hurt on Ramón's face anyway. "I thought you'd understand. Or at least try to," he replied, his voice laced with exasperation. "You know both of us. And, I mean, why do you even go to North if you don't believe change is possible? What are you working so hard for if you don't think we'll ever be equal to them?"

Now it was my turn to have the breath knocked out of me. I tried several times to speak, a choked sound the only noise I could summon. Closing my eyes, shielding myself from the probing way he was watching me, I took a deep breath and tried again. "That . . . is not the point," I said, not entirely sure I believed it. "The point is, what you are doing is *dangerous*. Remember Ernesto Velásquez? And have you heard about what they did to that poor boy Emmett Till? They found his *body* yesterday, Ramón. He was *younger* than us." I grimaced, thinking of the newspaper article I'd seen just this morning. "All they're saying he did was whistle at a white lady. Have you even thought about what they'll do if they find out what you've been up to with Julianne?"

He ran his hand along his jaw, his eyes boring into me. "That's different, Rosa."

I gave the subtlest nod. "Maybe. You're a different kind of brown, and this isn't Mississippi. But just because it's different doesn't mean it's not dangerous." Sometimes the differences—the unknowns—made it even more perilous and hard to predict, but for some reason, I couldn't bring myself to utter that bit out loud.

"What you do is dangerous too, you know, going to school over there," he said, his voice barely above a whisper. "Aren't some things worth the risk?" There was a pleading look in his eyes—a desperation to be heard and understood and seen in all the ways we'd been there for each other throughout the years. The kind of look that underscored a friendship like ours. A silent hope for unwavering support and love.

But I couldn't do it. Not this time.

I looked down at the dusty road beneath my feet and shook my head. "I'll see you around," I said with almost no conviction at all. "I've got to go."

INTEGRATION MANDATED IN ARIZONA SCHOOLS, ACCORDING TO COURT RULING

Arizona Sun—The Voice of 60,000 Negroes in Arizona
March 5, 1954

According to the 1953 ruling in *Phillips v. Phoenix Union High Schools and Junior College District*, all Arizona schools will integrate beginning with the fall term.

"This is not the South," Sheriff Callihan said at a recent Phoenix Union school board meeting, where he and his deputies offered support to the large crowd of parents with questions about the decision. "Arizona is the Wild West, and we have always done things our own way—including integration."

Though the ruling was initially intended to end the segregation of black students, it will, in turn, prohibit all discrimination based on race or color within Arizona schools. Mexican schools, or classes where Mexican students are often sent due to cultural or linguistic differences, are also expected to be integrated.

Eleven

Friday, September 2, 1955

I sat in the library, not reading the biography of Thomas Jefferson that was propped up in front of me. My sandwich lay on the table, concealed by the book, but I hadn't touched that either.

"Psst," a voice whispered to my right. "Don't you usually eat with Julianne Callihan?"

I jumped, nearly dropping the book, and looked up to see Tim Buckles peering at me from across the table. I wasn't sure how long he had been there, but the abundant arrangement of notebooks and pens around him suggested that he hadn't just arrived.

Though I'd never spoken to him before, I knew who he was. We had math class together, both this year and last, but perhaps I noticed him for the exact reason most people didn't.

Tim was on the football team, which in and of itself was

enough to get a little notoriety around here. With his wide shoulders and thick forearms, he was built like people had been talking to him about football since he learned how to walk. But still, he wasn't quite like the other boys. Tim was quiet and sweet, unimposing in an unexpected way.

He was the kind of person who could be sitting at a table with you for thirty minutes and never once draw your attention, even though he was just about the same size as a small grizzly bear. I was pretty sure every boy in our school would have loved to look like Tim. But to me, he always seemed a little uncomfortable in his own skin. Like he was worried he was taking up too much space.

"You know, the sheriff's daughter?" he continued, as if I wouldn't know who he was talking about. "Blond hair, blue eyes? Last year's Spring Queen, though most folks think she's a shoo-in for the crown at the fall dance too." His chair gave a loud groan as he shifted in it and waited for me to jump in. I noticed a faint blush creep across his broad face as he looked down at his notebook, murmuring, "Never mind. Sorry to have bothered you."

"She's president of the Latin club too," I said finally. "And a writer on the school newspaper. And an artist." I was frustrated with her, sure, but I still knew how bothered she'd be by only being known for her appearance and what other people thought of her.

He tapped his pencil on the table thoughtfully, accepting this correction as answer enough. "You two have a fight?"

I couldn't escape the notion that whatever was going on between me and Julianne—and Ramón, I suppose—was already a pretty perilous situation on its own. I was sure inviting strangers into it wouldn't help a bit.

And Tim was a stranger. A seemingly sweet stranger, but a stranger.

I shrugged. "I just have a lot of schoolwork already, I guess."

He nodded again, but it was clear by his impassive expression that he didn't really believe me. It wasn't that big of a school; he likely had a lot of the same teachers as me in addition to the math class we shared. Besides, it was only the second week. We didn't have that much homework. Not enough to necessitate locking myself in the library on my own all of a sudden, anyway.

Which made me wonder why he was hiding in here too. Shouldn't he have been eating lunch with the other football players at their table right smack-dab in the middle of the cafeteria where everyone could see them?

He was silent for a moment, as if debating whether to press for more information. "Is it because of Peter? The reason you two aren't sitting together?"

I tilted my head.

"Everyone knows he likes her. He's going to ask her to the dance. Wants to give her his letterman jacket. He was talking about it in the locker room yesterday after practice."

I considered this. I shouldn't have been surprised Tim wondered the same thing I had a few days ago. Most people would be delighted to see Peter and Julianne—two good-looking and popular kids from good families—get together. "Why would we be fighting about that?"

I watched Tim's face take on several different expressions as he searched for his answer. "You know, because Peter is . . ."

I waited for the end of that sentence, clamping my mouth shut tight to keep myself from trying to finish it for him. Obnoxious? A bully?

There was a conflicted strain on his face that made me sure I wasn't too far off the mark, even if neither of us was bold enough to say it out loud. Finally, he just shrugged and gave me a bashful smile. "I don't know, I guess," he said, though the tone of his voice suggested otherwise. "Hard to explain," he added quietly.

Hard to explain, indeed.

Twelve

Friday, September 2, 1955

"Can we talk?"

I swung my locker door closed to find Julianne standing beside me, gnawing on her lower lip. She flinched, almost imperceptibly, as I made eye contact with her.

First Ramón, now her? I shook my head.

"Rosie." The word caught in her throat, and I wondered if she was considering whether she should call me by my real name now that she knew it. Was I Rosa to her now?

Why go on pretending?

Why should she keep up with my charade when she and Ramón were tugging at the edges every time they saw one another, threatening to expose me each time they locked lips?

She clearly knew where I came from, who I really was. If she was spending so much time with Ramón, there was no way she hadn't pieced it all together.

There was a lump in my throat that was making it hard to breathe or speak—or even think straight.

"Unless you and *Ramón*"—I whispered his name, unable to stop myself from casting a furtive glance around me to make sure no one was eavesdropping—"have called it quits on this whole thing, I'm not sure there's anything you can say that I want to hear."

Her jaw tensed, as if to stop her lip from trembling. She was trying awfully hard to appear firm and resolute—but there was a flash of vulnerability in her round blue eyes that betrayed her.

"We wish you'd hear us out," she murmured. *"Please."*

"Why does it matter?" I asked, intending it to come out more snappish, like a quick retort. But instead, a warble found its way into my voice—a hint of my own inner anguish. "If you two are going to keep on doing . . . *whatever* it is you're doing, what does it matter what I say? What I think of it?" I gulped down a breath of air that felt tight in my throat.

This question seemed to pain her in a way I wasn't sure I understood. Something beyond frustration or worry. "Because we care about you and what you think," she said, continuing even when she noted the wariness on my face. "And we thought you'd understand."

There it was again. Where on earth did they get the idea that this reckless little romance was something I'd relate to? That it was even remotely similar to the calculated risks I took here in order to go to college?

"Why would—"

To my relief, the tardy bell cut me off, signaling that we only had a minute to make it to our next classes.

"If you want to talk, I'll be around after school," Julianne said finally. "Around the corner, where you saw us—"

I nodded, not wanting to hear the rest of the sentence out loud. I jammed my padlock into place. "I know the place," I said, neither accepting nor refusing her offer as I walked away.

I should've guessed he'd be there too, but my stomach still tightened when I spotted Ramón standing next to Julianne. They were side by side, facing me, but their heads were tilted toward each other as they murmured something back and forth. Their boldness—their complete lack of concern about being seen together—made a chill run through me. What were they thinking?

A breeze rustled the tree branches above them, shaking free a flurry of bright yellow flowers that scattered all around them. Like neon-colored snowflakes, incongruous but lovely.

"Thanks for meeting us," Julianne said as soon as I was within earshot.

Ramón plucked a flower petal off the cap sleeve of her blouse, a gesture that struck me as strangely tender.

"So what did you want to talk about?" It was hard to look at them right now, and I found myself focusing on anything else. The flowers on the sidewalk. The country club down the street. The striped awning of the shoe shop. A gleaming blue mailbox.

Almost like if I refused to look at them—refused to see them—maybe no one else would take notice of them either.

"We just want you to know that we know what we're doing is not without risks," Julianne said, softly but firmly. "We know it affects other people. We know it affects you. And we know there are some dangers for us as well."

"Us?" I repeated with a snort that I couldn't suppress. My eyes landed on Ramón finally, and he turned scarlet.

"Okay, not us exactly," she conceded. "For Ramón. And you." They exchanged a look that was indecipherable to me. "The thing is, we're in love." They gazed at each other for a few seconds, savoring this sentiment before returning their eyes to me.

In love?

"You've known each other for a week."

Ramón thrust his chin in the air as he answered me. "Two."

I glared at him.

"Two weeks," he clarified, as if I'd misheard him. As if that was the reason I was so confused.

"I know it seems crazy," Julianne began.

"It *is* crazy."

Hurt flickered across her face, but she nodded at me. "Yes, I know. This is . . . It's crazy." A flush crept into her cheeks as she glanced at Ramón once more. "But, it's real. It's how we really feel."

"You can't be serious," I said, keeping my eyes on Ramón until he looked back at me. *"Ramón."*

I thought of all the girls he'd wooed over the years. All the other ones who had claimed they loved him. All the broken hearts he'd left after he moved on to the next.

I brought my hand to my temple, pressing my fingertips into the piercing irritation that was throbbing just behind my eyes.

"We hoped that if we could just talk to you, explain things," Julianne said, her voice so smooth and honeyed that it must've taken deliberate concentration. "We hoped that you might understand." My anger flared at this. At their repeated use of me and my understanding. I could feel myself shaking my head as she added, "And we wanted to see if you'd—"

"Well, you were wrong. I don't understand this. I couldn't possibly . . ." The sight of them like this, together, united—it stung in a way I refused to dwell on.

I sighed, turning around. Turning away from them without finishing my sentence.

Thirteen

Friday, September 2, 1955

My words still hadn't found me when I stepped off the bus. I didn't want to go home yet or even to Blanca's. Just the thought of facing my parents or my sister or the baby exhausted me.

The sky above me was an unapologetic shade of blue, the kind of color that made no pretense of being anything else. Crystal clear without a cloud in sight. The September sun beat down on me between the full branches of shade trees, hitting me in bursts of bright heat, but I didn't mind. I relished the solitude and the space from everything.

I wanted so desperately to push Ramón and Julianne from my thoughts. To pretend this romance of theirs didn't exist. That they'd never met. That this whirlwind crush wasn't about to unravel everything I'd worked for.

But instead, I found myself imagining every way it could

go wrong. The sheriff's buddies harassing Ramón and his family until he agreed to leave Julianne alone. Parents at my school demanding the principal expel me and send me back where I came from. College and hopes for a better life—gone like a wisp of smoke.

I was so lost in thought as I trudged along the dusty roadside that it took me a while to sense I was being watched. I paused, looking around until I found the scorching gaze of Marco Montoya aimed right at me.

He leaned against the Bashas' warehouse where he worked, a cigarette balanced between his lips. His blue button-down work shirt emblazoned with the grocery store's logo was open, revealing a white shirt underneath. He was sweaty and covered in dust, and the fabric of his undershirt clung to his muscled frame. Everything about him was loose and easy, *indifferent*—except for the way he was looking at me.

"Hey, princesa." It wasn't quite a shout, but his voice carried across the street anyway.

I stared back at him, using one hand to shield my eyes from the sunlight. Marco was not the type to engage in pleasantries or formalities, not the type to simply bid passersby a friendly hello.

"¿Todo está bien?" He pinched his cigarette between his fingers, still watching me with unsettling intensity. There was a distinct lack of curiosity to the way he asked if I was okay. Not exactly teasing, not like the night he'd called me a princess in front of all the neighborhood boys, but not inquisitive either.

I gave an irritated shrug, dropping my hand from my face so a flash of sunlight obscured his expression from my vision. "What do you care?"

He laughed dryly. "Guess you saw my brother, eh?" A few cars passed between us, blocking us from each other for a moment.

Once they'd passed, I responded with one slow nod, surprised by his question.

He stayed where he was, stock-still. Cigarette smoke wafted in front of him, and his shoulders slumped backward against the brick wall. I wasn't sure if he'd seen me nod, but I also wasn't sure if I cared. But before I could make up my mind, he shook a few black curls of hair out of his eyes—the bits that had worked their way out of his pomade—and stomped out his cigarette with a firm twist of his boot in the dirt. And then he walked toward me, straight across the middle of the road.

Marco had so many of the same features that made Ramón such a heartthrob. Or rather, Ramón had his older brother's features. I hated to admit it, but the closer he drew, the more aware of his appearance I became. Marco was a few inches taller, slimmer, leaner. They had the same thick hair, though Marco wore his a bit shorter, his curls succumbing to combing more easily than Ramón's, which crimped and coiled in every direction no matter what he did. And then, of course, they had those same light brown eyes, hooded under the thickest lashes. Ramón's eyes had a glittering quality that made you feel like he wasn't quite looking at you, but Marco's were the opposite. His eyes bore right through you.

"So you *know*, then." His voice was low and gravelly now that he didn't have to call across the street.

He had stopped unusually close to me, it seemed. A few inches nearer than a typical conversation between two people who were not even friends. I could smell him, for goodness' sake. Citrus and sunshine and sweat—unfamiliar, but not bad.

I straightened, throwing my shoulders back to put a modicum of extra distance between us.

"About la gringa," he prompted when I still hadn't said anything.

I rolled my eyes. "Yes."

"Not jealous, are you?" His eyes lit up with something I didn't fully recognize; it made my blood boil regardless.

"No."

He cocked a skeptical eyebrow at me. "My brother, he's a heartbreaker." He chuckled.

I shook my head. "He's a fool."

Though it came out a bit harsher than I'd intended, Marco didn't seem particularly surprised. He watched me with clear intrigue.

"You know how he is," I added hastily. Why I was even explaining myself to Marco of all people, I wasn't sure—but I heard myself continuing anyway. "You know just as well as I do that this is just another crush, right? He's going to ruin his life over *this*."

Marco's lips curled into a smirk. "You worried about him ruining his life or yours?"

Of course he was just here to mock me, I realized with a hot burst of humiliation. I wanted to tell him to get lost, to beat it, to leave me alone. And yet I found myself rooted where I stood, languishing under his fierce gaze.

He nodded as he tucked his hands in his pockets, like my silence was all the explanation he needed. "What are you doing right now?"

I blinked. "Um."

"I'm going to a meeting," he said. "You should come." His burning eyes rested heavy on my face. It was like being hit by a hot gust of wind, being stared at by him.

I huffed out a breath. "No."

Despite my tone—despite the immediacy of my refusal—he didn't seem offended. In fact, he smirked. Another beat of silence passed between us. His eyes roamed over my face in a way that had every piece of me on edge before I finally succumbed to my curiosity. "What kind of meeting?"

"Guess you'll just have to come and see," he quipped.

"No," I repeated with a roll of my eyes.

The corner of his mouth turned, less of a smirk and more of a scowl now. "Figured as much," he muttered as he started to turn away from me. He moved slowly, like he was waiting for me to interject.

"And what's that supposed to mean?" I couldn't stop myself.

"La princesa wouldn't dare step outside her ivory tower, eh?" He wiggled his eyebrows at me as he said the word "ivory."

"Because I don't want to spend time with you, I'm a snob. Is that it?"

The lazy one-shoulder shrug he gave me was answer enough.

"Fine," I said, my annoyance short-circuiting inside of me. I was so angry at everyone who refused to see my side of things, who insisted they knew better than me. I stepped toward him.

He arched one eyebrow. "Fine?"

"Fine. Let's go. Take me to this 'meeting' of yours." I threw one hand in the air, gesturing for him to lead the way.

"Your wish is my command, princesa," he drawled infuriatingly, as if this hadn't been his idea in the first place. "It's just this way." A tilt of his head toward the right sent a few of his silky curls bouncing, one lock catching in his lashes. He swept it away without hesitation and reached toward me. Our hands brushed, and I jumped at the sensation of his rough skin against mine.

"What are you doing?"

"Take it easy. Just trying to lighten your load." His fingers wrapped around the two books I was holding—my history textbook and my beloved notebook of newspaper clippings. He gently pulled them toward him, and I realized he was offering to carry my books for me.

I guess I must have let go, but I was still standing with my arms outstretched when Marco began walking.

Fourteen

Friday, September 2, 1955

I'd come to the Sacred Heart Church more times than I could count since my family attended Mass every Sunday. We'd been parishioners since before the church itself was even built, back when Father Al would preach from underneath a ramada of palm fronds.

Even so, I had never seen the place quite like this.

Over the past few years, the church had risen from the ground brick by brick, mostly from volunteer labor organized by the American Legion post. After St. Mary's, the big cathedral on the north side of town, kept pushing out all the Mexican parishioners—first to their own Spanish services and then to the basement and finally out altogether—there was a loud cry for a church of our own. It was nearly complete now, though it was still missing a roof and floor, so we gathered on the dusty earth with the sun beating down on us.

But all this I was accustomed to.

What stunned me now was the boisterous crowd of people who had gathered here on a Friday night. Our makeshift pews—bales of hay and old milk crates—were arranged in a circle rather than the usual rows facing the pulpit.

I snuck a glance at Marco as he led me through the crowd. He nodded hello to a few people as he walked by but didn't crack a smile. He kept his head bowed slightly, even as a large man clapped him on his back and called him hijo.

"What are we doing here?" I asked him. "What is this?"

"El Foro," Marco said, leading me toward a hay bale on the outer edge of the circle and motioning for me to sit. There was a glimmer in his eyes that said he knew just how cryptic his answer was. "You haven't heard of it?"

The Forum? I shook my head.

"You see that man over there? With the mustache?" He jerked his chin toward our right. "He's with LULAC—you know, the League of United Latin American Citizens? And the guy in front of him is from Alianza. Oh, and this woman toward the front with the glasses, she's working with Friendly House." His eyes narrowed as they returned to my face, gauging my response. "Do those names mean anything to you?"

My cheeks burned hot as I shook my head once more.

Marco snorted. "Well, you'll soon see, princesa."

Before I could push for more information—and before Marco could fire off any more condescending comments—a low voice began to disrupt the scattered conversations all around us. It was hardly a commanding voice; it was barely loud enough to get the attention of this many people, and it took several attempts for everyone to quiet down.

Standing in the center of the circle was a short man who wore an old-fashioned zoot suit that appeared to be just a little bit big for his narrow frame. "Buenas tardes," he said as the crowd slowly settled and heads began to turn in his direction.

As he spoke, thanking everyone for being here, I caught sight of people nodding and murmuring responses, as if he were addressing them personally rather than a whole room of people. His voice was familiar, though it was hard for me to place it. I was certain I'd never seen him before, but there was something about him that resonated deep inside my memory.

Marco leaned into me. "That's Victor Verón," he whispered. "He founded El Foro about two years ago," he added before I could ask.

I nodded slowly, hoping my confusion wasn't as clear on my face as it felt inside of me. What *was* this place?

"I would like to dive back into our conversation on the Mexican American identity," Verón was saying. "It's imperative that we—"

"Ay, enough with the culture mierda," an old man sitting on the other side of Marco interjected, throwing his hands in the air. "What about the important things, eh? What about fair wages?"

"There haven't been enough opportunities since all these Operation Wetback roundups, and you know that!" another man bellowed, arms folded across his wide chest. "And what jobs there are left for us, they don't pay near enough."

Several people clapped and made noises of agreement.

Verón patiently waited for the comments to subside, but his face was stern when he resumed talking. "I hear your frustration, I do. But so many of our issues as Mexicans in this country stem from a lack of cultural identity." A few murmurs of protest began to bubble up, but he continued. "How do we resolve this unequal racial hierarchy if we don't have a consensus on where we fit into it all?"

The old man sucked his teeth. "How do we have time to sit by and talk about who we are when we can't even put food on the table? We need to organize, like they're doing in California!"

"Mm, I see the man from CSO has been talking to you, then," Verón responded.

Marco leaned over to me, and though I didn't turn to face him, I could feel his eyes on me. "Community Service Organization," he whispered.

"I *know*," I lied.

"Listen, I hear what you are saying. I do. I have been speaking with CSO as well. What they are doing out West, it's promising. Registering people to vote. Preparing to strike. But what they are doing, it is not without risks. I want to make sure we are prepared for those risks, and part of those preparations include coming together as a unified force, ¿entiende?" The old man nodded begrudgingly, and Verón continued. "I thank you, Hidalgo, for bringing this topic up, though. That is, of course, why we are here: to discuss the issues that impact our communities. Gracias, amigo."

Suddenly, it hit me. I put my hand on Marco's arm, noting the way he jolted at the sudden contact. "Wait, that's *Victor* from *En este momento*?"

He eyed my hand resting on his forearm before he nodded.

I returned my attention to Verón, dropping my hand back into my lap, fingertips tingling. This man, with his thin hair and determined gaze, was the man on the radio that I'd heard *countless* times. Every single morning! Despite the radio show being a staple in most households in our barrio, he had never shared his full name, referring to himself just as Victor, "su amigo en este momento."

"As we discussed last time, so many of our hardships are difficult to prove, in a legal sense, because under many laws, Mexicans are classified as white. However, as we know, we still face discrimination." He paused, surveying the room as people nodded in agreement. "We've been weighing the benefits and consequences of identifying ourselves as white for some time now. It's a complex conversation. LULAC is here with us today to talk about something called the Chicano Movement—another thing that's happening out in California. Manuel, are you ready?"

I stole a glance at Marco as the guest speaker joined Verón in the center of the room. Marco's customary smugness was still there, but it was barely hanging on. His clear interest couldn't be concealed by even his best attempts at apathy.

As I listened, a thousand questions raced through my mind about this group of people. About El Foro. About the issues they were discussing and the groups they represented and the goals they had for people who were both Mexicans and Americans. For people like us.

But perhaps the most persistent question, the one that kept popping up every few minutes, was why Marco had thought to bring me here.

Fifteen

Friday, September 2, 1955

The sun approached the top of the mountains in a dusky cloak of purple and orange as we left the redbrick church behind us and began our walk home.

"How did you find out about this place?" I asked Marco. "El Foro?" The name felt unfamiliar on my tongue.

"I *listen*," he said pointedly.

I glared at him. "Why did you even bring me if you're only going to tease me for my questions?"

He considered this with a frown before giving in. "Some guys at work told me about it," he said vaguely. He cleared his throat, running one hand along his hair as if it wasn't already slicked back into place. His other hand still held my books, hanging casually by his side. "What is it?" he asked suddenly, his tone far less aloof this time. He sounded caught off guard.

I looked over at him, somehow getting the impression that

he'd been watching me as we walked together. "What do you mean?"

His brows furrowed, and he gave a little shake of his head, like he was going to ignore my question—even though he'd started that line of inquiry. But there was the faintest touch of concern to his voice when he finally said, "You just . . . you look like you're thinking pretty hard over there."

I made a face. "I *like* to think."

"Oh sure." He laughed dryly. "Who doesn't?"

"I *do*," I insisted, hearing the childish hitch in my voice even as I said it. I felt my cheeks warm. Why was I bothering? Why did I care what Marco thought?

"Okay," he said blithely. "Want to talk about whatever it is you're thinking about?"

I lost my footing at this, stumbling slightly. "With you?"

This time the sound that came out of him was much more than a chuckle. A full-throated laugh. I wasn't sure I'd ever heard him laugh like that. He made a big show of looking around us for someone else, but the farm-lined road we walked along was vacant aside from the two of us. "Gee, it sure seems like I'm the best option you have," he drawled. "I'm betting your pal Ramón is a bit too tied up to chat with you right about now, if you know what I mean." His eyes gleamed deviously.

I cut a glare at him, clamping my mouth shut to hide my curled lip. I let a frustrated breath out of my nose. "Why . . ." I spat out, irritation making it hard to speak. I shook my head.

"Why what?" His voice was gentler now, but when I chanced a glance at him, he still had that unnerving quality about him, like he was just waiting for me to say something he could pounce on. Something he could hold over my head.

"Why did you bring me here, Marco?" I supposed that was as good as any place to start.

"You seemed angry."

"What do you know about how I'm feeling?" I snapped, heart racing. What I really wondered was when *how* he'd noticed this, but I wasn't going to ask him that.

He gave me a knowing look that only fueled my annoyance.

"So what if I'm angry?" I mumbled.

"Well, that's why I started coming to El Foro," he admitted. He tipped his chin, as if anticipating what I was about to say. "I've been angry for a while, but after I left school . . . I don't know. It got worse after I dropped out, I guess."

"And El Foro helped?" I asked, searching my memory for some marked change in the brooding, mysterious Marco Montoya who had always lurked in the background of my memories.

He shrugged stiffly. "Some days, I suppose. Other days it's all a bit square; it's a lot of talking, more talking than I'd like. But it's also given me new ways to think about the things that make me angry."

"And you think I need that?" I fought to keep my voice flat, determined not to let him know how vulnerable it made me feel that he'd noted my feelings without me even realizing and had come to this conclusion.

The only answer I got was the crunch of our shoes on the dusty roadside.

The thing was, I was angry. I was angry at Ramón and Julianne, there was no question about it. But maybe there was more to it. Perhaps my anger had more to do with this whole situation. The predicament we were forced into. The circumstances that brought me to North in the first place—that necessitated my lies—and the same circumstances that kept Ramón out.

This realization settled itself in my chest like a piece of food I hadn't chewed properly.

"The workers here have been trying to unionize, like the farm workers in California," Marco explained slowly. "It's been a big topic around here, as you might have figured out. Verón, he knows everyone, so he was helping connect them to different groups and leaders—and that's how El Foro got started, really. A place for all the groups doing community work to come together and discuss issues and hopefully unify."

I nodded, wondering if Verón was the same organizer Papi had been complaining about at dinner the other night, accusing him of stirring up trouble. "And has it helped unify people?"

He sighed, shaking his head. "Verón says this is a starting point, whatever that means."

"I see." If I understood anything, it was starting points. The kind of imperfect beginnings that often preceded messy and slow-moving endeavors.

"So, princesa, what *do* you think?"

"Hmm?"

"Of the meeting," Marco said with an arched eyebrow. "Of El Foro. What are your thoughts?" He tapped his temple with his forefinger.

"Oh," I said. "It was interesting. And confusing."

I braced myself for some jab about me being silly or naive or spoiled, but it didn't come. He waited, tilting his head for me to continue.

"I guess . . ." I chewed on my lip, thinking of Papi's endless lectures on how I had to blend in, how I had to do things the right way in order to make a better life for myself in the future. He was always so certain about that, and I'd believed him, but now, it gave me pause. "I didn't know there were so many ways to look at all these issues," I said slowly. I wasn't sure if those were the right words, but I said them anyway, letting them hang in the air like a fine mist.

Marco nodded, and though it looked like he was doing his best to not appear smug, he wasn't entirely successful.

I stopped walking suddenly and looked at him head-on, squaring myself directly in his path. Dusk was upon us, the sun tucked behind the mountain peaks, and Marco's face was all shadows and contrast. "What do you think about Ramón and my friend Julianne being together?"

His lips twisted in surprise.

"They said they're in love," I added with a feeble laugh, but he didn't laugh back.

"Then I suppose it doesn't much matter what I think." He shifted my books underneath his arm as he reached into his back pocket to get his lighter and a squashed box of Lucky Strikes. As he placed a cigarette between his lips, he glanced at me. "What do *you* think about it?" he asked, his words slightly garbled. He'd asked me about my opinions more in the past hour than he had in our entire lives.

"I suppose it doesn't much matter what I think," I parroted back, not trusting his sudden interest in the inner workings of my mind.

That did get a small chuckle out of him as he touched the flame of his lighter to the butt of the cigarette.

"Do *you* think they're in love?" I pushed.

Marco took a long drag. "You know my brother as well as I do," he said. "He's got a lot of love to give."

I found myself nodding. "Maybe too much love."

Marco considered this. "Maybe," he said, the cigarette bobbing between his lips.

"The way they're running around, they're going to get caught, and then who knows what will happen?" It made my chest ache just thinking about it. "It's so dangerous, don't you think?"

Marco flicked some ash onto the ground with a sigh. "It is. A lot of things are dangerous, though. Isn't going to school there dangerous? But you think it's worth it, right?"

"Ramón said the same thing to me, you know."

He nodded. "Well, it's true, isn't it?"

I bit down on my lip and nodded reluctantly. "Yeah, I guess it is. But . . . it's different."

"It is," he agreed. "It is different, but who's to say it wouldn't be worth the risks too?" We stood in silence as he finished his cigarette, the thin stream of smoke drifting up toward the darkening sky. "Come on," he growled, tossing the remaining bit into the dirt and squashing it beneath his heel. "Let's get you home, your royal highness."

I rolled my eyes. "I can get myself home."

"I don't doubt that," Marco quipped. "But I've got your books." He waved them at me as he began walking. After a moment, I joined him.

"You're home late, querida," Mamá said as soon as I walked in the front door. I barely heard her. My mind was still roaring with all the questions from this evening.

I offered her a thin smile as I tried to set everything from El Foro aside, for now at least. I wouldn't want to worry her. I tried to ground myself with the smell of enchiladas and the sound of baby Guillermo cooing happily and the open newspaper Papi held in front of him in the living room.

Mamá glanced up at me from the stove, where she stood wearing her floral apron with its frayed edges and faded pockets.

Blanca was seated at the kitchen table holding the baby in her lap, and she shot me a pointed look. I realized a little guiltily that she had probably been expecting me to come to her house after school, like I normally did. I had been planning on it, but obviously nothing about this afternoon had been typical.

I set my bookbag on the empty chair next to my sister. "I had a school project to work on," I lied, tickling one of Guillermo's bare feet to avoid meeting Blanca's gaze.

Blanca shifted in her chair to look at me straight on, her brows furrowed. I noticed the weary circles under her eyes and the fine lines forming around her mouth.

Papi gave an approving grunt from behind his paper. "Our Rosa, what a smart girl you are."

"Mm," Mamá agreed. She turned in our small kitchen, stroked my hair, and placed a soft kiss on my forehead.

Across from me, Blanca stiffened. Abruptly, she got to her feet and began singing softly to Guillermo, bouncing him gently with her back to us.

Smart. Right. I wasn't so sure he'd say that if he knew the kind of mess I'd gotten myself into with Ramón and Julianne—and even with Marco and El Foro.

The briefest pang of remorse struck me, but I found if I didn't look at my mother or sister for too long, if I just focused on the grooves of wood in our kitchen table, I could squash it down small enough to ignore.

Sixteen

Tuesday, September 6, 1955

"All right," I said, sitting down next to Julianne at our normal lunch table in the courtyard.

She paused with her sandwich halfway to her mouth and frowned, mouth slightly agape. "All right?" she repeated in puzzlement, head cocked to one side.

"You and Ramón are *in love.*" I hoped I sounded cool and breezy. Modern, progressive, enlightened. I hoped she couldn't hear my lingering fear and skepticism. "You have my . . . *support.*" It sounded strange, that word—but I tried not to dwell on it.

Her eyes brightened for a moment before she seemed to catch herself. She set her sandwich down on the paper sack before her. "You're serious, aren't you?"

I hesitated before I nodded. I was. I was scared and confused and all sorts of things—but I was serious too. I'd given it a lot of thought over the weekend, ever since the El Foro meeting.

"Can I ask why you've had a change of heart?" I could see the mix of worry and hope swimming in her deep blue eyes.

"It wasn't so much a change of heart," I admitted. "I changed my mind. Or at least I'm trying to keep an *open* mind." I considered briefly telling her about Marco and the community groups. I was certain she'd be interested. In fact, she'd probably want to come with me next time. But I didn't even know if there'd be a next time yet, let alone if that was a place for her. So I bit my tongue.

There were so many unknowns in my life right now, and the more I could keep under wraps, the better.

Julianne made a soft humming sound, clearly curious but not bold enough to push for more information. At least not yet. "Well, all right, then. I suppose now I should tell you the next bit."

My heart lurched. "There's *more*?"

She leaned toward me even though we were already sitting fairly close to one another. "You see, I agree with a lot of what you said about people not liking me and him together. So we've come up with a plan."

"A plan?" I repeated, unable to keep the dread out of my voice. "What sort of plan?"

Her denim-blue eyes glinted, and she suddenly had the scheming demeanor of an aspiring bank robber. "We're going to go to the Silver and Blue Ball together."

"What?" I nearly shouted. *"Why?* Why would you want to

bring him here for that?" I struggled to keep my voice low, both to avoid being overheard and to conceal my terror at this notion. I couldn't begin to fathom why they'd want to flaunt this romance like that, to throw themselves in the crux of scrutiny and scandal.

"We want to use our love for one another as a force for good," she said, flushing instantly at the disbelieving look I gave her. "Like I said, I know it's not without risks, which is why we want to take a stand. To speak out against the stigma of a relationship like ours. There shouldn't be anything wrong with what we're doing, and yet—"

"Julianne, is that what this is really about? Is this all some sort of protest or rebellion—"

"No!" she interrupted, eyes wide. "No, of course not, Rosie. We truly care about each other. Really, you have to believe me. I *love* him." Her voice caught a bit at this, like just talking about her feelings for Ramón was enough to make her tearful. "We both believe in a better world. A more equal one. And we both want to be a part of making it happen. It's something we talk about all the time. We think this thing between us, it could be meaningful for others as well. Maybe if we show up together, somewhere that's a big deal to folks, then we can make a statement. But we'll need your help."

I couldn't stop myself from snorting. It was ridiculous and silly and idealistic and exactly the type of thing Ramón would be drawn to.

Maybe they had more in common than I'd thought.

Maybe there was something here.

My pulse raced as I considered this plan. I tried to see it all from another angle—from *their* angle—like El Foro had shown me. I tried to keep my fear from boxing me in.

But it wasn't easy.

"Julianne," I said slowly. "I just need to hear you say it. That you know all of this . . . it really is dangerous. Especially for Ramón."

She nodded quickly, emphatically. "Of course. I *do* know that."

"I know you've said it," I conceded. "But this is all happening so fast, don't you think? Have you really stopped and thought about what's at stake?"

She opened her mouth to jump in with another swift assurance—another grandiose proclamation—but caught herself and let me speak.

"If you really do care about Ramón the way you say you do"—at this, she gave a decisive nod—"you'll think about the risks he and I are facing."

She worried her lower lip before speaking. "I do, Rosie. I care about you both."

"Interracial marriage is illegal in this country, you know that. Miscegenation—"

"No one's talking about getting married," she said in a light, hurried way that made me certain that it had come up between the two of them. I could just picture sweet, romantic Ramón whispering questions of white dresses and gold bands in her ear.

"I know," I said anyway. "But my point is, this is serious. A lot of folks will think the idea of the two of you in love is *wrong*. They don't want people like me and Ramón in their schools, for one. Or their restaurants or neighborhoods or anywhere, really. And they certainly don't want us going steady with people like you."

She was quiet for a moment, her lips pressed into a thin line, and I realized this was the first time I'd openly acknowledged who I really was to Julianne.

My pulse pounded in my temples as I waited to hear if she'd try to brush off my concerns or downplay it or . . . well, I wasn't sure. But she didn't do any of that. Instead, she sat with what I said, really thinking about it, and just gave me a simple, slow nod.

"All right," I said with a sigh. "Tell me more about this plan of yours, then."

Friendships could take you to unexpected places. I think that was true for most people.

I thought about my father and Ramón's father, Roberto Montoya. They met in basic training. I was only three when Papi left for the Second Great War, so I didn't really remember a time before their friendship was woven into the very fabric of our family.

They weren't in a segregated unit, like the Puerto Rican and black soldiers were, which I guess had its own challenges. Though they both spoke English well enough, there was still something isolating about being the only person from your culture in a large group, so I think they were thankful to have each other, even before they truly understood the value of having someone to count on through the war.

At the time, the Montoyas lived near Tucson, two hours away from Golden Gate and the rest of Phoenix, not far from the Mexican border. Like my parents, Señor Montoya was a farmworker, though Señora Montoya didn't work back then. She stayed home and cared for Ramón and Marco, who were three and four, as well as her mother-in-law, who was ill and lived with them. Señor Montoya's mother passed away shortly after he and Papi arrived in Europe, and though it freed Señora Montoya up to get a job—something she desperately needed—it was obviously a troubling loss that haunted Señor Montoya more than he ever fully let on.

At least that's what Papi said. It was one of the very few things he said about that time of his life.

Within a year of the war ending, the Montoyas moved to Phoenix in search of more opportunities. I was almost eight, which meant I was old enough to notice things but not quite old enough to understand them. I remembered there was a weary hopefulness to my father and his new friend. They always looked tired, even first thing in the morning, but they talked animatedly about the future. There were dark circles under their eyes, but they both had a relentless gleam in their gaze.

"Can't you see it?" Señor Montoya would say to us, waving his hand in the air. "A dance hall, just like the Riverside Ballroom—except ours will let Mexicans in *every* night, not just once a week."

Ramón and I would nod at this, like we understood why it mattered.

"Hector will take care of the business," he'd say, gesturing to Papi. "And me? I'll be in charge of the music." He'd strum a little song on his guitar or spin Señora Montoya in a dance at this part.

It was a beautiful dream. I loved listening to them bicker about paint colors and headlining bands as they fantasized about one day seeing their own marquee lit up on the roadside. Looking back, even as a small girl, I understood it was just a fantasy. An escape. It must've been something Papi did that gave me that impression. Something in his voice or face that told me those nightly conversations after dinner about music and dancing and moneymaking were just make-believe. Though, try as I might, I couldn't put my finger on how exactly I knew.

Or how the Montoyas could've missed it.

For them, it wasn't pretending. Despite all the outlandish details we'd drum up in the early evenings, Señor Montoya and his boys *believed* it would all come to fruition one of these days. Marco saved up to buy a bass of his own to accompany his father on the stage, and Ramón would practice his singing for us almost every single night.

I wasn't sure when exactly the fantasy fell apart for them. When Señor Montoya realized, even as veterans, they were not going to be able to scrounge up the kind of money or connections necessary to open a club. When he realized that perhaps Papi suspected this all along.

I'd never had the courage to burden Papi or Ramón with

my questions about what happened, but I was pretty sure this realization was connected to Señor Montoya's death somehow. Everything from the war, plus the disappointment of realizing his wildest dream was never going to be anything more than that—well, that was a heavy load to bear. A crushing load that he couldn't survive.

I knew that this thing with Julianne—as much as it didn't make sense to me—had the potential to crush Ramón in the same way. And I knew I had to do my part to make sure it didn't.

SEEKING ADVICE: HOME OWNERSHIP IN NORTH PHOENIX. IS IT POSSIBLE?

El Sol, Spanish-language newspaper
January 17, 1954

My family and I are hoping to purchase a home in the Willo neighborhood of Phoenix near North Phoenix High School and the Phoenix Country Club. Though we might not be able to access all the amenities yet, as a new lawyer with a young family, I believe this part of town holds more opportunities. However, many of the houses we have been interested in have racially restrictive covenants that prohibit the sale to persons with, as one deed called it, "perceptible strains of Asiatic, Mexican, Mexican-Indian, Negro, Filipino, or Hindu races." As a Mexican family, do we have any hope of purchasing a home in this area? Is our only option going to court?

Sincerely,

Hopeful Homebuyer
of Phoenix

Dear Hopeful Homebuyer,

Moving to the Willo neighborhood—or any other wealthy, predominately white area—is possible. But at what cost?

Seventeen

Wednesday, September 7, 1955

"So I see you made up with your friend," Tim whispered to me as we sat down in math class. I shot him a confused look as I opened my textbook. He had never sat close enough to me to talk before, not here.

"I haven't seen you in the library this week," he said by way of explanation.

I nodded warily. It almost seemed like Tim had missed me this afternoon. That couldn't be it, could it? I tried to keep my expression neutral as I told him, "Um, yes, we talked."

Tim slung his bookbag over the back of his chair. He was quite a bit bigger than most full-grown men, and it was hard to ignore how out of place he looked in his desk. When he was in the back of the classroom surrounded by other bulky football players, he was tucked out of the way, and his large, muscular frame was far less imposing.

"I'm sorry you had to eat lunch alone," I said, watching him as he gingerly set his homework in front of him.

He responded with a smile and an easy shrug that pulled at the crisp fabric of his neatly pressed oxford shirt ever so slightly. "I'm used to eating lunch alone." It might have sounded like a complaint coming from anyone else, but he said it with a lightness that made me wonder, yet again, why it was that someone like Tim Buckles didn't eat lunch with a crowd of friends or teammates. "I did like getting to sit with a fellow outsider for a little bit, though."

It took me a heartbeat to realize what exactly he had just said. He said it so freely, so openly. But when it did hit me, I froze in a flash of fiery panic. The room suddenly felt too small, too stuffy, too cramped.

Fellow *outsider*? What on earth did that mean?

It felt strange to keep a secret from my family, but I knew I had to.

We'd always been close, the four of us. Our tiny little casita didn't leave much room for distance. Blanca and I didn't even have our own room until I was twelve, when my parents had finally saved up enough to tack on a spare bedroom.

But it was also more than that, much more than forced closeness. Family felt like all I could count on in a world that made no sense to me—a world that was often capricious and unfair and cruel. A lot of families in Golden Gate were huge, with branches and roots that wound their way throughout the south side. Families like us and the Montoyas—small ones without aunts, uncles, cousins—were far less common. Usually, it meant our family trees had been cut short by tragedy.

Papi was the youngest of seven boys, and his parents had long since passed by the time I entered the world. My tíos were spread across the Southwest, some in Texas, some in California, some in New Mexico. They were all in farmwork, just like Papi and just like their parents. A few of them were migrant workers who traveled with different crops in different seasons, and they would visit occasionally. Papi's side of the family was more like a vine.

But Mamá's family? Well, that was where I could see the axe that had cut into our family tree. The sharp blade of injustice and violence hacking away at our limbs.

They called it repatriation, but I didn't think that term made sense. Not that any of it was based on sense, of course. Mamá and her brother and sister were born in Los Angeles, after all. The United States was their homeland.

But *home* was one of those arbitrary things people didn't pay much attention to in times of crisis. The crash of 1929 hit a lot of people hard, but when it came to people like her family, who were already just scraping by, it hit them the worst. President Hoover summed it up pretty clearly with his slogan: "Real American jobs for real Americans."

It started with pushing Mexican people out of jobs to free up some work for white folks. But when things didn't improve, people wanted more. Wanted Mexicans out of here in general.

They called it voluntary repatriation. Discounted train tickets across the border, stuff like that.

But it quickly escalated. People were dragged onto buses. Threatened. It didn't matter if they could prove they were citizens.

Though it happened all over the place, not just in the border states, from what I'd read, Los Angeles had some of the worst raids. People were deported from hospitals and schools and parks and just dumped on the Mexican side of the border with nothing. Nada.

They'd swarmed Mamá's barrio in East Los Angeles, blocking off exits and snatching people right off the streets. Mamá and her brother, Miguel, somehow got out, sneaking through alleys and backyards, running as if their lives depended on it.

But their parents and their younger sister, Rosario, hadn't been as quick or fortunate.

They never made it back to the US. Part of it, I thought, was the hassle of appealing their deportation. Fruitless paperwork. But part of it was also their pride. They'd been betrayed by their country, and they couldn't bring themselves to endure the humiliation of trying to return.

Mamá and Tío Miguel stayed, though, mostly at their parents' insistence. They may have been barred from the life they'd planned for themselves and forced to start over, but there was no reason their eldest children had to do so too.

It was hard on both of them. Tío Miguel, just fifteen and only three years older than Mamá, wasn't prepared to raise himself, let alone his younger sister too. Mamá dropped out of school at the age of twelve to work. They exchanged countless letters with their parents and little sister, but they never risked a border crossing.

Mamá never saw her parents or sister again.

Shortly after she married Papi, when she was pregnant with Blanca, she'd received a letter from one of her parents' neighbors saying her parents and little sister had been killed in a bus accident coming home from church. Mamá and Tío Miguel were not just the only ones left in the United States, they were the only ones left at all—until Tío Miguel was drafted about three months after Papi left for the war. He died in a remote village in Italy.

Unlike Papi, Mamá talked about her pain regularly. She said it was her job, as the last one in her family, to keep their memories alive. To make sure the cruelty that robbed her of them would never be forgotten. To remind us how important it was to hold each other close, to protect one another at all costs.

Eighteen

Thursday, September 8, 1955

"Why do I even need a date to the dance?" I asked Julianne over lunch, running my fingers along the pasted-down edges of the plan in my notebook. "This is about you and Ramón, not me." My eyes lingered on the military times she jotted down—a habit she'd picked up from her father—the coded initials, and the ominous question mark where the name of my date should be.

Julianne rolled her eyes, not at me necessarily but at some larger, unseen annoyance. "If my mother finds out you don't have a date, she'll try to fix you up with someone. And trust me, no good will come of her meddling," she muttered.

"We can't just say we're meeting our dates at the school?"

She shot me a look. "My mother has been prattlin' on about this dance since the Fourth of July. There's no way she's missing a chance to snap my picture and make a big fuss at the house."

"Okay, well, why can't you just meet me at the school, then? You and Ramón can have your pictures and fuss and what have you, and I'll be here . . . alone." I cringed even hearing myself say it. Waiting around at the ball by myself was hardly any more appealing than figuring out who should escort me.

She made a face. "My folks would never allow me to be in a car with a boy, just the two of us," she admitted. "Besides, I thought we were in this together, right? The whole thing?"

I took a deep breath, trying to quell my uneasiness before I nodded. "Yes. Yes, you're right. We are." She smiled at this. "It's just, who am I supposed to go with?" I asked her, feeling my cheeks warm as I said it. It was a lot easier to accept that no one was likely to ask me when I didn't plan on going.

"You said Tim Buckles has been friendly with you, right?" Her voice was light and innocent, but there was a calculating gleam in her blue eyes. She ran her fingers along the bow that adorned the top of her pink pullover.

My blushing deepened as I strategically avoided her gaze.

"I think he's just being nice," I said hastily. "Tim's a nice guy. That doesn't mean anything. It definitely doesn't mean he's going to ask me to the dance." My chest tightened as I thought of him calling us outsiders last week.

"He's *very* nice," she agreed with a knowing smirk. "Which is why he's perfect. You should *hint* at it. Suggest it to him?" She batted her eyes prettily at me, playful.

"Julianne, you do remember this isn't just a dance," I said, lowering my voice but keeping an edge to it. "This is more than putting on a fancy dress and fox-trotting with a boy who may or may not like me."

Julianne cleared her throat, her smile falling. "Of course I do."

"Do we really want to get Tim mixed up in all this?"

She tilted her head. "What do you mean?"

"Do I really need to bring him along as my date is what I'm asking."

A flash of emotions crossed Julianne's face, none of which I was prepared to decipher. "Yes. I think to keep it all a secret until we get to the dance, we need Tim there. And it would be swell if it was Tim since my family already knows him. I can tell my folks that Tim is my date, and Ramón is yours, and then we'll be able to keep it all under wraps until we get to school. Until it's too late for my parents to stop us."

"You think they'd try to stop us?" I asked. "I mean, I thought your father was a moderate. When President Eisenhower said he'd use the National Guard to enforce integration, didn't your dad make a big show of pledging officers to support?"

Julianne nodded slowly. "He did."

"So isn't there a chance he'd be supportive of this too? In the name of progress and all that?"

I wondered if it was pity in her eyes the longer she looked at me. "Maybe. But you said yourself that people were going to have some strong feelings about this."

I didn't understand this sense of caution when we were planning something so risky anyway. It was such a fine balance, and it just wasn't clear to me when to be bold and when to tread softly. Or why.

I wasn't sure I was cut out for this sort of thing.

"It would just be best if it all came to light at the dance," she insisted. "More meaningful."

More meaningful? It was more public, certainly. And more dangerous.

In Julianne's and Ramón's minds, it was a demonstration. Ramón had said it was really about the power of love, about love and equality. But I couldn't ignore that it was also a charade and a spectacle, layers of ambiguity and deceit. Would their good intentions matter if things went awry?

"We'll go to the dance as a mixed couple. Everyone will be surprised, sure, but they'll see how happy we are. And then you'll write a newspaper article about it that will enlighten others and change minds and—"

"That's the other thing, Julianne. How do we know Simon will even publish what I've written?"

"One thing at a time," she said, trying hard to maintain her chipper tone despite all my concerns. "You'll talk to Tim, won't you?" she said finally. Quietly.

So much of this plan hinged on me and my ability to do things I'd never done before.

The bell chimed, and around us, people began to rise, idly collecting their lunches and books and knapsacks as they chatted and laughed. I could feel Julianne watching me, willing me to look at her. A knot coiled itself in the pit of my stomach.

Maybe it was silly. In the grand scheme of things, whether

I flirted with Tim Buckles was inconsequential. It wouldn't go down in history books. It might not even register as a memorable life event for Tim or me when we were old and gray, looking back on our pasts.

But I also couldn't ignore what it would lead to. The essential part it played. It felt like a defining moment. It would set our plan in motion. And our plan, just maybe, would end up mattering. In some way, at least.

Finally, I nodded and got to my feet.

A girl could hope, right?

Nineteen

Thursday, September 8, 1955

I didn't know how I expected Tim to act when I brought up the Silver and Blue Ball.

Surprised?

Confused?

I never once thought that he'd seem relieved, but that's what he was. Relieved.

He let out a puff of air, like he'd been holding his breath for weeks, and wiped away a bead of sweat. We were standing just outside the math room. The hallway was nearly empty save for a lone straggler stooped over the drinking fountain and a pair of sophomores holding hands and gazing into each other's eyes by the janitor's closet.

"I think that'd be really swell if we went together," he said, his words tumbling into one another in a half chuckle. "*Really* swell." His cheeks had a rosy roundness to them that made him seem particularly boyish despite his size.

"As . . . friends, right?" I ventured nervously. I wanted him to say yes, of course, but I liked Tim, and I knew I had to manage the false pretenses of this whole evening as much as I could. Maybe I couldn't tell him about our whole plan, but I could spare him some extra heartache.

Again, he surprised me with his reaction, nodding eagerly as his grin widened. "Sure. Yes. That'd be great, Rosie."

"Oh, good. That's good to hear," I told him. "I was hoping we could go with Julianne?"

His smile faltered slightly, but he nodded. "Oh. Oh, sure. I mean, a lot of the football guys are going together, but I guess you don't know too many of those fellas, do you?" I shook my head. "So that probably wouldn't be too much fun for you, then."

I thought about shaking my head again but caught myself. He didn't seem to be too close of friends with any of them, but he still might have thought it was rude.

"I guess we'll see them all there, anyway." He seemed like he was talking to himself, like he was working something out in his head. He rubbed the back of his neck. "Is she, um, going with Peter, then?" This time I did shake my head. "Oh," he said with a thoughtful frown. But he didn't ask who Julianne's date was, and I didn't offer any additional information. We just stood there, smiling at one another. "Great."

"Great," I repeated.

There was an eager glimmer in his eyes that I felt flickering inside of myself too. A curiosity tinged with just the tiniest bit of unease about what was to come.

Only in hindsight would that feeling strike me as fatefully disastrous.

Twenty

Monday, September 12, 1955

I got off the bus a stop early. Just like I had the day of the El Foro meeting.

I tried to tell myself that I did it without thinking, that I wasn't sure why I'd done it.

But I found my eyes glued to the other side of the street the second the bus doors swooshed shut behind me. And it wasn't until I realized no one was standing outside that my disappointment registered with me.

I was looking for Marco. I was hoping to see him.

What was wrong with me? One mildly intriguing afternoon with him did not make up for years of being ignored and taunted, did not make up for the last couple years of clear contempt.

I tried to shake away the fizzle of frustration as my eyes

searched for any sign of him. But the parking lot was empty, save for an idling Bashas' truck, likely awaiting a load of produce to be packed inside.

I'm just wondering about the next El Foro meeting, I told myself. *That's all.*

I supposed I could go without him, now that I knew about the meetings. In fact, maybe I'd see him there

My heart lurched suddenly when I spotted two figures toward the front of the truck who had been concealed from view until I walked past. I slowed, peering at them from across the street.

It was Marco. And Verón.

I couldn't hear them from this distance, certainly not over the rumble of the truck engine, but the way they stood told me they were arguing. Or at least Marco was. He was so rigid as he threw his hands up in the air, as he shook his head, as he refused to meet Verón's eye.

Verón moved toward him, bowing his head down even though they were almost the exact same height. He tried to put his arm around Marco, but Marco shook it off. Verón said something else to him before trying again. Marco hesitated, but he eventually let Verón pull him into a hug.

I looked away, quickening my pace down a side street that would put me out of their line of sight.

There was something so sweet about that embrace. So paternal. I had no idea they were so close. The way Marco had spoken of him at the meeting had been respectful, yes, but also disgruntled. A little wary.

But the nearness of them here at Marco's work, the obvious emotions being exchanged . . . I wasn't sure what to make of it.

But I was sure I wanted to get out of there before Marco saw me.

Twenty-One

Friday, September 16, 1955

"I think what this piece needs is a quote," Simon said as Walter and I pored over my notes and his draft of the pep rally article. We were both within earshot, but he looked at Walter as he spoke.

Walter grunted in agreement. "Maybe a football player?"

Simon snapped his fingers. "Yeah, that'd be perfect. Rosie, why don't you pop out to the football field real quick? See if you can grab one of them on their way to warm up?"

Instinctively, I turned toward Julianne's desk to exchange an exasperated eye roll but caught myself as I remembered that she wasn't there. That she'd been skipping out on all her afternoon activities to meet up with Ramón.

I sighed. "Sure thing." I grabbed a notepad and pencil from my bookbag as Simon and Walter began discussing the article's lede.

Maybe I'd be able to find Tim. But as I opened the classroom door, I stumbled upon someone else pacing just outside in the hallway. Someone sporting shoulder pads and an anxious frown.

Peter Duke.

He startled as he spotted me but quickly wiped away any traces of surprise as he straightened his shoulders. "Is J-Julianne in there?" He held his football helmet against his hip, and I noticed the white-knuckle grip he had on it.

"No," I said slowly, carefully, as I watched frustration darken his expression.

He shifted his weight on his feet. "Do you know where she is?"

I shook my head. I knew *who* she was with, of course, but I had no idea where the two of them made off to during their afternoons together. I wasn't sure I wanted to know.

Peter's mouth clamped down into a grimace as he appeared to weigh his next words. Several seconds of silence passed, and he moved to turn away. I assumed he'd decided whatever was so clearly on his mind was not worth asking, but instead he paused, turning to me with his eyes fixed on the floor. "I heard she's already got a date to the dance," he said, voice low. "Is that true? Do you know who it is?"

I started to shrug before I realized he wasn't even looking at me. His eyes were still downcast, like he was embarrassed to be having this conversation at all.

"I think he goes to another school."

Peter's sun-kissed cheeks blanched as he looked up at me,

finally, with a scrutinizing stare that bore right through me. "A college guy?"

"No, I don't think so."

His face remained stern as he nodded and again turned to walk away.

"Um, Peter?" I called out.

He stopped, casting me a curious and impatient look over his shoulder.

"Do you think you could give me a quote about the pep rally?" I held up my notepad. "For the paper?"

He gave me a preoccupied nod as he fixed his helmet on his head. "Sure. It was swell. Go, Mustangs!" He started jogging off before he even finished talking, calling the last bit out so it echoed back down the hallway.

Twenty-Two

Friday, September 16, 1955

I'd cut out of newspaper club early, right after I'd gotten that silly quote from Peter. I'd blamed a stomachache that started out as a lie but turned genuine when I heard three of the other staff writers burst into laughter as they took turns making fun of Desi Arnaz in a recent episode of *I Love Lucy*, their fake Spanish increasingly ridiculous.

Because of all this, I'd caught an earlier bus home. And this partially accounted for my surprise at finding Marco Montoya waiting for me as soon as I stepped off the bus.

Or at least I guessed he was waiting for me. Why else would he have been there?

And, perhaps most perplexing of all, why exactly was I so pleased to see him?

That was the thing about Marco. It seemed that everything he did roused up more and more questions. Nothing was straightforward. He was a winding path of a person that could lead me off the edge of a cliff at any moment.

He sat on the ground, his back against the brick wall of the Chinese grocery, legs outstretched. A paperback rested in his hands, his eyes peering over it as I approached.

"*1984?*" I asked as I walked toward him.

"You read it?" He folded the corner of the page to mark his spot before getting to his feet. His dark cuffed jeans had some dust on them, but he didn't move to brush it off.

I shook my head. "No, our school library doesn't carry it. All the parents and teachers were pretty worked up, making sure it didn't end up anywhere near the school. They say it's not appropriate."

He gave a knowing snort, folding the book into a roll and stuffing it into his back pocket. "I'll bet."

"What's it about, anyway?"

"Resisting an oppressive government," he said. "And of course, a bit of communism and sex to get the nice, decent folks really 'worked up,' as you said." His smirk turned completely wicked, and I suspected he noticed the blush I felt hitting my cheeks.

"Oh," I choked out awkwardly, searching frantically for a change of subject. "Marco, about the other day . . ." Even as I said it, I wasn't sure what the end of that sentence was.

He shook his head with a dismissive grimace. "What are—"

"What am I doing right now?" I finished for him, dropping my voice to a husky, teasing impression of him.

His lips fought a smile. "Yes."

"You're awfully interested in the day-to-day activities of 'la princesa' all of a sudden," I pointed out, equally fascinated by this crack in his dark demeanor. I couldn't help but wonder what other reactions I could coax from him.

"You're right. Forget it, your highness." His tone didn't sound serious, but he also didn't say anything more. Didn't keep teasing. He started to turn away.

Before I could stop myself, I reached out for him. My hand grazed his upper arm. Half on the soft sun-worn cotton of his white shirt and half on the firm tawny skin of his bicep. I recoiled almost as soon as I made contact.

I wasn't sure which of these caught his attention—me grabbing him or jolting away like I'd been scalded—but he paused and turned to face me again regardless, eyes glinting with intrigue.

"There's another El Foro meeting today," he said. His gaze dropped down to my hand, which now hung by my side. Could he sense the way it was tingling too? There was no way, but still, the expression on his face suggested he sensed *something*. "Thought you might be interested."

"All right." I nodded. "But it's barely four o'clock."

He shrugged. "Maybe we could go for a walk." He shrugged once more, as if to really make it seem like an idea that had just occurred to him spontaneously, though somehow it had the opposite effect.

I thought briefly of my conversation with Blanca just a few

weeks ago, when I'd promised her I'd keep my head down and stay out of trouble. But I was already embroiled in trouble—trouble that wasn't Marco's making either.

And while I didn't know for certain whether that made it all right, I heard myself saying, "Sure. Let's go for a walk."

Twenty-Three

Friday, September 16, 1955

Normally, a walk alone with a boy under the shaded seclusion of the canal would have been ill-advised at best. Though Ramón and I had spent at least half our childhood splashing about in these waters, it was generally accepted that past the age of twelve, boys and girls shouldn't be unsupervised together.

I could only imagine that rule was doubly serious for boys like Marco Montoya.

There was something undeniably wild and unpredictable about Marco; I'd always known that. What was new, however, was my growing curiosity about him and everything that made him so wild and unpredictable. Instead of writing him off for being unruly and shameless and cavalier, I caught myself stealing glances at him as we walked, wondering what was going on in that head of his, wondering what he was thinking about . . .

Wondering if he was second-guessing everything he thought about me too.

"What's with that notebook of yours, anyway?" He said it like it was part of a conversation we were having. Like we hadn't been walking side by side in a rigid silence.

He held out his hands, nodding his head at the books I was holding and motioning for me to hand them over. I pulled them closer to me.

"What do you mean?"

He pursed his lips, as if anticipating my hesitation, and gently tugged them out of my hands. "This ratty old thing," he said, waving my notebook at me. "You always have it with you, except for that night at your school, of course." His eyes cut over to me, simmering, before settling back on the notebook. "And it looks like it's taken a beating or two. Its pages are all thick and crinkly." He was clearly curious, but I was relieved he made no move to open it or thumb through the pages.

"So?"

"It's not schoolwork, is it? It doesn't look like it is." He lifted one shoulder lazily, as if to conceal how much thought he'd apparently put into this.

"It's hard to explain," I admitted.

He seemed to think I was trying to dismiss his question, because he just nodded stiffly, kicking at the dusty path, his eyes sweeping over the glittering turquoise water to our left.

"It's a bit of everything," I continued, not without reluctance. "Newspaper articles, notes, even some pages from books. Things I think are important or interesting. Sometimes it's things I want to remember, sometimes it's things I don't. It helps me make sense of the world in a way."

This time his nod was slower, somehow gentler. I had no idea how someone could express so much without a single word, but I felt how deeply he was listening to me now.

"I want to be a writer," I said. "Someday."

"That's why you go to that fancy school, hmm?"

"Yes," I said. "I want to go to college and write about things that matter." It wasn't until the words had escaped my mouth that I realized their connection—North Phoenix High School and the future I wanted—might not be obvious to someone like Marco.

"Mm, and you have to do what the white folks do for that to happen?" I waited for another jab—for another "princesa" comment—but it didn't come.

"I . . ." I didn't know the answer to that. I thought I did, but the way he was looking at me sent a spike of doubt straight into the nape of my neck.

He made a satisfied grunt.

"How long have you been going to these El Foro meetings?" I asked. If he was going to prod into my business, I was going to return the favor. What I truly wanted to know more about was him and Verón—about that moment I caught a glimpse of him by the grocery truck—but I suspected it would take time to work up to that.

"A year, I think? A while." He ran his free hand along the back of his neck.

"I had no idea anything like that was happening here."

He waggled his eyebrows at me. "Of course you didn't, princesa."

There was the taunt I'd been bracing for, though surprisingly it didn't hit with the same force. The way he said it was light. Tender. Affectionate, even.

"So this is what you do every Friday night," I said with a laugh, thinking about all the nefarious activities Ramón and I had imagined him getting up to. "Sit around talking about culture and civil rights."

He smirked in response.

"And you and Verón . . . ?" I tried to keep my voice breezy as I watched his face for a reaction.

"I met him when he was handing out flyers about fair labor laws to some guys at work," he said plainly.

I couldn't shake the notion that there was more to the story than what he was willing to share, though. "He seems to be a very influential person," I ventured.

Marco nodded, his face so neutral it had to be deliberate. "I guess you could say that. He's . . . he's a good man." The silence that followed this statement had a finality to it that I wouldn't question any further. For now, at least.

"Ramón's never gone with you?" I asked, even though I was pretty sure I knew the answer.

Marco kicked at a small stone as he walked and sent it tumbling into the otherwise serene water of the canal. "Ramón? No. Never."

It was hard to imagine Ramón attending weekly meetings of any sort, to be perfectly honest. He scarcely made it to his classes on a consistent basis, and that was with his mother haranguing him. But a Friday night gathering where people sat around talking about serious issues regarding the future of the community? Ramón wouldn't have lasted five minutes, I'd guess.

"So." Marco's voice came out an octave higher than it had been moments before. He looked at me to gauge whether I'd noticed the scratchy sound, and I did nothing to conceal my amusement.

He cleared his throat. "*So*. This gringo who's taking you to this dance..."

I stopped walking, unsure what to make of this comment. He must've found out about Tim from Ramón, but I tried to picture that conversation. Had Ramón offered it up, or had Marco asked? Curiosity pinged around inside me like a bottle rocket.

It took him a few steps before he stopped too, dropping his head backward between his shoulders in exasperation before he turned to face me.

"*Tim*," I supplied.

He nodded, his jaw clenched. "Tim," he growled. "Is he your boyfriend? ¿Tu novio?" His scowl deepened; he appeared to hate how the question sounded in both languages.

I shook my head, fascinated by the play of emotions on Marco's face. The clear interest and trepidation as well as the half-hearted attempt at nonchalance.

"Do you want him to be?" His brows furrowed deeper with every word.

I pressed my lips together to keep myself from breaking out in a full-on grin. I shook my head, not trusting myself to speak.

"And Ramón?"

A burst of laughter ripped through me. "What about Ramón?"

He groaned, as if it were obvious.

"Marco."

His expression remained taut, though his eyebrows rose slightly.

"Marco, you can't be serious! He's in love with Julianne. Head over heels. You know that as well as I do!"

He glared at me, not one bit amused by the levity in my voice. "Everyone has always thought the two of you would . . . you know."

I knew precisely what he was getting at, but I was still utterly fascinated by this strange, flustered version of him. This was Marco Montoya *jealous.*

It was astonishing and riveting and . . . endearing.

Part of me wanted to tease him a bit more; he'd certainly poked fun at me enough over the years to earn it. But I could see the vulnerability he was trying to tamp down in his copper eyes, and I thought better of it.

"It's never been like that between us," I assured him. "I know what everyone says, but they're wrong. We've only ever been friends. Only ever wanted to be friends." I thought of how Ramón had always chased romance at every chance he got and how I'd actively avoided it. We couldn't be more different, more wrong for each other.

"No Tim, no Ramón," Marco said quietly, meditatively.

I shook my head, and our eyes locked on one another. "Just me," I said.

The stern line of his brows softened, the faintest hint of a smile playing on the corners of his mouth. He waved my notebook at me. "Just you and your words, right?"

I felt a pinch in my heart as I considered what he said. Were they really my words? They were other people's words. Words I'd stolen and borrowed. There was nothing in there that I'd actually written myself. Nothing that was truly my own.

But I nodded anyway.

A warm breeze stirred around us, the leaves of the lush cottonwood branches swaying overhead. One stray curl had worked itself free from Marco's pomade, fluttering just a little bit against his forehead as he watched me.

"That's good" was all he said before we both began walking again.

Twenty-Four

Friday, September 16, 1955

"I invited a representative from the NAACP to speak with us today," Verón said as he opened the meeting. "But he was unable to join us, unfortunately."

Next to me, Marco made a soft snorting sound.

"I think our time might be well spent exploring *why* that is." Verón stood with his hands in his pockets, his gaze drifting across the room without settling on anyone in particular. It was almost like he was thinking aloud to himself rather than soliciting input.

"Selfish is what it is!" someone called out anyway.

Verón didn't turn in the direction of the voice. He maintained his same detached demeanor as he stroked his chin. "It might feel that way, yes. But our history, our relationship with colored folks . . . it's complicated, isn't it? Our oppression and discrimination, though perhaps stemming from the same prejudice, are quite different. And while I hoped we might be able to learn from their triumphs in the civil rights movement, to partner with one another, I think bearing our differences in mind might be useful. Instructive."

No one protested, but the quiet that followed was uneasy.

"I'd like to speak to this." A woman a row in front of us stood. "From a legal standpoint."

For the first time, Verón's gaze seemed to focus, and he turned to her. "Please." He motioned for her to come to the center of the circle as he took a seat on a crate.

She gingerly stepped into the opening and smiled demurely at the crowd as she smoothed the skirt of her neat gray suit. Something about her reminded me of Miss Shaw, though they didn't look much alike. Dark hair, I supposed. Smart clothes. Perhaps it was more in the way they carried themselves. The squared set of their shoulders and the brightness in their eyes—like they didn't miss much. Like they were always ready for *something*.

"My name is Pilar Palomente, and I am a law student," she said, her voice clear and even. "I have been studying a case for one of my classes that I think is pertinent to this discussion." She paused, perhaps expecting the same interjections that often punctuated Verón's speeches, but the room was quiet. "*Hernandez v. Texas*. A recent case." There were a few nods, a few murmurs of recognition. Verón leaned forward and propped his head up on his hands.

"You see, it's about jury selection, but the rulings from the Supreme Court from last year relate to this discussion of our race as seen by the law," Pilar said, making eye contact with each of us as she spoke, leaning into our focus in a way that was both inspiring and terrifying to me. "In this case, a man named Pete Hernandez was convicted of murder for allegedly shooting his employer, and the Supreme Court reversed his conviction after finding he was discriminated against during his trial."

There were some clearly confused faces listening to her. A man a row in front of us elbowed his neighbor with a scowl, but no one interrupted her. The room remained breathlessly silent. Undeniably interested.

"There were no Mexican Americans on the jury, and therefore it was impossible for Hernandez to truly be judged by a jury of his peers, as our Constitution requires," she said. "As many of you likely realize, it is important to be judged by people who understand your circumstances and experiences. None of the white people on the jury could fully comprehend the way we are often regarded as second-class citizens—how we face so many of the issues we discuss here. However, the reason this case was brought to the Supreme Court is what Señor Verón was talking about." She nodded at Verón, who gave her a small smile. "Mexicans have often been categorized legally as white. Which is no accident, of course. For the past fifty years or so, activists have been campaigning to be seen as white in order to have access to the same rights and privileges white people have. However, we now see that that plan was deeply flawed because no matter what the law says about our race, we are still very often treated as 'other.' As foreigners, even if we were born here. *We* know we've faced hardships due to our identity. But because of the law, it is hard to prove. It is not documented in the same way Jim Crow Laws are, for example. And in some ways, we are fortunate for that, I suppose. Our discrimination is not as widely accepted, not quite as rampant as what colored people experience. And that is part of the issue with the NAACP. That we have not had the same experience but also that we've had the benefit to claim whiteness in some scenarios."

My cheeks warmed at this, and though I knew it was impossible, I felt like Pilar's eyes rested on me. We didn't know each other; she couldn't know that I lived my life doing the exact thing she described, could she? Though I guessed my light skin wasn't exactly hard to spot. It wouldn't take a lot of work for someone as smart as she clearly was to figure out that I used this trait to my advantage.

"We are at an in-between point," Pilar concluded. "We are not white, but what color are we? The law does not say much about 'brown.' It is so often black and white. And that is the key challenge we face as we work for civil rights, in my opinion. Maybe someday, we will be able to collaborate with Negro groups to work for mutual equality. But I believe, before that happens, we must figure out where we fit. Who we are as a people."

Pilar sat down to a palpable silence. Even Marco seemed a bit stunned by what she'd had to say. His arms were no longer folded across his chest; instead, he leaned forward, elbows resting on his knees, running his hand along the edge of his jaw idly.

After a minute, Verón stood and continued the meeting, though my eyes kept wandering back over to Pilar, her words echoing in my mind as Verón spoke.

At the end of the meeting, I told Marco he could leave without me as we got to our feet. He frowned, amused and curious, as he pulled his pack of Lucky Strikes out of his pocket. "How about I wait for you out front?" he said simply, making his way toward the back door.

As soon as Marco turned, I eyed Pilar where she stood collecting her shiny black briefcase. Bashfully, I drifted toward her. I wasn't sure what I wanted to say, but I knew I wanted to speak with her.

She looked up as I approached, as if she sensed my wide-eyed apprehension, and to my relief, she offered me a friendly smile that I readily returned.

"I—I wanted to say how moving everything you shared was," I stammered quietly. "The way you spoke . . . and just . . . I had never thought about our circumstances that way. Perhaps I knew those types of things were true in some fashion or another, but to hear it spelled out like that . . ." My rambling was a stark contrast to how eloquently Pilar had spoken, but she nodded as if I were making perfect sense.

"That's certainly how I've felt, now that I'm studying these cases," she admitted. "That's why I need this group—why we all need this group. I love digging into these topics from different perspectives. These issues we've long accepted without examining. It's very important work."

I nodded fervently. Perhaps too fervently. "Well, thank you," I concluded, but I didn't move. I didn't have anything else to say, but I also wasn't quite ready for this exchange to end. I longed to bask in her insight, in her wisdom, in her quiet confidence for a moment more.

"Here," she said, reaching into one of the leather pockets of her briefcase. "This is my card. I clerk part-time at a law firm downtown, about a block from the Hotel San Carlos. In case you ever have any questions or just want to talk, mujer a mujer."

Eagerly, I accepted the crisp white card she was holding out to me, and I admired the neat print. I was already looking forward to pasting it into my notebook. "Gracias," I told her.

"You're new to El Foro, ¿verdad?" she asked.

I nodded. "Yes, I've just started coming with . . . my friend Marco." Again, a flush of sheepishness rose in me. Had I ever referred to Marco as my friend before? *Was* he my friend now?

"Ah, yes, I know Marco Montoya." She nodded thoughtfully, pausing before speaking. "Verón has quite a soft spot for him." Her mouth moved like there was more to say about that, but she just lifted her briefcase, moving to leave. "You just be careful, okay?"

"I—"

I stopped as Pilar's eyes found something just over my shoulder. The back door had swung open as someone left, revealing a fleeting glimpse of Marco before it shut. His back was toward us. He could've been virtually anyone in that brief moment. Any greaser from the south side in a white shirt and cuffed jeans, dark hair slicked back, cigarette smoke drifting above him.

But the way he stood . . . It was unmistakably defiant, even from a distance. Like he was not only braced for a fight but looking for it. Shoulders back, legs rigid.

I glanced back at Pilar as Marco disappeared from view. "I'll see you around . . ." She tilted her head, curious.

"Rosa," I supplied. "My name's Rosa."

"Hasta luego, Rosa."

Twenty-Five

Friday, September 16, 1955

"You're quiet," Marco said as we walked home.

I looked over at him, our shoulders nearly brushing, our steps synchronized. I gave him a quick nod, a thin smile on my face.

"Quiet, even for you," he amended with a soft laugh. "Thinking?"

"You know how much I like it."

I could feel his eyes on me for a few moments before he spoke again. His breathing changed slightly, and though I kept my eyes on our feet crunching through the dusty roadside, I imagined him opening his mouth, searching for what he wanted to say. And I was surprisingly warmed at the idea of Marco speechless.

"This dance" is what he finally spit out, gruff and quick.

I waited a beat before I let my eyes flit up to him, noting the frustration on his face as he dragged a hand along his chin. He was still preoccupied with the Silver and Blue Ball? "Yes?" I prompted.

"I know what Ramón wants out of all this," he said. "But what about you?"

I frowned. "What do you mean?"

"What are you hoping this *demonstration* achieves?"

Now it was my turn to struggle for words. Notions of equality and change and acceptance swirled in my head—as they always did when I thought about the world and my place in it—but in a way that was hard to explain. Even given the new closeness El Foro had brought between the two of us, I wasn't sure all these new ideas were things I was ready to unravel with Marco just yet.

"It seems a bit out of character for you," he said somberly.

My cheeks heated—with hurt or anger, I wasn't sure. "What does *that* mean?"

He stopped walking suddenly, but I proceeded until he squared himself directly in my path. The sun was long gone by now, and there were no streetlamps on this side of town, so the only light that fell on him was from the moon and the glowing windows of the carnicería two doors down. The shadows and lines of his face were hard to ignore, especially this close. The warmth in my face traveled straight down to my chest. To my toes.

"I just mean you're quiet."

I snorted, looking away from him. "So you've said."

"Reserved," he continued, ignoring the dismissiveness in

my tone. "Thoughtful. Practical. To me, it seems you're better suited to El Foro than to what Ramón's got planned."

I tried to focus on what he was actually saying rather than getting caught up in the implication that he'd devoted so much thought to me and what I was like. That was far too distracting. My voice was tight when I finally managed to speak. "You're probably right. But they're my friends. And I want to do more than hide in my ivory tower." He tensed, recognizing his own words echoed back at him. "I want to—"

"Put yourself out there?"

Our eyes found each other, his burning even in the moonlit darkness. He tipped his head toward me ever so slightly, and before I could even begin to wonder what he was doing, he whispered, "Have you ever been kissed, Rosa?"

I leapt back like he'd electrocuted me. *"What?"* I hissed.

I wasn't sure I'd ever heard him say my name before. I was always princesa. I'd certainly never heard him say it like *that*.

A flash of apology crossed his face, but he did not attempt to take back this question. If anything, his gaze remained insistent and curious.

I scoffed, avoiding his eyeline once more. The light in the butcher shop flickered off as the shopkeeper pulled down the shade in the window. "What does that have to do with anything?" I asked, trying to hide how wounded I was by this line of inquiry. How spot-on he was in wondering.

"You've just always been so . . . remote," he said softly, and again, my mind raced, trying to determine how—*when*—he'd arrived at this conclusion. "Holding yourself apart from everything." His eyes dropped to my leather notebook, still in his hands.

I thought of how lonely I'd been at North those first few weeks, before Julianne and I became friends. I thought of Ramón assuring me no one at South Mountain was gossiping about me transferring, that the rumors of me being stuck-up were nothing at all, that I was imagining the scrutinizing glares I caught at church. I thought of an entire childhood of being several shades lighter than everyone in my family for no apparent reason other than what Mamá called my "Spanish blood."

What on earth did Marco know about any of that?

I shook my head. "I'd better get home."

"I'll walk you."

"You don't have to—"

But he was already heading in the direction of my house. "Vámonos, ¿eh?"

We were silent the rest of the way, and though I did wonder if he should stop a few houses down like he did last time to avoid questions from my parents, I didn't suggest it.

We stopped at my front gate, still not looking at one another. "I'll see you—" he began.

"Are you going to the meeting next w—" I started at the same time.

But we were both cut off by the sound of my front door bursting open forcefully. We turned to see Mamá's figure standing in the doorway, arms folded across her chest.

"Hola, Marco," she called out. I could tell by the way he

flinched that he also heard the disapproving edge to Mamá's voice.

"Buenas noches, señora Capistrano." He didn't look at her as he spoke, kept his eyes fixed on his feet. On his dusty work boots.

Mamá didn't say anything else, but she didn't move from her position in the doorway either.

"I'd better go," I said to Marco. I could feel my mother looking at me, beckoning me, like her glare was a lasso around my heart, tugging me toward her.

"I was just going to say—oh, sure. Right." He cleared his throat. "Claro que sí."

I cast one last curious look in his direction, watching him as he reached in his pocket for a cigarette, his eyes anywhere but on me or Mamá.

I thought back to that image of him outside the church, alone. Of Pilar warning me about him. *Have you ever been kissed, Rosa?*

"Rosa." Mamá's voice barreled between us. A command and a reproach.

"Good night, princesa," Marco said, turning away from me as he spoke.

The front door had scarcely shut behind me before Mamá began scolding me.

"Rosa, hija, you know I don't want you spending time with a boy like Marco Montoya."

"Yo sé," I muttered, and she tsked at my tone without missing a beat.

"The Montoyas are like family, I know," she conceded with a guilty expression. "And you and Ramón—you're so close. But Marco . . ." She couldn't seem to find the words she wanted, so instead she reached out to stroke my cheek, concern on every inch of her weary face. "I pray for him. I pray for Marco to find peace. But that boy . . . he's trouble, Rosa. Stay away from him, hmm?"

WETBACKS FROM YUMA COUNTY: HERE TO WORK OR STEAL?

The Arizona Republic
Wednesday, October 21, 1953

When will the wetback invasion end?

Customarily, Mexican laborers return to Mexico after their given farm season. However, it appears many workers are remaining in Arizona illegally in hopes of gaining permanent employment.

There are what appears to be two types of wets: those seeking good, honest work and those with more nefarious intentions. Court records show that over a six-month period of time, 75 percent of the crimes committed were by or against a wetback.

The official word from the Maricopa County Sheriff's Department and Sheriff Callihan is for residents to be vigilant, especially around unknown wetback males and youths.

Twenty-Six

Saturday, September 24, 1955

It was a dance. At the end of the day, that's all it was. Just a school dance.

Something for enjoyment. For fun and flirting and fancy dresses. For music and punch and jitterbugging.

This is what I told myself, anyway, as I caught the three o'clock bus uptown to Julianne's house.

I climbed aboard, taking a seat toward the middle behind a mother and two young children. I was soothed by the stop-and-go rhythm of the bus leaving behind the lush farmlands and dirt roads of South Phoenix and making its way toward the technicolor city center. I sat there, awash in the sound of the rumbling of the motor, the chattering of other passengers—the singing of the pigtailed girl in front of me—and the steady beating of my pulse, which raced just a tad faster each time I thought about what I was doing. Each time I really considered it at all.

Because it was so much more than just a dance. It really was. I knew, at my core, what was at stake.

I stared out the window, not really seeing the drugstores or cinemas that flew past.

Instead, I thought of walking home from Blanca's a few nights ago, later than normal because I'd stayed after she'd laid Guillermo down and helped her wash and fold all his diapers. I'd been passing the Montoyas' when I saw a shadow slipping out the back door of their sleeping porch. I'd caught myself hoping it was Marco, but instead Ramón's eyes met mine in the darkness. He'd put his finger to his lips as he darted toward me, stealth in every step.

"What are you doing?" I'd asked.

"Heading out to see Julianne," he'd said, like it was obvious. Like it was something he did all the time. "My ma fell asleep listening to the radio." He grinned conspiratorially.

"Be careful," I'd begged, and he'd brushed it off with a wink before sliding into the driver's seat of Marco's car.

The brakes of the bus whined as it came to a stop in front of a flower shop, the windows full of roses and lilies and tulips, big waxy ribbons tied around each glass vase. One more stop. I took a deep breath as my heart beat faster.

In front of me, the little girl sang, "Hickory dickory dock. The mouse ran up the clock."

I closed my eyes, the thumping in my chest growing faster and louder.

I thought of Marco, who'd been waiting for me at my bus stop the previous afternoon before the meeting. He had just walked alongside me, holding my books, hardly saying anything at all, really. But watching me in a way that made my stomach turn fizzy, like a bottle of Coca-Cola all shaken up.

I thought of how I'd passed a newspaper stand with Sheriff Callihan's picture on the front page of the paper as I walked to school on Wednesday. The headline had read MARICOPA SHERIFF CALLIHAN TO SENATOR MCCARTHY: LET ARIZONA RUN ITSELF I'd be in that man's home today. In a matter of minutes.

I thought of everything at once, it felt like. Everything that was happening, everything that could happen. Everything . . .

The bus lurched forward, back into motion, and I opened my eyes.

Twenty-Seven

Saturday, September 24, 1955

Julianne was waiting on the front lawn of her house when I walked up, hand tented over her eyes to shield her face from the sun. I wasn't sure how long she'd been outside, but the sweat on her hairline led me to believe it'd been a while.

The Callihan house was a bungalow, which was a popular style on the north side. I thought the name was a bit misleading, making it sound a lot more modest than it really was. Because, in actuality, the Callihan residence was a sight to behold.

With its charming gabled roof and wide porch and stone pillars and immaculate rose garden, it was beautiful to every last detail. Every brick, every stone, every blade of grass. Absolutely perfect. Completely picturesque.

Julianne's posture went rigid as I approached, her hand dropping to her side as she met me where the sidewalk and her front yard touched. She wore a pair of bright yellow pedal pushers, a white sleeveless pullover, and canvas espadrilles—an outfit that was bright and casual, especially compared to the stony look of unease that marred her neat features. Her mouth was pressed into a thin line, with just the corners of her lips turned upward. She clasped my hands in hers as soon as I was within arm's length, and I was instantly struck by how hot and clammy her palms were.

Then I realized she was just as nervous as I was. Which was equally reassuring and horrifying.

"You made it," Julianne said breathlessly as she led me inside and up the stairs. She'd said something to that effect twice already. "You think Ramón will be able to find it? I believe Tim knows where the house is . . ."

"I'm sure it'll be just fine," I said meekly, all too aware that the Callihan address was the least of our concerns.

She nodded thoughtfully as she opened the door to her bedroom, a girlish oasis of pinks and flowers and lace. With its rosebud wallpaper and ruffled throw pillows, it looked too childish to be the bedroom of a girl who would be heading off to college in less than a year.

A girl who spent her evenings wrapped in the arms of Ramón Montoya.

But at the same time, it suited her somehow. It was a reminder that many things had two sides to them, contrasting and complex. Julianne could be young and girlish but also passionate and strong.

I'd been in here once before, the previous year, with a group of girls who worked on the school newspaper. We were brainstorming ideas for an advice column Simon wanted to add so the female students had more reason to read the paper, as he put it. Etiquette questions, fashion tips, suggestions for ladylike behavior.

We had to fake the first few letters until students actually started sending them in. So the five of us had sprawled out on the plush rug in Julianne's room with our notebooks, a few copies of *American Girl* and *The Arizona Republic* spread out between us for inspiration.

I recalled being awestruck by Julianne's house that day, a feeling that still lingered with me. The gleaming wood floors were just one piece of evidence of the household staff who cared for this home. The glamorous details like the crystal bar set and mustard-yellow velvet throw pillows were simple touches that dazzled me more than I liked to admit.

That was also the first time I'd seen the sheriff up close. I remembered him pulling into the driveway in his patrol car as I was walking down their front steps. Most of the other girls had already been picked up by their maids or parents or older siblings, and I'd been mulling over how to make my exit. No one would be coming to pick me up, after all. I'd need to take the bus, but I also wasn't sure I wanted anyone to know that. I worried someone would offer to drive me, and what a fix I'd be in then. I knew my best bet was to just try to slip out without anyone noticing.

Which is what I'd almost managed to do until Sheriff Callihan spotted me as he swung his long legs out of the car.

He was so much taller than I'd expected, lanky and spindly

like a scarecrow. The way he carried himself was like he was unfolding toward you. Every motion deliberate and unending.

"Where are you off to, young lady?" he'd called across the yard, turning his lean body in its khaki uniform to face me. The tone he'd used was mock authoritative, like he was poking fun at himself. Like he knew just how he seemed—peering at a schoolgirl in his yard with his gun on his hip—but he couldn't resist the opportunity to interrogate. I remembered how the metal of his badge gleamed in the sunlight.

"We're done with our schoolwork, sir," I'd said simply. And then I'd just kept walking. I'd called out a thank-you as I turned and hurried down the street, ducking out of sight at the first chance I had.

The trepidation I'd felt coming face-to-face with him had taken me by surprise. I'd been following his career for well over a year, collecting pieces of news about him. A small part of me had looked forward to meeting him.

But there was something about having those dark, scrutinizing eyes on me that I couldn't explain. Something that stuck with me. Something that made me feel like there was a factor we weren't accounting for in this plan of ours.

"He's so busy lately," Julianne assured me when I asked about her father one more time. She was examining her dress, which hung on the back of her bedroom door, and she ran her fingers along the powder-blue skirt, not looking at me as she spoke. "He's hardly ever home anymore." There was something odd in her voice—a heaviness that was hard to decipher.

But before I could give it too much thought, she turned to face me. "Can I ask you something?"

I couldn't stop the dry laugh that spilled out of me. "I suppose we don't have many secrets between us now. Why not?"

She flushed at this, unamused. "Is it . . . really awful where you're from?"

I frowned. "What do you mean?"

"The south side," she clarified with a hint of embarrassment. "And Phoenix South Mountain. Are they terrible? Is that why you're here?"

"Oh," I said, the weight of this question reverberating in my chest. "No, it's not. Not at all. South Phoenix—Golden Gate—it's beautiful. I love it," I told her without hesitation. "And I've never been to South Mountain High. I switched here the year it opened, when they closed the colored schools. But even before, when I was in the Mexican classes, it wasn't awful."

"It wasn't?"

I shook my head, looking down at the floral bedspread upon which I was perched. "I mean, the buildings were bad sometimes. In kindergarten, we didn't have air-conditioning, and that was not good. And, you know, the books and supplies were often in rough shape. But the teachers were great. They were people I knew from my community, people who spoke Spanish, who cared about us too."

I could see the confusion on her pretty face. "Then why do you do this? If it's so dangerous and if you liked it before you got here?"

I thought of Papi instantly. The weariness on his face at the end of each day. "Well, the classes at South Mountain are more technical. They're to help us become workers, mostly. The offerings at North are better suited to college."

She shook her head in disbelief, touching her fingers to her lips. "So no one you grew up with will go to college?"

"No, no, that's not true. Some do," I jumped in. "It's just a difficult path. Harder to convince colleges that a Mexican student with mostly technical courses on their transcript is prepared for college courses. Not to mention earning any scholarships or finding people to write letters of recommendation. It's just . . . it'll be easier this way." Or at least that's what we'd always thought.

She crossed the room quietly and sat down beside me, her sunshine-yellow pants up against my cream-colored shorts. "It doesn't seem easy," she murmured.

"No," I admitted. "It hasn't been."

"And no one's found you out? No one's suspected you?"

Immediately, I thought of Tim's comment—calling us outsiders. He hadn't mentioned it since then, but it lingered with me anyway. "Other than you, no."

"But your last name?"

"You never thought much of it," I reminded her. "I think most people assume it's Italian, like Anthony Damato. Once, last year, Mary Sue Lewis asked me a bunch of questions about Europe and whether I ever made it back there." I shrugged.

She considered this before placing her hand on mine. "It

makes me so angry, how unfair it all is. How *ridiculous* people are about color," she said. "I—I'm sorry."

The sincerity in her voice made my cheeks warm suddenly. "It's hardly your fault, Julianne," I said.

She hummed thoughtfully. "I don't know if that's true. I feel like all white people are *complicit* in some way. Don't you think?"

I opened my mouth to respond—but words eluded me. I'd heard the sentiment before, even recently from Marco, who frequently muttered a "if they aren't with us, they're against us" standpoint at El Foro. But I hadn't expected to hear this kind of comment from Julianne.

"Well, I'm terribly glad you're here," she said. "Regardless of the circumstances. You're my dearest friend, Rosa."

I hadn't heard her say my name—my real name—before. All I could do was nod, stammering out, "Me too."

She fixed a bright smile on her face as she walked over to her record player and flipped it open. "It's awfully quiet in here, don't you think? Let's put a record on. Pick something, won't you? Something happy." She gestured to a stack of records on her bookcase.

I rose and began perusing the stack of brightly colored sleeves. The Fontaine Sisters. A collection of hymns. The Four Aces. Dean Martin.

I settled on Bill Haley and His Comets. There wasn't a happier song than "Rock Around the Clock," I thought.

But when I slid the record out, I noticed it wasn't Bill Haley's name written on the round piece of paper at the center. It was Nat King Cole. With a frown, I returned it and selected a different one. But inside Doris Day's case was Pérez Prado. Little Richard was tucked inside Perry Como's. Every single record was mismatched.

Every single sleeve that bore a white face on it had a colored singer's record stowed inside.

I cast a perplexed look at Julianne over my shoulder, but she had wandered over to her vanity, examining a few bottles of Cutex nail polish in various shades of pink.

Julianne Callihan. When would I stop being shocked by all the mysteries and contradictions wound up inside of her?

I pulled the record out of Kitty Kallen's sleeve and set it atop the record player. I positioned the needle, and Etta James's voice came crackling out with a rhythmic drop beat. I watched Julianne for a reaction, some forgetful guilt or embarrassment. But she just started bobbing her golden head along to the melody.

When she turned to face me, there was a mischievous gleam in her eyes.

Twenty-Eight

Saturday, September 24, 1955

Mrs. Callihan came home just as Nina, the Callihans' maid, was helping us step into our dresses, having spent the last thirty minutes powdering and hot curling us into glossy perfection. Julianne was snugly fastened inside her bodice by the time Mrs. Callihan's clicking heels approached her bedroom. When she threw open the door, Julianne and Nina were crouched behind me, trying to coax up the zipper of the chiffon dress I was borrowing.

Julianne and I were *about* the same size, though the strained noises coming from Nina as she battled the dress said we'd underestimated my bust and hips.

Of all the worries I'd spent the last week stewing over, it never once crossed my mind that Julianne's dress wouldn't fit me. My outfit seemed like such a silly detail but, however ridiculous, it was necessary. I couldn't go without a dress.

"Oh *my*," Mrs. Callihan said by way of greeting, her perfectly lipsticked mouth puckered in displeasure. "Nina, pop into the bathroom, won't you? Grab a bar of soap. That should loosen it up." She immediately shooed Nina out of the room and stepped toward me. I was suddenly awash in the floral scent of her perfume.

She smiled at me courteously, her crimson lips curling into an expression that was pure etiquette, if not genuine warmth. She was pretty and polished in her olive shirtwaist dress, a smart belt fixed around her narrow waist. Her hair, shimmering gold just like Julianne's, did not move from its perfect curls as she flitted around me. "Don't you worry, dear. I've used this trick many times myself when I've had one too many desserts the week before an event." She gave me a conspiratorial wink, her thick lashes brushing up against her alabaster skin, and though I doubted a woman as petite and immaculate as her had ever had to slick a zipper to fit over her frame, I appreciated the gesture all the same.

Finally, she turned to Julianne. I thought all she wanted was a good look at Julianne's dress, but her focus caught on her daughter's peculiar expression. Mrs. Callihan frowned, and though she smoothed out the wrinkles in her forehead almost as soon as they appeared, it was enough to cause both me and Julianne to stiffen.

"Well, goodness, Jules, what's going on?" she asked with a baffled shake of her head. "You look like you're about to go in front of a firing squad, not off to a party!"

Julianne forced a shaky laugh, waving away the comment as Mrs. Callihan continued chattering.

"I'm *so* glad you went with the blue dress. It really does just look so nice with your eyes." Mrs. Callihan appraised her, gently sweeping a flyaway tendril of Julianne's flaxen hair so her shoulder-length curls, rolled under in a sleek curve, were absolutely flawless. "Don't you think so ... Rosie, isn't it?" She didn't pause long enough for me to confirm. "Ah, Nina! There you are." She took the bar of Ivory soap out of Nina's outstretched hand and busied herself behind me. "All right, see, you place the soap just here. Pay attention, girls. This is a handy trick to know now that they're using zippers on more evening wear. We'd be in a real bind if this dress had buttons, like the ones in my day." I felt her tugging on the closure behind me, and the next thing I knew, I was tightly encased in the dress, like a mummy wrapped in gauzy red fabric. She placed her hands on my shoulders and gave me a quick spin, so I was now looking at myself in the floor-length mirror that stood beside Julianne's bed.

If the sudden force of the restrictive zipper hadn't knocked the wind out of me, the reflection that greeted me certainly did. There I was, in a full tea-length skirt propped up by three crinkling layers of crinoline, with sweeping pleated ruby-red fabric winding its way up my torso and coming to rest in an off-the-shoulder neckline.

There was no mask. No scarf. Nothing obscuring my face. In fact, with the lower neckline, this dress revealed more of myself than my normal clothes did. And yet . . . I scarcely recognized the girl staring back at me in the mirror.

I just hoped whoever she was, she was capable of what we'd come here to do tonight.

"Now, Rosie, you just be careful not to make any sudden movements, of course!" Mrs. Callihan laughed good-naturedly, giving my skirt a good fluff. "Your night would be absolutely ruined if you busted a seam."

Twenty-Nine

Saturday, September 24, 1955

Julianne was spritzing our necks with her mother's bottle of Chanel No. 5—the same flowery scent I noticed when she was tampering with my dress—when we heard the doorbell and froze. She was still holding the square little bottle to my wrists as she drew in a sharp breath.

We heard the front door open and Mrs. Callihan's voice echoing throughout the house. "Oh, hello, Tim, dear. Don't you look nice! Who's your friend?"

It was my turn to gasp, my pulse thrumming around my temples.

They were here. It was truly happening.

There was no turning back now.

I gently took the perfume bottle out of Julianne's unmoving hands and set it on her dresser.

"We'd better get down there," I said. I could hear Tim's

deep vibrato responding to Mrs. Callihan, but his voice was too low for me to make out exactly what he was saying.

Mrs. Callihan was grappling with Ramón's name as we descended the staircase. "*Ray*-man, is it?" she said, her vowels flat and terse.

Mrs. Callihan glanced up, eyes fixed on her daughter. "Julianne," she said, her voice unsteady with undeniable confusion. She clasped her hand to her chest, right over the neat little buttons that fastened her dress. "I don't believe I've ever met this young man. Have I, dear?"

Ramón shot me an uneasy smile, and I tried my best to return it. Tried my best to calm the waves of trepidation I felt roiling inside of me.

"You attend North Phoenix?" she prompted, though she clearly wanted to say that she'd never seen him at our school. "That's how you know Rosie?" Her gaze flitted between Ramón and me with a shadow of thinly veiled disapproval.

Standing next to broad, blond Tim in the bright lighting of the Callihan home, Ramón looked particularly brown, his tawny skin impossible to ignore. He looked nice, though. Somber, but *nice*. His thick dark hair was swept to the side, the unruly tendrils of his curls slicked back into mild obedience. His black sport coat wasn't quite as fitted as Tim's. It hung just a little awkwardly on his frame—a little too loose around his shoulders, a little too long in the sleeves—and it occurred to me that it was probably borrowed, just like my dress. Was it Marco's? It was hard to picture Marco wearing a sport coat, though my imagination instantly rushed to piece it together.

Julianne stepped onto the landing, pausing halfway between her mother and the boys. She gave Mrs. Callihan a quick nod but offered no other explanation as to Ramón's presence.

"Well," Mrs. Callihan said in a strained voice, like she was trying to clear her throat. "I'll grab the camera, then. And you kids can be on your way, how's that?"

"Sure thing," Julianne murmured, eyes locked with Ramón's as her mother's shoes clicked past us into what I assumed was the study, based off the bookshelves and plush armchairs.

She returned a moment later, a black Kodak camera held in front of her. "Let's see if I can recall how to use this contraption. Ah, there it is. All right, Julianne dear, why don't you and Tim come stand here by the stairs." With one dainty wave of her hand, she ushered Julianne and Tim to the staircase and relegated Ramón and me to the corner by the coatrack.

"Actually, ma'am—" Tim began to interject, but Julianne linked her arm with his, cutting him off. He cast a confused look over his shoulder at me. The only explanation I could offer him was the slightest shake of my head, but he seemed to understand not to say any more.

"Oh, don't you two look just *darling*," Mrs. Callihan cooed, the camera pressed to her face. I caught the stricken look Julianne shot across the room at Ramón as the flash illuminated her face. "*Smile*, won't you? For Pete's sake!" I'd never heard a laugh sound as frustrated as Mrs. Callihan's did.

Julianne dropped Tim's arm as soon as Mrs. Callihan moved the camera away from her face.

"Your father will be so pleased to see these pictures. I know he's sorry to miss you kids," Mrs. Callihan said. "Tim, tell your parents we said hello, won't you? We'd love to have them over for dinner sometime soon, especially if the two of you are going to be spending more time together." She smiled affectionately at Tim, causing his ears to turn bright pink. "Oh, what a smart match you two make!"

I didn't have to even look at Ramón to sense the way he bristled at this. I bumped my arm against his as a silent reminder to play it cool.

"Have her home by ten thirty?" she continued, sweeping her arm toward the doorway.

"Mama, won't you take a picture of the four of us? The whole gang?"

The way Mrs. Callihan froze at this question, you'd have thought she'd forgotten Ramón and I were here at all. She tilted her head at her daughter, halfway to the front door already.

Ramón and Julianne exchanged a look. One I couldn't decode. But one I was pretty sure Mrs. Callihan caught.

"It's all right." I tried to brush it off. The sooner we got out of there, the better.

Julianne shook her head. "I'd like a picture with *all of us*."

Mrs. Callihan's irritated laugh tumbled out again. "Of course. Ra—the two of you, won't you join them?" I didn't miss the clip in her voice as she stumbled over how to address us.

Wordlessly, we shuffled to reorganize ourselves, Julianne and Ramón in center, with Tim and me flanking them. Tim took a half step toward me at first, but another shake of my head had him rooted to where he was.

"Smile!" Mrs. Callihan called out, scarcely giving us a chance to obey before the flash dazzled us into starry oblivion.

I blinked my eyes, resisting the urge to rub them since Julianne had put eyeliner on me. When my vision refocused, the front door was open.

And the sheriff was standing in the doorway.

Thirty

Saturday, September 24, 1955

It couldn't be. He wasn't supposed to be here. Julianne had said he wouldn't be here.

I blinked again.

"Well, hello there," he said in that booming voice of his.

"Darling," Mrs. Callihan choked out. "You're home early!"

"I raced home," he continued, stepping into the foyer and swinging the door shut behind him. He finally came into focus now that the stream of dusky sunlight that had framed him was extinguished. There he stood, still in his tan uniform, just like he was in all the newspaper clippings I'd collected. Hands on his hips, his gun holster resting just below his right hand. And though he smiled at the four of us, his eyes were scrutinizing as he took in the scene. "Didn't want to miss this."

"We were just about to leave, Daddy—"

He silenced her with an upheld hand. "Now, hold your

horses. I'd like to make everyone's acquaintances." He strode forward, holding that same hand out toward Tim. "Tim, my boy. Hell of a season you're having, huh?"

"Um, yes. Yes, sir," Tim said, shaking the sheriff's hand, a soft tremble in his throat that I was somehow certain the sheriff noted too.

"I'm quite pleased you're taking my Julianne to this shindig," he said, his grin widening as the rest of his expression hardened. Like a veiled warning of sorts.

Tim glanced at me out of the corner of his eye, but Julianne jumped in. "Daddy, really, we should be—"

He turned his attention to me and Ramón, chewing on his lower lip. "Now, I remember you." He wagged a finger at me as he thought. "From newspaper club, isn't that right?"

I nodded.

"What's wrong? Cat got your tongue?"

Julianne and her mother both let out that same strangled laugh of theirs.

I started to shake my head but caught myself. "N-no, sir." I cursed myself for the stutter.

He nodded slowly. "You're a quiet one. A fast walker too, if I remember correctly." His eyes flashed at that vague mention of me slipping out of their house last year, and it took everything in me to keep from dropping my gaze down to my silly little satin shoes. "Rosie, was it?"

I made a soft sound of agreement.

"Right," he said slowly, his eyes lingering on me for a beat before he slowly dragged them to my left. To Ramón. "And *you*."

A pause followed this that knocked the breath out of all of us—even Mrs. Callihan, it looked like.

"Daddy, this is—"

He held up his hand again, and again, Julianne fell silent. "Can't this boy introduce himself?"

"Ramón, Sheriff Callihan." He straightened as he held out his hand to the sheriff, shoulders back and chin held high. "A pleasure to meet you."

It was almost imperceptible the way the sheriff recoiled at this. Almost. But I clocked the way his eyes narrowed, the way his lip curled, the way his own hand twitched. I was certain Ramón and Julianne had noticed it too. He quickly schooled his expression into his customary coolness, but still, he made no move to shake Ramón's hand.

The silence grew thicker the longer he waited; it was almost suffocating, but Ramón would not back down. He kept his extended hand steady, his head up, his eyes on the stoic man before him.

After what might as well have been an eternity, the sheriff huffed out an indignant breath just as Mrs. Callihan and Julianne sprang into action.

"Sweetheart, let me fix you a drink," Mrs. Callihan said, placing her hand on her husband's shoulder.

"Daddy—" Julianne's voice cut in simultaneously, barely a breath above a gasp.

"Now, now," the sheriff said with a light chuckle as Ramón's hand finally dropped to his side, fingers now clenched into a tight fist. "Don't get worked up over nothin.' I'm just a bit *surprised* is all." His eyes swept across the four of us, catching once more on Ramón. "I didn't realize that school of yours had such a . . . colorful crowd, Julianne."

Instantly, I was bombarded with a scorching mix of outrage and bewilderment. I wished desperately that I'd been smart enough to anticipate this—to expect this kind of reaction from a powerful white man discovering a brown-skinned boy playing dress-up with his daughter—but I was struck dumb with incredulity. I couldn't help it.

Surely he was surprised, but still, I couldn't make sense of the look of contempt on his face. How could this be the same man who criticized the meddling McCarthy and praised Arizona schools for integrating a year before *Brown*? This man was a hero. A leader. A renegade. Someone I admired.

Wasn't he?

"*Daddy*," Julianne snapped, stepping in front of Ramón in a flurry of petticoats and defensiveness. "Would you like to know another thing you didn't realize?"

"Julianne, don't," I heard myself whisper, dread snaking its way through my rib cage.

"*Ramón* is my date," she spat, folding her arms across her chest. "In fact, he's more than that. He's my boyfriend. He and I are *in love*—"

The sharp clap of his hand against her flushed cheek thundered around the room. Julianne let out an anguished, throaty cry as she stumbled backward from the force of the blow.

Mrs. Callihan screamed.

I gasped, my own hand clasped to my mouth.

Ramón did not hesitate, throwing himself over to her. Pushing past the sheriff. Or at least trying to.

The sheriff was an immovable force as he gaped at the pile of taffeta and tears that was his daughter. He was frozen for a moment, disbelief written all over his face. He did not strike me as a man who typically lacked control—of himself or others or anything. And yet here he was, his world unraveling all around him.

Ramón crouched next to Julianne, his back to the sheriff as he murmured soothing sounds. I watched her rise, lifting her head from her hands, her tear-soaked cheek an excruciating red. She glared at her father as she moved to put her arms around Ramón's neck.

But she never quite made it.

In a flash, the sheriff seemed to reawaken to the scene. He seized Ramón, grabbing him by the arms and wrestling them behind his back like a criminal he was preparing to handcuff. Ramón tried to wrench himself free and yelled for the sheriff to take his hands off him. But it didn't matter. His struggle had no effect on a man who wrangled opponents to submit to his will for a living.

With minimal effort and grim resolve, the sheriff dragged him across the foyer and thrust him out the front door despite the screams of both Julianne and Ramón. It took only a brief glare in our direction for Tim and me to scramble after him, out onto the front porch. I glanced over my shoulder in distress at Julianne, who was still sprawled on the ground and reaching toward us.

"Stay the hell away from my daughter," the sheriff growled the second we'd stepped outside, slamming the front door and silencing Julianne's sobs behind him.

Thirty-One

Saturday, September 24, 1955

"Should we . . . go?" Tim asked, indecision and distress flickering in his round eyes. I spotted his car keys clasped in his large hand.

I couldn't blame him for wanting to flee.

Ramón hadn't moved from the porch, his gaze still fixated on the Callihans' front door.

I was caught between the two of them—both figuratively and literally.

I didn't want to abandon Julianne here to contend with her father's anger all on her own, but really, what other options did we have?

It felt like we should do something, of course, but I hadn't the faintest notion of what that could be.

Why was it so clear when something was wrong but so hard to figure out how to do something right?

This wasn't the plan. It wasn't supposed to happen like this.

I found myself wishing Marco were here, a deep-in-my-gut desire that snuck up on me as I gazed at Ramón's silhouette, statuesque on the Callihan porch. Perhaps he'd be able to see past the shock and humiliation and uncertainty of all this. Perhaps he'd know what to do.

"Ramón," I said, my voice hoarse with unease. "We should . . ." I trailed off as he turned to me.

Though darkness was falling on us quickly, I could see his bright brown eyes ablaze with something I didn't recognize.

Behind me, I heard Tim opening his car door. He called out something about dropping Ramón off wherever he wanted. But despite the desperate hitch in his voice, neither Ramón nor I responded to him.

Instead, Ramón cut across the Callihans' lawn, his steps harried and uneven, like he was trudging through desert sand rather than immaculately cut grass. Without thinking—without even a glance back at Tim—I followed.

Ramón paced a few yards in front of me, his head angled upward, a scowl fixed on his face as his eyes searched the darkening sky.

No, not the sky.

The house.

He was staring at the second-story windows of the house.

I could hear Tim's car roar to life in the distance, but it didn't move from where it was parked. Maybe Tim meant it to get our attention. Maybe he wanted to be ready for a speedy getaway should he need it. Again, I couldn't blame him. I shouldn't have dragged him into this.

"That's her room," Ramón murmured. I craned my neck so I could see where he was pointing.

The window on the side of the house was brightly illuminated even though night hadn't fully set in yet. The lace curtains fluttered out toward us, the gauzy fabric caught in the gentle summer breeze.

Of course he knew which window was hers. Even if this was the first time the sheriff had laid eyes on him, this was not the first time Ramón had been here. Who knew how many nights he'd helped Julianne slip out of that window or perhaps even climbed through into her bedroom?

"Ramón."

He glanced at me distractedly. There was a grisly determination in his eyes, an unyielding way his body was moving. I didn't like it.

We both looked up in time to see a shadow pass somewhere inside the room. She was up there.

Or someone was up there.

Ramón sprung into motion again—away from the window this time. His eyes were downcast as he stalked toward the edge of the lawn, toward the plants and rocks that bordered the neighboring yard. He stooped clumsily, nearly losing his balance halfway down, and collected a handful of rocks. He held them to his stomach, dropping a few with his rushed movements.

"Ramón, what is it you're going to do?" I asked, though I really meant please don't do this. Please, let's go home. *Please.*

He looked at me, a single stone grasped in his right hand and the others held to his body with his left. His crisp white dress shirt was now dusty along his stomach. I could see beads of sweat glistening along his hairline and temples. "I can't just leave her here."

"You don't seriously want to go to the dance still, do you?"

"It's not about the dance," he barked. He remained focused on Julianne's glowing window, and with a fluid movement that was so natural and unremorseful it seemed as if he were always destined to do it—as if this entire night were somehow about this rather than the dance—he launched his stone upward and sent it clattering against Julianne's shutter.

"Ramón—"

However, before I could reach out to stop him, he'd already cast the next rock.

The shadow in her bedroom drew closer, becoming a darker silhouette rather than a vague shape in the distance. We froze, straining for any sound that might reveal who inside the house had heard us.

The dark figure above paused too.

Was it Julianne, like Ramón clearly hoped it would be?

Maybe it was Nina or Mrs. Callihan, consoling Julianne and reprimanding her for this doomed plot of ours?

Or could it be the sheriff?

My breath caught in my throat as the silent evening air gave way to the soft creak of the window being pushed farther upward. The curtains were parted ever so slowly, and the dark figure emerged, leaning out toward us. Suddenly not so dark at all.

Suddenly . . . Julianne.

Her curls were slightly mussed, but she still wore her shimmering blue gown. Framed by her bedroom light, with her glistening cheeks, she had a distinctly ethereal look.

"What are you still doing here?" she called down, her voice thin and hushed.

Ramón's entire body straightened, as if drawn toward her by a gravitational pull. I heard his breathing quicken at just the sight of her. A star burning bright in the dark night of his heart. "I'm not leaving without you."

Julianne shook her head, but even as she did it, a tearful smile spread across her flushed face. "What? No. Ramón, that's crazy."

"You can't stay here."

Julianne nodded without hesitation, as if that point were painfully obvious.

"Where do you plan on going?" I hissed at Ramón at the same moment Julianne said, "Okay. Let me just grab a few things."

Ramón let out a breath of relief, a hopeful and greedy look settling on his face as we watched Julianne disappear back into her bedroom. He released the remaining rocks he had clutched to his body. It was so silent, I could hear each of them *plunk* into the soft grass.

Things hadn't gone as planned, but what would running away with Julianne accomplish?

Wouldn't that only make things worse?

Oh God, what if we got caught trying to whisk her away?

This had all been a calculated risk, a danger with an overarching purpose. It had been something I could understand. Something I could rationalize. It was something much like my situation at school. But stealing away into the night together? What would that achieve? And what were we risking in doing so?

Julianne reappeared, shoving the curtains aside hastily and unleashing a burst of brightness from her bedroom. She had her bookbag slung over her shoulder, a strange contrast to the gauzy folds of her party dress.

"Rosie," Tim called from behind me.

I'd nearly forgotten Tim was here. Reluctantly, I tore my eyes away from Julianne to look at him peering at me urgently from his car.

"This is a bad idea," he said, shaking his head. "I—I should go. *We should go!*"

I couldn't bring myself to do anything but shake my head back at him before turning to Julianne once more. The sound of Tim's car slowly accelerating only distantly registered with me as I watched her balance herself on the windowsill. She started to sling her leg over, bunching up her pale blue dress in the process. She wobbled precariously, the full skirt making her movements clumsy and uncoordinated.

"Maybe I should change?" she whispered. "I'm not sure I can climb down in this thing."

Ramón cast a dubious glance at the front door and shook his head. "No, better we be quick."

I could see the reluctance on her face, could see her stamping it down with a deep breath. She nodded.

"I'm right here," he said, stepping toward her, his arms outstretched. "I won't let anything happen to you."

It struck me as a rather grand promise, an impossible thing to say, but Julianne appeared comforted by it as she swung her other leg out the window. She was perched on the ledge, facing us.

Ramón nodded eagerly. "That's it, mi amor. Now just turn as you step down, and use the trellis for support. I'm right here. I'll catch you, okay?"

"Okay." Her whisper was far quieter this time.

I could hear the rustle of her skirt as she moved. The vines bristled as she shifted her weight along the latticework, the structure thumping against the house as she approached the ground level. Ramón stepped toward her as she drew closer to the ground, his arms outstretched and waiting.

Then I heard the forceful bang of the front door being flung open.

And because I was still standing at the edge of the yard, and Ramón was hidden by the row of shrubs, I saw the sheriff about a half second before Ramón did.

But it wasn't enough time.

It wasn't enough time to call out his name.

It wasn't enough time to warn him.

It wasn't even enough time for my terror to fully wash over me.

The shock was still rippling through me—my eyes trying to tell the rest of my body what they saw—when Sheriff Callihan charged toward Ramón and Julianne with his gun drawn.

Thirty-Two

Saturday, September 24, 1955

Five.

There were five gunshots.

Which felt like too many.

Any gunshots at all were too many.

But five.

They rang out with a blast that could've split the world right in half. One after another.

Bang. Bang. Bang. Bang. Bang.

There were five gunshots.

Gunshots?

Oh no. It couldn't be, could it?

Gunshots.

Five gunshots.

And two bloodcurdling thuds against the ground.

Thirty-Three

Saturday, September 24, 1955

I pressed my hands to my eyes, but I could still see the flashing lights. Their strobing brilliance was penetrating. Inescapable.

It was fully night now. Not even a glimmer of sunlight along the mountaintops.

But there was still brightness. Somehow. It didn't make sense.

Nothing made sense.

Flashing blue and red, glowing, pulsing.

Police lights.

And of course, the light from the Callihan house. From Julianne's bedroom, the lace curtains still wavering through the window.

I was slumped on the ground, the skirt of my dress splayed around me like a melted puddle of fabric. The cement was still warm to the touch. The sidewalk felt toasty and cozy against my bare legs. I could feel the night air on my back, like the hot breath of someone just behind me. I realized—dimly, distantly, detachedly—that my seam must've burst open, just like Mrs. Callihan warned me, when I rushed toward my fallen friends.

Ramón was on the ground.

Julianne too.

But I couldn't see them from where I was. Couldn't understand how this—*any of this*—had happened.

A small crowd of people milled about the yard, talking to each other in somber tones, dressed in all sorts of uniforms. Police. Paramedics. There were so many of them—maybe ten? When had they gotten here? I wasn't sure. There were so many of them, I couldn't see past them.

Besides, Ramón and Julianne's bodies were covered.

Their *bodies*.

Dizziness seized hold of me, and even though I was seated firmly on the ground, I felt like I was about to fall. I steadied myself with my hands, the grittiness of the cement pressing into my bare palms.

The world around me spun and blurred. The flashing lights. The stars. The muffled chatter. The *blood*.

Tim patted my back. I'd heard him drive away, hadn't I? When had he come back? As I felt his hand against my exposed skin, I realized I was trembling underneath his touch. I was shaking.

I was crying.

I was crying because Ramón and Julianne were dead.

I was crying because I watched them die.

I was crying because I watched Sheriff Callihan kill them.

Thirty-Four

Saturday, September 24, 1955

"Do you . . . do you want me to take you home, Rosie?"

Tim squatted next to me, his skin an ashen color. His dress shirt was rumpled and sweat-stained, his swoop of straw-colored hair mussed and flattened. The vacant roundness in his eyes gave the impression that he'd been awake for days.

He had wanted to leave right from the start. He had tried to. Why hadn't we listened to him? We should've gotten in his car, just like he wanted. We were so *stupid*.

No one addressed us. No one seemed to notice us at all. None of the officers. Certainly not the Callihans themselves. We were invisible in the impossible aftermath, Tim and me. Two sole figures on the perimeter of this scene—witnesses, bystanders, ghosts in our own way. The gruesome chaos churned on without looking outward. It was both a relief and a betrayal.

How could I possibly face everyone with this news?

How could I have let this happen?

I pictured Mamá and Papi. Señora Montoya. Marco.

"Rosie?" Tim repeated gently.

What other choice did I have, though? I had to contend with the consequences. That responsibility had fallen to me. I was the only one left.

I shook my head. "Will you take me somewhere else?"

I could tell by the slow, cautious way he drove that Tim had never been on the south side of town before—especially not at night. It was a daunting drive after the sun went down, even under normal circumstances. No streetlights, unpaved roads, shade trees, and farmlands, dark and rustling and rattling with all sorts of ominous sounds.

It *felt* late, like the entire neighborhood should be asleep and closed down. But despite everything that had happened tonight, I realized it was barely nine o'clock. The Chinese grocery down the street was still brightly illuminated, a line at the checkout counter visible from the window as we drove by. The dance hall a few doors down thrummed with music. Several clusters of passersby ambled along the roadside, meandering and aimless and carefree.

Life went on. Obliviously and miraculously and tragically, life went on.

The Montoya house, though, was quiet. Almost lying in wait, it seemed. Only one light was visible from the street—the bedroom Ramón and Marco shared.

Or used to share, rather.

My limbs were suddenly heavy as Tim's car eased to a stop.

"Do you want me to go in with you . . . to tell his parents?" Tim offered with the kind of instinctive politeness that was so deeply ingrained in him, it seemed unscathed by the horrifying evening we'd just shared.

Even though I wasn't looking at him—I couldn't look at anything besides the dark house that Ramón would never enter ever again—I knew Tim was praying I wouldn't ask this of him.

And I wouldn't.

This was my responsibility and mine alone.

Ramón was my friend, his family was part of my world.

His death was on my hands. Both of their deaths.

I shook my head. "That's okay, Tim. You should go home. Get some rest. I'm so sorry you got pulled into this." My voice broke.

He exhaled, his breath trembling. "I'm really sorry, Rosie."

I couldn't look at him. I couldn't be in this car a moment longer. I gripped the car door handle and pushed it open with far too much force. "Me too," I managed to say. I pushed the door closed behind me before he could say anything else.

He waited as I inched my way up the Montoyas' overgrown walkway. I wished he wouldn't, but I wasn't surprised. He was kind and respectful, and that's what kind and respectful boys did. They made sure girls made it safely to their destinations.

Even after they'd witnessed a murder.

Marco must've heard the car because the front door popped

open only seconds after I'd knocked. His eyes flitted away from me almost instantly and narrowed as they landed on Tim's car behind me.

I heard Tim pull away, the sound of his car fading down the street before Marco had a chance to ask me about it. When his gaze returned to me, the suspicion and wariness in his eyes disappeared, replaced by concern and alarm as the color drained from his face.

I was not sure what I looked like, but I could tell it wasn't good.

Even though we'd never embraced before, he reached for me and pulled me into a hug without a word, without even the briefest trace of hesitation. I felt incapable of doing anything besides melting against him, my entire body going limp in his arms.

As I let my head fall against him, I noticed his hair was damp. The cloud of smoke that usually lingered on him was gone. His skin was cool and fresh with the scent of soap. He must've just gotten out of the shower; perhaps he'd just gotten home from work. He usually worked the early morning shift, but sometimes he would take the evening one for extra money or to cover for someone.

Was he rinsing soap off his body as blood pooled out of his brother's? Was he scrubbing the dust of the warehouse from his skin as Ramón's soul left this earth?

It was too horrible to contemplate. And yet I couldn't stop thinking about it.

I clung to him. I'd never touched anyone like this, except for maybe my parents when I was very young. So unguarded. So openly in need of him. My hands pressed into his back, clutching the thin fabric of his T-shirt like it was my only lifeline.

I felt his hand on the back of my head, stroking the haphazard remains of my bun gently. He tilted his head down toward me, and suddenly it was the moment I'd been dreading.

We were eye level.

His vibrant golden eyes were staring right into mine, blazing with distress.

"Rosa," he croaked, tender and strained. "Are you okay?"

My lip trembled as I inhaled. I wanted to close my eyes and bury myself back in his arms. I wanted to feel the comfort of his shirt against my cheek again. I wanted to wonder what kind of soap he used.

I didn't want to talk about what had just happened.

I didn't know how I possibly could.

But this was what I'd come here to do.

I forced myself to return his gaze, and I shook my head slowly. I wasn't okay. No one was.

Marco's expression hardened. "What happened? What did he do to you?" He held my shoulders as he tried to peer around me once more, and it occurred to me he was looking for Tim, even though I knew he saw his car disappear already.

He thought this was about him.

I shook my head again and reached out for Marco. My hand rested on his upper arm as I tried to steady myself. To summon my courage. "He didn't do anything," I said.

Neither of us did anything.

We did nothing to stop Ramón and Julianne from doing this stupid, reckless thing.

We did nothing to save them.

Marco's eyebrows dipped in confusion underneath the moist spirals of his curls. They were uncombed, free of the pomade he usually wore. The pomade Ramón likely borrowed for tonight. He lifted one hand from my shoulder and stroked my cheek with his thumb. It was a sweet gesture—one I was certain I did not deserve. He was staring at me with such unease, searching my face for any clue as to why I was here. What had happened to bring me to his doorstep in the dark of night looking like *this*.

I could almost pinpoint the exact moment the alarm bells went off in his head.

His posture suddenly stiffened; his right hand fell away from my face as he staggered backward. His left hand remained on my bare shoulder, but his arm locked, as if he was holding me away from him so he could get a good look at me. So his eyes could fully take in the state of my dress.

My blood-splattered dress—the dried stains just a few shades darker than the crimson fabric.

When he finally found his words, they came out hoarse and whispery, but I heard them in my bones. They'd stay with me forever.

"Rosa, where's my brother?"

Thirty-Five

Saturday, September 24, 1955

I wasn't sure what time it was or how long I'd been sitting in stunned silence with Marco when the Phoenix Police Department cruiser pulled up, quietly and inconspicuously. No sirens, no flashing lights. Just two stone-faced officers.

A moment later, Señora Montoya turned the corner from her bus stop. She took in the police cruiser. Then me and Marco on the front steps. I saw as she put it together before anyone had said a word to her. She steadied herself against their fence as the grief washed over her.

"¿Es Ramón?" she asked us, already seeming to know the answer. To understand.

I could only manage a slight nod in response as she sagged to the ground. "¡Mi bebé! ¡Mi bebé!" she wailed.

Marco didn't move from the front step, his head in his hands. I stood and took his mother by the arm, leading her inside the house as the police exited their car. I helped her step around Marco, her grip on my arm viselike.

"Won't you come inside too?" I said to him from the doorway.

He didn't even look up as he shook his head. I tried to pat his shoulder, but he shifted away from me.

"All right," I said. To myself. To no one. I turned to the two officers lingering in the front yard, hands on their hips. They looked sympathetic but uncomfortable. "I suppose you two should come on inside, then." I didn't have the energy for the courtesy or deference I'd normally show to police officers. But I couldn't just ignore them like Marco.

Señora Montoya would need answers. It was the very least I could do.

They nodded at me and followed me inside.

"Were you the young man's sister?" the taller officer said to me as he walked into the kitchen.

I shot him a confused look as I helped Señora Montoya into her chair, her entire body shaking. *Was I Ramón's sister?* What kind of question was that? And then I realized these officers didn't know that I'd been there. That I'd seen what happened. That I was more intricately involved in this situation than they could imagine.

They didn't seem to notice the blood on my red dress in this half-lit room. They knew nothing of the blood on my hands.

"Something like that," I mumbled.

I glanced out the front door as the officers sat down across from Señora Montoya. It had been left slightly ajar. I could see Marco's hunched silhouette from the kitchen table, but he didn't move at all the entire time we spoke.

I listened as these two officers explained to us what happened in slow but impatient tones. I wondered if they'd drawn straws to decide who had to come all the way down here to deliver this dismal parcel of news.

They were very sorry, they said without looking at Señora Montoya.

They were still uncovering the details, they said.

It appeared Ramón was attempting to break into the home of Sheriff Callihan, they said.

He was shot in self-defense, they said.

He was killed instantly, they said.

They were very sorry, they said again, but they needed someone to come down to the station to identify the body and sign some papers.

Except they said all of this in English, which Señora Montoya did not understand.

So I said it all, interpreting each sentiment in Spanish.

Or almost all of it. I couldn't bring myself to repeat some of their misunderstandings to Señora Montoya, of course. The parts about "self-defense" and Ramón being "suspected of breaking and entering." Parts that were clearly false, that would surely get resolved in the light of day once the chaos had settled and the evidence stood clear.

Thirty-Six

Monday, September 26, 1955

As Mamá sat at my bedside and told me that I needed to stay home from school today, I thought of the perfect attendance certificate I'd gotten last year. It still hung on the fridge.

They usually mailed them home, but we didn't have our address on record. The law may not have forbidden Mexicans from going to North, but it did say we were supposed to go to the school closest to where we lived, which I most definitely did not. So the secretary had just handed me my certificate in a special folder so it wouldn't get bent in my bookbag.

Mamá stroked my hair as she spoke to me. "Mi pobre niña," she said. "My poor, poor girl."

"No, I should . . ." The words burned as I struggled to get them out. Everything—my eyes, my cheeks, my throat—was swollen from crying. Everything felt tender and raw from the inside out. I took a shaky breath as I felt more tears welling up.

I knew Mamá was right about school. I couldn't face the questions and the stares from my classmates. Not yet. Perhaps it was cowardly, but I didn't care at this point.

I didn't know why I bothered arguing. I didn't know what I should do, that was for certain. I couldn't even lift my head from my pillow, I was so weighted down with guilt and grief. I had hardly gotten out of bed since she tucked me in late Saturday night. This kind of idleness would never be tolerated under normal circumstances. Blanca and I often shook our heads remembering how many times we'd been sick and simply lathered with Vicks VapoRub so we could complete our daily chores.

But, of course, this was anything but normal. This wasn't just a cough or an upset stomach. This was . . . I didn't quite know what this was. But it hurt.

"Besides," Papi added from where he stood in my doorway, "the officers want to speak with you at the station today. Since you were there." He grimaced a little bit as he said that last part, rubbing his chin as if to conceal his discomfort.

I closed my eyes, drawing my blanket closer around me. My blood pounded in my ears as I thought of the flashing lights of the police cruisers that night. The officers in the Montoyas' kitchen. The sheriff as he ran across his lawn. The five shots he'd fired.

Julianne and Ramón. There one moment, gone the next.

So the police had remembered that I was there after all.

Perhaps I could help. I thought of what they'd said about Ramón breaking and entering and how wrong they were.

Maybe it was good that they'd found me. I could help them understand what had really happened. I could bring truth to the situation. Either way, I knew there was no way around it. If the cops wanted to talk to me, I guess I had to go.

It wasn't as if I could argue with the police, right?

Thirty-Seven

Monday, September 26, 1955

The sheriff's office was downtown, only a couple of miles from school. I'd seen it a handful of times when the bus had to take a detour due to an accident or construction, but I'd never actually known it was there. Probably would never have known if the deputies we talked to on the telephone weren't clear to point out that their headquarters was in the Wells Fargo bank building, of all places.

We were directed to the elevator by a stout mustached security guard who scowled at us when we walked in. After we told him who we were, he straightened up, eyeing us with undisguised curiosity. He offered to escort us all the way up to the sheriff's offices, but I guess I wasn't the only one who suspected that this gesture was more an act of investigation rather than courtesy because Papi assured him we'd be fine without him in a tone I found impressively brusque.

And it didn't stop there. The blatant staring.

The elevator operator peered at us as he opened the door to a room that instantly fell into an eerie, tense silence as soon as we appeared.

Julianne used to talk about this kind of probing hush. After her father was elected sheriff and started appearing in the newspaper every week, she said she felt like rooms were just waiting for her to walk into them.

I had never understood what she meant by that—until now.

Papi stepped out of the elevator first, and though I desperately wanted to mimic his confident posture, I felt like nothing more than his shadow as I trailed after him.

As we crossed the room, a thin woman with a beak-like nose and bouffant hairstyle rose at her desk. She held the telephone receiver in her hand, halfway between the base and her ear, like we'd interrupted her in the act of making a phone call, though we hadn't said anything yet.

"How may I help you?" she asked, thrusting her pointy nose in the air as she spoke.

I should be the one to answer, I realized. This was about me, after all.

But to my utter relief, Papi jumped in. "We are here to meet with the sheriff."

The woman pursed her lips knowingly and spoke as she was already turning away from us. "Very well. I'll let him know you've arrived."

She didn't even ask for our names, but I supposed she knew just by looking at us. Everyone did.

There was an office directly behind her desk. The door was closed, but the walls were made of tinted glass. My eyes followed as she got up and walked over in her modest heels and stiff pencil skirt. As she delivered a curt knock on the door, my gaze suddenly found the sheriff through the glass panels. He was standing behind his desk, his blue eyes—exactly like Julianne's—already fixed on me.

Waiting.

Thirty-Eight

Monday, September 26, 1955

Papi had said I'd be meeting with the sheriff. That's what he had been told. I'd assumed that was just a manner of speaking. I thought we'd be meeting with *someone* at the sheriff's office. Not necessarily the sheriff himself.

I was stunned to see him. I didn't expect him to be here—at *work*.

I thought he'd be at home, grieving.

Over his daughter.

Who died just two days ago.

By his own hand.

Nothing made sense right now. It figured I'd misunderstood this too.

The man who greeted us was a dried-out husk of the Sheriff Callihan I saw the other night. A version of him that had been left out in the sun too long and was now cracked and faded and worn along the edges. As we entered his office, I saw his eyes were red-rimmed and glassy, drooping at the corners. An uneven brassy stubble coated his jaw and sunken cheeks.

"Thank you for coming," he said curtly. He motioned for his dawdling secretary to leave the room, and with noticeable reluctance, she obeyed.

He gestured at the two chairs arranged in front of his desk. I looked at Papi and sat down only after he did. The sheriff remained standing behind his desk.

"You are welcome to wait in the lobby, of course," he said to my father. "I just have some questions for Rosie." The way he said my name made me sit up straighter in my chair.

Out of the corner of my eye, I saw Papi shake his head. "No, no. It's okay. She is only seventeen. I want to be here."

"Mm." Sheriff Callihan placed his hand on a stack of papers on his otherwise immaculate desk. The only other items adorning its surface were a metal pencil cup with exactly three pens and a silver picture frame featuring Julianne's school picture from last year.

He still didn't sit, but he did lean against the desk slightly, shifting his weight to his arms.

"What happened the other night," he began, his voice steady despite the gravelly, tired edge to it, "was a tragedy."

He didn't look at me.

He *couldn't* look at me.

He just stared at the desk. Its glossy surface. I wondered if he could see his own reflection. His bottom lip began to tremble as he searched for his next words.

"An unfortunate tragedy."

I saw Papi tilt his head, and for a moment I thought he was going to say something, but instead he just exhaled as he uncrossed and recrossed his legs, seeming to swallow whatever thoughts were forming inside of him.

"I'm . . . I'm sorry you had to experience that." Sheriff Callihan's words came out calculated and cool, like chess pieces being placed in front of us. "I imagine that had to be very confusing for you."

"Confusing?" I hated the way that word sounded, first from him and then echoing out of my own mouth. But still, I nodded. I *did* feel confused. I couldn't understand why—how—any of this was happening. Woven inside of me along with the agonizing remorse and guilt was deep, undeniable bafflement. Of course, the sheriff knew that. He could probably read it plain as day on my face. "Confusing," I repeated once more, this time softer, but it still didn't sound quite right.

The sheriff grunted, drumming his fingers along his desk.

I didn't know much about law enforcement, I supposed, but I still couldn't believe he was the one here talking to us. *That* was confusing. Could that be what he meant? Since he was there, since he fired the gun, shouldn't there have been someone else to speak with us? Someone less involved? Someone impartial?

Someone who wasn't mourning the loss of his only child?

Someone who hadn't cut two young lives short with his own weapon?

Why *was* he here?

I guess I didn't even know why *we* were there either. I had hoped it was to provide a statement, for me to answer questions about what I saw. But he hadn't asked us anything yet. He didn't even seem curious.

The sheriff took a deep breath, and he started to look at me before he caught himself. I stared at the wispy, coppery top of his head, his eyes still hidden from view.

"Yes," he drawled at last, the word sliding out between gritted teeth. "It is common for bystanders in events like this to display a certain misunderstanding of what happened. Without proper training, why, it is quite easy to misconstrue what's occurred, mix up the sequence of events, misremember people involved, et cetera. It's completely normal."

"But you haven't even asked me about what I saw yet." The words fell out of my mouth without a thought. Papi bristled next to me, and for the briefest instant, it felt like we all stopped breathing. All three of us. "Sir," I added feebly.

The sheriff cleared his throat. "Of course," he said with an unmistakable bite to his words. "Go ahead, *Rosa*." The way he said my name this time—my real name—was a warning. I was sure of it. At long last, his eyes rolled upward. He stared at me, head lowered like a predator.

My insides—my blood, my bones, my breath—turned ice cold. With fear, but also with realization. With the first wave of understanding I'd felt since I watched Ramón and Julianne's bodies come crashing to the ground.

Suddenly, the terrifying reason we were here became clear to me.

He was trying to take hold of my confusion—my shock and desperation. He wasn't interested in investigating at all. What he wanted was a cover-up.

It was so obvious, and yet . . . it couldn't be. Could it?

I could feel Papi watching me.

I took a deep breath, but the air that entered my body was stagnant and unsettling, and it only made me feel even more queasy. "Shouldn't there be someone here to take notes? Or record my statement?"

The entire time we'd been in his office, the sheriff's mouth had been shrinking into a thinner and thinner line. At this point, his lips had all but collapsed into themselves in displeasure.

"Rosa." He said my name again. My real name. "I suppose I thought that we might be able to settle this informally, if you will. Since you are—*were*—a friend of Julianne's." Her name caught in his throat, but despite the brief shudder that rippled through him, he barreled through to his next point. "This is an ugly affair, and I want to be on the same page about moving forward without rehashing it all in the spotlight." He ran his hand along his jaw, tugging at the pallid, unshaved skin. "Now, I've seen how things like this play out. Many times. Once the press gets a hold of it all, it's not pretty. I'd hate to see folks like you dragged into this."

Hadn't I already been dragged into this? I was *there*. I watched it happen. If I could remove myself from it all, erase the gunfire and the screams and the blood from my memory, I would. I *absolutely* would.

But I couldn't. It had happened, no matter how desperately I wished it hadn't. Out of all the things that perplexed and astounded me, that remained excruciatingly clear.

I couldn't deny it. The horrible truth of it.

"But if you want to do it the hard way," Sheriff Callihan said with an ominous shake of his head, "I suppose that is your right." He straightened, no longer leaning against his desk. "I'll have Mrs. Peabody set up an appointment for you. We'll call up our friends at the Phoenix PD. They'll be the ones to handle the case since it's within their jurisdiction. We'll collaborate on the effort. You can meet with some detectives in the interrogation room in the next couple of days if you like, as part of the formal investigation."

I could feel Papi's eyes on me as I nodded, a quick jerk of my chin that I hoped didn't reveal the tremor of nerves I felt inside of me. "I think I'd like to speak with the detectives, please." The sound of my own words made a chill race down my spine.

His eyes flashed as he tipped his head in a gesture that was somewhere between acquiescence and affront. "Mm, well, don't say I didn't warn you, young lady."

Thirty-Nine

Wednesday, September 28, 1955

Tim was waiting for me in front of school on my first day back. How he knew I'd be returning today, I wasn't sure. Had he been waiting for me like this all week?

I thought of my conversation last night with my parents as I drew closer to him, crossing the crowded front courtyard. I thought of how they'd reacted when I told them I needed to go back to school.

"I don't know," Mamá had said. She was exhausted. There were dark circles under her eyes, and her hair was frazzled. She'd been spending every night at the Montoyas' with other women from our church, helping with the cleaning and cooking and consoling her friend through this disaster.

"She has to go back sometime," Papi had replied.

"Does she?" Mamá countered.

"I can't just do nothing." I knew I had startled both my

parents with this. But I couldn't hide at home, surrounded by the anguished buzz of whispers from my neighbors. Couldn't listen to Verón addressing our community on the radio as our friend Victor, with messages of loving one another and streams of somber love ballads. Couldn't keep praying that I wouldn't have to face Señora Montoya or Marco again.

"Oh, Rosa," Mamá had whimpered, a tear streaking down her cheek. "Ay, what are we going to do?"

"What can we do?" Papi fired back. "We carry on."

So here I was. Carrying on. Or trying to.

I noticed Tim was holding something. A small stack of newspaper clippings. I couldn't help but eye them as I greeted him. He'd cut them out with painstakingly straight lines, unlike the jagged little edges most of my articles had from me frantically tearing them out. He handed them to me in a neat little stack. Paper clipped together, like Polaroid photos or coupons. I hadn't told him about my collection. I guess he just knew somehow I'd want them.

"It was on the front page yesterday," he murmured, shoving his hands in his pockets. For several moments, I was too fixated on the secretive way he was hunching toward me and the disquieting hush that had fallen over the courtyard to fully register what he'd said. Finally, I let my eyes fall on the papers clenched between my fingers. The blocky letters were fuzzy and unfocused. My mind caught on the sound of my name being whispered somewhere behind me.

"The front page?" It came out louder than I intended.

Tim's eyes widened as a cluster of girls to my right turned

around to peer at us. He nodded, jaw tight. "At first, in the Sunday paper, it was just a tiny article, a couple pages in. A quick something about a disturbance near the sheriff's house. Only a few sentences. You'll see. No details or anything, really. It took a couple of days, but then there was something about a suspected kidnapping and a fatality." The way he said the word "fatality" sounded so unnatural, like he'd been mulling the word over for a while now, but this was the first time he'd ever uttered it out loud. "No one had been named yet. But today . . ." He waved his hand at the papers, and for the first time, I forced my eyes to take in the text before me, blinking until the swirling black symbols became letters.

The bold script of *The Arizona Republic* stared back at me. There were two large pictures right below the headline. On the left was the Callihan house. Bright and tidy, unmarred by corpses and blood and police sirens. And on the right was Julianne. Just Julianne.

It was her school portrait—the same one that was on the sheriff's desk.

Her shy smile, not quite enough to show her teeth or to give her cheeks their full roundness. Just the slightest sparkle in her eyes, the subtle upturning of her rosebud lips. Her golden hair, even in gray tones, was radiant in flowing curls. Pearl earrings studded her earlobes. The top of her collar and cardigan peeked out at the bottom of the picture. The very epitome of an all-American teenager.

It made my stomach lurch as I involuntarily compared this version of her to my last disordered memories of her . . .

Tearstained and flushed in an evening dress, arguing with her father.

Stumbling backward in her heels after the force of his blow had hit her powdered cheek.

Panicked and heartbroken, reaching for Ramón as she was dragged upstairs.

Crumpled and lifeless on her lawn, red blood flowering against her baby-blue bodice.

I shuddered.

"It mentions a witness at the end. Not a name," Tim said, tilting his head toward me, as if that made any difference at all with everyone's eyes on us like they were. "I—I think most people know it's you, though. That you were there. Julianne was so private, you know. Kept to herself. But most everyone at school knows you two were close, that you were planning on going to the dance together."

I knew this before he said it, of course. We used to be two girls just trying to get through the day without everyone looking at us. And now? Look what this quiet friendship had led to.

It was too much.

"Tim, I'm so sorry," I sputtered, my throat tight with the threat of oncoming tears. "We shouldn't have—*I* shouldn't have . . . You . . . I'm so very sorry."

The words on the page started to dance in front of me. Clammy, flushed pangs of emotion hammered along the back of my neck. On my palms. At my temples.

It was too much.

I couldn't do this.

Why had I thought I could do this?

With a shaky breath, I glanced at Tim once more, but I didn't really see him—just his shadowy outline, just the sense that he was watching me with growing wariness.

I thought I heard him say my name, but I wasn't sure if that thin, echoing sound was real or a figment of my imagination.

I needed silence. Peace. A respite. I didn't deserve it, but I couldn't bear a moment longer with people looking at me and talking about me and . . .

I bolted.

The house was empty when I got there since my parents were at work. I rushed in, dropping my bookbag on the floor. I slumped against the door, head lolled back and eyes clenched shut.

I searched for quiet, my pulse pounding, my breathing ragged. I could hear the low, disinterested tones of all the officers I'd spoken to at the interview yesterday. I could hear Señora Montoya crying. I could hear gunshots.

I opened my eyes.

It was still early. I hadn't been awake all that long. And yet weariness took hold of my body, a bone-deep exhaustion that was about more than the fitful, nightmare-ridden sleep I'd gotten last night. Everything from my eyelids to my legs suddenly felt heavy, overburdened, and I barely made it to our sofa before sleep dug its claws into me and dragged me into an all-consuming silence.

Forty

Wednesday, September 28, 1955

"Hermanita, ¿qué haces aquí?"

It was Blanca's stricken voice that began to draw me out of sleep, but it was Guillermo's little fingers in my hair, tugging powerfully, that brought me fully awake. My sister crouched above me, an alarmed frown creasing her face. Guillermo was slung against her hip, making several full-body moves to escape from her grasp. I could see one of my dark hairs wrapped in his chubby hand as he reached out toward me for another fistful.

I sat up, returning Blanca's frown. "I *live* here."

She clicked her tongue and hoisted Guillermo a little higher. "You know what I mean. Why aren't you at *school*? Mamá said this was your first day back since . . ." She trailed off, and instead of trying to find a way to finish that sentence, she busied herself with tugging down Guillermo's shirt, which had risen to expose his round belly.

I shrugged, avoiding her discerning gaze.

"Did something happen?" She set Guillermo on the floor as she took my hands in hers, forcing me to look at her. Her eyes were red and shining and swimming with fear.

I shook my head. Of course something had happened. The unthinkable had happened. But that wasn't what she meant, I knew that.

"Pues, háblame, Rosa." The sharp snap of her Spanish made her sound so much like Mamá, it would've almost been funny under any other circumstance. She gave my hand a squeeze. "What's going on? Mamá told me you talked to those detectives again yesterday. Was it something they said?"

"No, it's not that," I mumbled, and it wasn't a lie. Not really.

"No?" She wasn't going to let this go. My sister was nothing if not stubborn.

"Yesterday . . . it didn't matter," I told her, still trying to piece together how that could be. How something like that could be so dull and insignificant. It was an interrogation about the murder of two teenagers, and yet it hadn't felt that way at all.

They'd gone through the whole routine, of course. A big production. A private room. The big fancy recording machine; they'd waved the microphones around to show them off like it was a treat for me to be this close to them. There'd been two officers, one from the sheriff's department and one from the Phoenix Police Department.

"Rosa," Blanca said soothingly.

"They hardly asked me anything at all, Blanca. I'd spent the whole night before going through everything I could remember from that night. I mean, it's all I can think about anyway, but I tried to pull out the important things. Tried not to let my sadness and my fear cloud the facts, you know?" Soberly, Blanca nodded. "I thought about what Julianne and her father had said to each other, what he'd said to us. About the order of everything, who was where . . ." My throat started to sting. "I just wanted to be able to remember everything, like I was supposed to."

I could see tears in my sister's eyes as my voice warbled. "Oh, Rosa. Of course."

"But all they wanted to talk about was Ramón. About where he was from, whether he was born here or Mexico. Where his parents were, where he lived, whether he was a good student or a troublemaker. They even questioned *Papi*! He wasn't there that night, but they asked him all those same questions about Ramón anyway."

I could hear the officer's voice even as I spoke, a droll echo in my imagination. I saw him leaning back in his chair, pen tapping along the side of a blank notepad, saying, "I'm just wondering what kind of fellow shows up uninvited like that to a man's home *and* thinks it's a good idea to break in after being asked explicitly to evacuate the premises?" I thought of the way the officers had chuckled at that, like it was almost too ridiculous to answer.

"What does this have to do with the shooting?" I'd asked at first.

"Sweetheart, we just need you to answer the questions," said the first officer, the one with the police department.

Then the other man had leaned toward me, cocking his head like we were pals. Like I was on his team. "You do want to cooperate with this investigation, don't you?"

"Of course, I just—"

The officers had exchanged a quick look before the sheriff's deputy continued. "How was it that this boy knew Miss Callihan in the first place?"

"I—"

"It seems like you were acquaintances with both of them, is that correct?"

I gave the slightest nod, watching as the deputy jotted his first note down. Illegible from my angle.

"I go to school with Julianne. She and I, we're friends. We're reporters for the school newspaper." Again, the officers' gaze had flitted to each other's. "And I grew up with Ramón," I said, selecting my words as carefully as I could. "Our families are friends. Our fathers served together in the war. I am not quite sure how Ramón and Julianne came to know each other, though." My stomach flipped at this not-quite lie, the image of the two of them at the pep rally flickering in my brain like a torn piece of film caught in the projector reel. I didn't know how that one moment had led to any of this, really. I'd been too angry to ask at first, and then... then things had moved so quickly.

I felt Guillermo's fingers toying with the hem of my skirt, trying to bring the fabric to his mouth. I reached down to pat his head, savoring his downy soft hair for a moment before I continued relaying my disappointment to my sister. "We didn't talk about anything that truly mattered, Blanca. It's all so *unbelievable*."

"Unbelievable?" she said softly, almost as if it were to herself. She let out a puff of air. "Sad, yes. But not unbelievable, hermanita."

I looked at her, though she was watching her baby. Or at least her eyes were downcast in Guillermo's direction. But, I realized, she had a faraway look, like she was seeing something distant. Something only she could see. A mournful thoughtfulness marked her face, her full lips twisted into a pout. It took her several moments to notice me watching her, and she gave a melancholy snort as she met my eyes. "What? You may be book-smart, Rosa, but . . ."

"But what?"

The look she shot me was the same face she'd make when we'd team up against Ramón playing hide-and-seek. Like we were in on a big secret together. But unlike all the times I spied her crouched behind an oleander bush or stooped underneath a table, now I wasn't sure what her unspoken truth was.

She sighed regretfully. "You can be a bit naive sometimes."

"*Naive?*"

Blanca nodded, glancing at Guillermo, who had crawled toward the table near the kitchen that held the radio. "Just sometimes. It's not a bad thing, truly."

"Oh right, that sure sounds like a compliment," I scoffed, the tears I'd felt clumped in my throat earlier now spilling down my cheeks.

"Oh, Rosa," she said, scooting even closer to me so our legs were pressed up against one another. "I'm sorry. I didn't mean to upset you. You have so much going on right now, I know that." She paused, considering her words. "All I meant was, the way you see the world isn't how it always is. Or at least it isn't how the world is for a lot of us."

For a lot of us.

People like her and Ramón. People who didn't have the benefit of being light-skinned. People who were forced to contend with the harsh capriciousness of the world every single day. People without the choices that I had.

I wanted to tell her I knew that. I knew that things were difficult and unfair. After all, that's why I went to school somewhere else, why I lived this half life, why I wanted to go to college and write about these important things. But did I *really* know? How much of it had I actually experienced firsthand before this?

I knew nothing of the true ugliness of the world—of the violence, of the apathy, of the pain. I'd been utterly blindsided by it all. I'd said I understood, said I was being careful and smart, and yet . . .

I *was* naive.

The tears fell faster now, dripping off my face and into my lap. "I just want to do what's right, Blanca," I said between sobs.

"What's right, hmm?" She pulled me close to her body, her arm tight around my shoulders, and rested her head against mine. "All right. Then let's go, hermanita."

I turned my head to look at her. "Go where?"

"You're going to come with me over to the Montoyas'—"

I jerked backward, shaking my head. "No, Blanca. I can't."

She held up an admonishing finger, as if she were telling Guillermo a simple no-no. "Have you even seen her since that night?"

I swallowed as my imagination plummeted back to that night. To the kitchen table. "No," I said hoarsely.

"Well, then," Blanca said, like that settled it. "Mamá and I have been helping with her laundry. I've got a load of hers that I need to take off the line out back and return to her. You can help me carry it over."

"*Blanca*," I pleaded.

"I know it's hard," she said. "But, Rosa. You've lived so much of your life in the in-between, where things are unclear. It's not your fault, but it becomes easy to hide there. You can't hide. Not from this. You're being forced to face it, and you may as well do it on your terms. A lot of hard things have happened to you—things that were perhaps out of your control—but you get to decide what to do next. Where to go from here." When I didn't respond, she softened her tone. "You know she'll want to see you. Señora Montoya loves you."

"But what if she doesn't? What if she blames me?"

Blanca was quiet for so long that I began to wonder if I'd managed to say those questions out loud. Perhaps I'd only thought them. But then she got to her feet and said, "I suppose there's only one way to find out. Vámonos."

Forty-One

Wednesday, September 28, 1955

I froze on the Monotyas' doorstep, laundry basket clutched so tight that the wicker bit into the pads of my fingers. To my right, the mulberry tree Ramón and I used to climb rustled in the breeze. It was the same tree where we'd sat that afternoon in August, him singing and me agonizing over my first day of school. My stomach churned at this memory, at once vivid and remote somehow. Right before me, clear as day, and gone forever at the same time.

I cast an uncertain glance at Blanca, who had paused at the base of the front steps to remove Guillermo from his stroller. Lips pursed, she moved past me and opened the front door without knocking—something I'd done countless times in my life. Something I couldn't even fathom doing now.

With a gulp, I followed her inside.

Father Al from church was seated on the couch with Señora Montoya, whose eyes were closed in prayer. He didn't stop reciting his prayer as his gaze flitted up warmly to us. Blanca murmured, "Hola, padre" as she led me to the kitchen, which was crowded with women cooking, cleaning, consoling each other.

"Put the laundry over there, won't you?" Blanca said to me as one of the older women reached out to her to hold Guillermo. He squealed happily as he was transferred.

My eyes drifted around the cramped space, noting Mamá's friends from church, girls from the neighborhood, and grandmothers who sat on their front porches in the evenings, trading chisme.

One person, however, was painfully absent.

"He isn't here," my sister whispered to me, somehow reading Marco's name in my expression. "He's out of the house a lot." I wasn't sure what that meant exactly, but it seemed Blanca intended to be vague.

Numbly, I set the laundry basket just inside Señora Montoya's bedroom. It barely hit the floor before Blanca tapped me on the shoulder. "Dishes. I'll wash, you dry."

And that's what we did. We allowed ourselves to be swept up in this current of domesticity, in caretaking as a form of love and salvation. And while I knew a tidy house wouldn't fix Señora Montoya's broken heart, it felt . . . not quite good but close to it, to do something. The rhythm of it all reminded me that I couldn't survive this on my own. I'd been forced into my own bubble by my situation at North, passing but not belonging, and it had been hard but manageable. But now? We needed each other. All of us. There wasn't a single one of us who could do this by themselves.

And when Señora Montoya pulled me into a hug as we were leaving, it didn't hurt like I'd expected. I'd worried that her pain would be overwhelming, that it would be a burden that would become entangled with my own guilt.

That it would break us both.

Instead, it felt like something we shared. Our grief, split between the two of us. Not quite a lighter load, but one we recognized in each other at the very least.

"Ay, mi nuera," she said in a half sob, stroking my hair.

I was struck with an excruciating stab of nostalgia as we held each other, thinking of all the times she'd playfully called me her daughter-in-law. Ramón and I laughing and rolling our eyes and teasing one another.

"Te quiero, Rosa," she told me.

I was crying so hard—with remorse, with relief—that I wasn't sure she heard me tell her that I loved her back.

Later that night, I slipped into my bedroom and laid my notebook out on my bed with the newspaper clippings Tim had brought. My hands trembled as I ran my fingers along the creased and crumpled rectangles of paper.

Blanca had been right. I was glad I'd gone to see Señora Montoya. And while I wasn't sure I deserved that kind of support, I was glad Señora Montoya had it. It's what Ramón would have wanted.

SHERIFF'S DAUGHTER NAMED VICTIM IN SUSPECTED KIDNAPPING GONE AWRY

Tuesday, September 27, 1955
The Arizona Republic

Sheriff Callihan responded to a suspicious noise outside his home on the evening of September 24th. According to a report from the sheriff's department, he drew his weapon upon seeing an intruder attempting to scale the exterior wall of his home to reach the window of his daughter, Julianne Callihan. Warning shots were fired initially, according to the report, but when the suspect was undeterred, additional shots were taken. The intruder was struck four times in the back. A stray bullet, appearing to have ricocheted off the storm drain, struck Miss Callihan in the chest.

Additional details regarding the fatalities, including the intruder's identity, are expected to be released at the sheriff's upcoming press conference on Thursday, September 29, at four o'clock in the afternoon at city hall.

Forty-Two

Thursday, September 29, 1955

I found Tim as soon as I got to school the next day. I was buzzing like a live wire, two words from the most recent newspaper article thrumming through my entire body. *Press conference, press conference, press conference.* I had hardly slept.

"We have to go to hear what he has to say," I told Tim.

"Who?" he said uncomprehendingly, and I didn't move, didn't even blink, until a flicker of understanding settled onto his pale, exhausted face. "You're talking about the sheriff?" His eyes, shiny and red like he hadn't been sleeping much either, went wide. He shut his locker slowly.

Everyone was still staring at me. Heads turned all around us. Mouths closed in on ears to whisper some comment or another. Was it more brazen now? It surely seemed like there was no effort to hide the fact that I was now the focus of their attention. Was I imagining it?

I nodded swiftly. "The sheriff's speaking today at city hall. That's not far from here."

He grimaced. His hesitation made my heart plummet. "I heard a lot of folks are planning on being there. A lot of people from school were saying they wanted to go in honor of Julianne."

"Exactly. For Julianne. *And* Ramón."

His entire face twisted into a mess of frown lines and trepidation. "I just don't know if that's the best idea for you. People are starting to talk, Rosie."

"That doesn't matter to me," I lied, hoping that as I said these words, they'd become true. "What's been reported in the newspapers—it's not the full story. Not even close." I could feel my resolve withering away inside of me, my fear chipping away at my bravado as I thought of the disparaging conversations at the police department. I took a deep breath. "I need to be there, Tim. I need to hear what he has to say about what happened that night. I need to . . ." I trailed off, not entirely sure what the end of that sentence was.

Tim ran a hand along the back of his neck, his eyes darting around us uncomfortably. "Well, Rosie, what *did* happen?"

Tim, poor Tim, had gone in blindly, expecting nothing more than a night of dancing in the school gym. I couldn't fault him for his confusion. I'd been battling my own lack of understanding—and I'd known what I was walking into that night.

And yet his reluctance still made my stomach sink.

"Tim, the sheriff shot my friends," I told him as evenly as I could manage. "Ramón was my best friend. We grew up together. Our fathers were best friends too."

Tim's expression softened with understanding as he undoubtedly pieced together what this meant about who I was.

"He and Julianne met because of me. Ramón came to the pep rally to see me, and they hit it off, I guess. That part has always been a bit hard to understand, but that's how Ramón was. Heart on his sleeve kind of fellow, you know?"

He gave me a sad, sympathetic nod.

"They . . . they were together. The two of them, they were a couple; they had been for a couple weeks before they hatched this plan. They had this whole thing about being bold and brave and telling the world about their love at the ball. And I thought it was crazy, but they were so hopeful, and I—I'm sorry, I should've told you. I should've. You deserved to know what you'd gotten yourself into, Tim." My voice began to crack, and he placed his hand on my arm to steady me. "Anyway, you know the rest, I suppose. The sheriff came home and was angry to find that Julianne's date was Ramón and not you, and, well, you know that part. Julianne was trying to sneak out, to climb out of her window, and that's when the sheriff shot Ramón—shot them both. And the thing is, I'm beginning to suspect no one would even care about any of this if Julianne hadn't been killed too." Even Tim's warm hand on my arm couldn't stop a fresh batch of tears from welling up. "They're trying to cover it up. To make it seem like . . . like nothing wrong happened."

I searched his face desperately for some sign of agreement

as I dabbed at my eyes. I wasn't sure if anything I said added up. I was still piecing it all together, of course. But I knew, in the pit of my stomach, that I was onto something. And I couldn't just let it go, even if I was still uncovering the bigger picture.

"But what exactly are you going to do?" He wasn't arguing with me, but he hadn't agreed either. "Are you going to stand up in the middle of the sheriff's press conference? Steal a microphone? Start ranting and raving about the plan a couple of teenagers cooked up to make some sort of showy political statement at a high school dance?" He kept his voice low, but I could still hear his skepticism. He was trying to dissuade me.

It stung.

A very large part of me wished I was brave enough to do what he was describing, but it seemed we both knew that wasn't me. "I—I don't know yet. But I can't just stand by and let it happen. I've got to at least be there and hear what he says."

Tim stared at me silently, his square jaw tense with clear indecision.

"You don't have to come. I know this was all way more than you signed up for," I conceded thinly.

The bell rang out to start our day, sounding over my last few words. Though there were still countless eyes on us, most of the students began drifting down the hall toward the classroom doors at the opposite end.

"I just thought you might want to," I added, readjusting the strap of my bookbag and looking up at him square in the eyes. "You know, as a fellow outsider."

Forty-Three

Thursday, September 29, 1955

People poured out the front doors as soon as the bell rang, like ants spilling from a crushed anthill. Everywhere you looked, students were racing to cars, scrambling for rides, dashing out to beat traffic. The sheriff was scheduled to speak at four o'clock. The man was notoriously punctual, so that gave us exactly a half hour to make our way downtown to Phoenix city hall.

    I missed Julianne so deeply in that storm of impatient energy. Missed having someone by my side in a world that often felt like it moved to a different rhythm, someone who would've rolled her eyes at the raucous jeering of the football players or pointed out that the paloverde trees still had their flowers this late into the year. But here I was. All alone.

    I paused on the final step of the school entrance. I supposed the bus was my best option, though I'd be ten minutes late at best. I'd definitely be in the back of the crowd, maybe even too far to be able to hear well. I'd likely miss the beginning, but it was better than nothing.

But just as I stepped down—before my foot even reached the cement landing at the base of the stairs—I felt a heavy arm drape itself around my shoulders, a warm figure cozying right up beside me.

"Come on, better hurry," Tim said without missing a beat, guiding me toward his car in the swarming parking lot. "Outsiders stick together."

Forty-Four

Thursday, September 29, 1955

There was a row of sheriff's deputies standing behind the vacant podium when Tim and I joined the crowd amassed in front of the imposing sandstone building of city hall. It wasn't far from the sheriff's office, I realized, but this building was much more impressive than the dowdy old bank building where the sheriff's department was tucked away. City hall, with its decorative bricks and vaguely Spanish colonial windows, was a beautiful place, built for the eyes of history.

Perfect for photos. A truly monumental backdrop. I could practically see it on the front page of *The Arizona Republic*.

"Over here." Tim tilted his head toward a vacant bench at the back as we approached the crowd. We'd had to park a few blocks away at a parking meter, but Tim's watch told us we were still a few minutes early. He was tall enough that he could see over most of the bystanders' heads, but he held his hand out to help me step onto the bench so I'd be high up enough to see and hear too.

My gaze swept over the crowd of faces, everyone bubbling with an unsettled curiosity. I recognized quite a few people from school. Tim pointed out some girls from the cheer squad, and I noticed a group of staff writers from the newspaper. My heart lurched as I spotted one unnervingly familiar face across the way.

Leaning against the narrow trunk of a towering palm tree was Peter Duke, arms folded across his chest, eyes locked on the setup in front of us all. A few boys from the football team stood near him chattering excitedly, arms waving with animated gestures, but it didn't look like Peter was listening to them.

It made sense that he was here. But the look on his face had my insides on a razor's edge. His features were settled into a pout—a handsome pout, of course—and there was a hardness in his eyes I had never seen before. Even from a distance, it was clear to me there was something dark ready to burst out of that boy. Something more than sadness. More than grief.

I hadn't thought of him much over the past few days, but now I found I couldn't tear my eyes away from him as I tried desperately to understand what I saw on his face.

Suddenly, he straightened, somehow sensing my gaze, and slowly turned in my direction. Seeking out his unknown observer. A shiver raced down my spine as our eyes met across the sea of bobbing heads. His lips curled into a sharp scowl, and for a moment I thought he was going to call something out to me. What he could possibly have to say, I had no idea.

He shifted, moving out of my view as he pivoted forward, a hush falling over the crowd. An expectant, stifled kind of silence that stopped us in our tracks simultaneously.

I looked up, and I understood.

The sheriff was ready to speak.

He wore his tan uniform, just like the other officers, but he must've given his badge a special shine because the star on his chest was blinding. It caught a spectacular gleam in the late afternoon sun, and I had to shield my eyes. His hair was much neater since I'd sat across from him in his office, and I wondered if he'd gotten a haircut. The idea of that man going to the barber in the midst of all this grief, days after the bloodshed he'd caused, made me queasy. It was exactly how I'd felt when I'd spotted him at work that day I'd gone into his office. It was so gruesomely routine.

There was the slightest tremble in his hands as he adjusted the microphone toward him. Like a leaf on a branch, quivering in a breeze.

In my peripheral vision, I saw Tim step toward me—glance up at me—protectively. But I didn't look away from the sheriff. I couldn't look away.

"Good afternoon. Thank you for being here," the sheriff said into the microphone in front of him, and the words reverberated with a tinny echo throughout the mass of people. He looked down. He was holding a small stack of papers in his hands, fidgeting with them. Running his fingers along the edges like the mere sensation was tethering him to this moment, to his purpose today. "It's with a heavy heart that I address you, but I feel it is my responsibility to provide you, my constituents, my community, with a factual account of the events that transpired the evening of September twenty-fourth." He cleared his throat and paused to let his gaze rake over the crowd. It seemed strangely deliberate. Rehearsed.

It was chilling.

"As you've likely heard, a terrible tragedy took place at my home this past weekend." His voice caught on these last words, and again he directed his focus toward his papers, his gaze dropping down while he appeared to take a steadying breath. He didn't look back up before he continued speaking. "The life of my daughter, Julianne, was taken during a series of horrible events surrounding a suspected kidnapping. This has been an incredibly difficult time for both my wife and me, so my remarks today regarding my daughter will be brief. However, I know there are many questions about what happened, and I wanted to deliver a few of the facts we've gathered at this time." He flipped a page. The crowd was so quiet that I could hear the paper rustle.

"At approximately six forty-five in the evening, shortly after I returned home from work, I heard a disturbance outside my home. Upon investigating, I discovered a man attempting to remove my daughter from her bedroom window. As both a parent and a trained officer, I responded accordingly, treating the issue with the utmost seriousness. I drew my weapon and fired a shot at the perpetrator. When he was undeterred, I proceeded to fire my weapon an additional four times." Here he drew in another deep breath, and though it seemed like he'd use this pause to return his gaze to the crowd, he didn't. His stare remained fixed downward. "After—" he warbled shakily. He paused once more, cleared his throat, and repeated himself with more firmness. "*After* the final shot, the perpetrator released my daughter and fell to the ground, likely due to the wounds he sustained. As I approached both him and my daughter, it became clear to me that one of the bullets had ricocheted . . . and my daughter had been shot as well." The last words tumbled out of his mouth, rushed and garbled.

The silence that had gripped us began to crack and crumble as a soft, horrified murmuring snaked its way through the audience.

"I—I . . ." His mouth hung open for a beat, as if he was searching for the right words even though they were likely right there in front of him. "I am *heartbroken* at what I can only describe as a tragic accident. I've dedicated my life to protecting and serving my community, and that has always included my family. If you are a parent, I hope you can empathize with my wife and me as we cope with our immeasurable loss."

I didn't remember moving at all as he spoke, but I found my hand clasped over my mouth. His sadness was so palpable. It tore through me, piercing and disorienting. It was so hard to reconcile his grief with his role in what happened. How was it possible that he was both the cause of this tragedy and a victim? It was physically excruciating to consider, making my entire chest throb in a way that rendered breathing difficult.

"The perpetrator has been identified as Ramón Montoya, a seventeen-year-old Mexican male, unknown to both my wife and me."

The pulsing ache inside of me sputtered to a stop at the sound of Ramón's name. Like a balloon blown up as big as it possibly could be. Stretched tight. About to burst.

Ramón Montoya. Ramón Montoya. Ramón Montoya.

I hated the way it sounded coming out of his mouth.

"We are currently in the process of investigating any known connections this man may have had to my family and encourage anyone with additional details to please reach out to the sheriff's office immediately." He paused, his skin shining with sweat. "With instances such as this, where a civilian bystander is struck down during an officer's response to an incident, the Maricopa County Sheriff's Department conducts a thorough investigation. This is our standard protocol, and I intend to fully comply with the investigation. Additionally, since this incident took place within Phoenix PD's jurisdiction, we will be partnering with detectives to uncover all available evidence related to this trespasser and the events that followed."

Finally, he looked up—a quick glance around, shifty and fleeting. It almost seemed as if he might elaborate on this final piece of information, but he did not. Instead, his jaw clamped down on unsaid words, and he turned his head. One of the men behind him stepped forward and said something in his ear, and the sheriff gave a slight nod.

"This is a very sensitive issue, as I'm sure you understand. Mrs. Callihan and I both appreciate your support and ask that you respect our privacy as we grieve." He lifted his hand in a feeble half wave, and as he began to turn away from us, the crowd erupted in questions—particularly the reporters clustered in the front, waving notepads in the air frantically.

"Sheriff Callihan, is there any legitimacy to the rumor that you plan to run for governor? How will this impact your campaign?"

"Is this event linked to rising crime rates in central Phoenix?"

"Did he have a criminal history?"

"Was he a bracero? Was he here legally?"

"Who was he? What can you tell us about this Ramón Montoya? Was he known to your daughter?"

The sheriff collected his papers, shaking his head. "Like I said, I will not be taking ques—"

"Sheriff, Ramón Montoya was unarmed. He was your daughter's *boyfriend*. Was he not?"

The question boomed out across the crowd. It didn't come from the row of reporters but rather somewhere in the middle. It was a familiar, steady vibrato. A confident, purposeful tone that I knew instantly even if my remorse-addled brain struggled to place it.

My eyes searched the crowd, seeking out the source. I startled when I finally found it.

Around him, people were starting to face him, to form a small circle a step away from him to stare. A few people clapped and called things like, "Let him speak!" or "Answer his question!" in both English and Spanish.

Standing right in the middle of all these people, in his own expanding spotlight, was Victor Verón.

"He was seventeen years old, Sheriff. A student, a young man with a life ahead of him. He and your daughter were *in love*."

With each word, Verón's voice grew louder, rolling across the audience like a giant boulder crashing down a mountainside. A few gasps, some charged whispering, but for the most part we waited, collectively breathless, for what came next.

Marco must've told him everything. Instinctively, I looked for him next—for that knowing scowl or those blazing eyes. But no.

No Marco.

A mix of disappointment and relief nipped at me.

When I returned my attention back to the podium, I was surprised to see the sheriff still standing there—angled away from us but unable to take more than a single step toward the building. Like Verón's words had frozen him to the spot. He stared right back at Verón with a wide-eyed, open-mouthed expression that gave him a vaguely skeletal look.

However, before he could say or do anything, a deputy appeared next to him and guided him away from the podium with an arm on his shoulder. As the sheriff walked away, another deputy approached the microphone. "As with any high-profile case, there are bound to be many rumors and unsubstantiated accounts. The investigation is still open, and I assure you that we, along with the police department, will consider all—"

"Ask *her*! *She* knew him! She was *there*!"

Even before I fully registered who had spoken up this time, my body seized in panic. My muscles and nerves sensed the danger a moment before my brain did. The crowd's attention was again diverted. Bodies twisted and turned away from the podium once more, away from Verón.

Peter Duke stood a few yards away from me, face flushed, his arm outstretched and pointing right at me. "Tell them! Tell them what you know, Rosie Capistrano!" he spat, his words jagged and uneven, barely restrained in his infuriated effort to be heard. "I saw that *spic* at school, looking for you! You're in the middle of all this, aren't you?"

Now I was the one rooted to the spot. Heat raced down my skin, each person's eyes on me burning.

"*Aren't you?*" he demanded again.

I started to shake my head, started to deny it, but my neck wouldn't cooperate. I couldn't do anything. Nothing at all.

Tim reached up and took my hand. Gently, he guided my rigid body down from the bench and tugged me away from the crowd. He marched toward his car, pulling me along behind him. I followed with clumsy steps, like my feet didn't belong to me at all. It was hard to keep up with his long strides, and I found myself stumbling, but even as I scrambled for balance, I was thankful for his speed, his urgency, his ability to act when I'd been struck senseless.

We were almost out of earshot, almost around the corner when I heard Peter's voice one final time. "*You're* the reason she's dead, Rosie Capistrano!"

Forty-Five

Thursday, September 29, 1955

As soon as we rounded the corner and put some space between us and the crowd—which had erupted into a riot of shouts and calls to order from the police officers—I instantly wanted to be alone.

Wanted silence. Wanted to think. Wanted to *hide*.

Even as the voices faded, they lingered inside my mind. Peter's accusations rolled on and on with the speed of my racing heart. Relentless and inescapable. *You're the reason she's dead.*

"I'll drive you home, Rosie," Tim said gently, just like he had that night.

I couldn't stop shaking. I couldn't catch my breath. I . . .

"We'd better hurry. I hate to think what trouble a crowd like that might get into," he added with a tone of apology.

I managed to nod as I sank into the passenger seat of his car, gazing forward. I watched a woman leave Woolworth's with a paper shopping bag dangling from her hands, smiling to herself before she popped into the men's shoe store next door.

I was no longer the quiet girl in the middle row hoping not to get noticed. I was no longer an anonymous teenage witness in the background of these events. I was no longer a high school rumor.

Now, because of Peter, I was at the front and center of a firestorm.

The drive to the south end of town was a quiet one. Tim made a couple polite, half-hearted comments about the radio, remarking vaguely on a song about a yellow rose, but I didn't think either of us were really listening—to the music or each other.

His car eased to a stop a few houses down from mine. I didn't want him to pull up directly in front of my house and risk Mamá and Papi seeing us. They were already so worried about my mixed-up world these days. I didn't want them to know how much worse I'd made it now.

Eyes trained ahead, I muttered a quick thank-you as I collected my books at my feet. I could feel Tim watching me, and it was with great reluctance that I finally looked over at him, my heartbeat sounding out every second that passed between us.

"You know that this isn't your fault, don't you?" he said, his voice soft and warm. I could see his Adam's apple quiver in his throat as he spoke.

I felt like I was on the verge of tears—I'd felt like that the entire ride home—but my body was too exhausted to cry. I just sighed, shaking my head in response as I swung the car door open and stepped out onto the sunlit roadside. Before closing the door, I caught myself. I stooped slightly so I could look at Tim once more.

"Of course it's my fault, Tim," I said. My voice was quiet but clear. Firm. Unflinching. "We're all to blame."

Forty-Six

Friday, September 30, 1955

The next morning, my parents were waiting for me at the breakfast table. More unsettling than the matching frowns that marred their tired faces was the fact that they were both seated. Still for once.

"Hija," Mamá began, but she couldn't say anything else before she broke into tears. She dabbed at her eyes with her dish towel, looking away.

Papi scowled in the direction of the radio, which I realized was off. Another oddity.

This couldn't be good.

"We heard about what happened yesterday," he said. "On the radio. The . . . the . . . what do you call it?" He waved his hand irritably as he searched for the word.

"Press conference," I finished for him. Of course they'd heard. Of course Verón had spoken about it on his show.

Mamá sniffled. "Victor didn't say her name, gracias a Dios."

Papi threw his hands up in the air at this. "That doesn't matter at this point. Don't you see? The world knows it was her."

Papi seemed to understand that even though Victor hadn't shared my identity with his followers, that didn't mean the other reporters had done the same. My name was probably being printed in papers all across the state.

This made Mamá cry harder, her shoulders crumpling as she buried her head in her hands.

"I had to go—" I started to say, my voice quieter than I'd intended, barely audible over Mamá's sobs.

"She can't go back to that school. Not after this," Mamá cut in. She lifted her head only to shoot a red-eyed glare at both me and Papi. "*They* know who she is now, and there are going to be a lot of grieving, angry people at that school who are looking for someone to blame . . ." She shook her head, unable to finish her sentence.

Papi nodded, rubbing his temples.

"But, Mamá," I protested, not entirely sure what my argument should be. How could I possibly make her see I couldn't run and hide *now*? I needed to stand up against what had happened. For Julianne and Ramón. For all of us. It didn't matter that I had no idea how to do that. I knew backing down wasn't the answer. I couldn't run from what had happened, no matter how desperately I wanted to.

I glanced at Papi, who was more likely to be persuaded. Going to North had been his idea, after all. "You understand, don't you?" I pleaded. "My college application is due at the end of the semester. If I leave now, then all of this—everything—will have been for nothing." I prayed he couldn't hear the thinly veiled desperation in my voice.

Papi grunted, mistrust written all over his face as he considered this. He closed his eyes and gave me one pained nod.

On the way to school, I opened my notebook, setting it in my lap as the city streamed past me through the bus window. Towering palm trees, pharmacies and soda shops, newsstands and mailboxes. A blur, a world apart from me, now more than ever.

My chest tightened as I ran my fingers over the neat edges of Julianne's obituary, pasted on its own page. I would've put it next to Ramón's if his family had been able to afford one.

The bus groaned to a stop in front of the Fox Theatre, a ghost town this early in the morning. The marquee read NOW PLAYING: REBEL WITHOUT A CAUSE. I hadn't seen it. I hadn't seen any movies since this summer. Ramón and I had watched *The Seven Year Itch*, the new Marilyn Monroe movie, on the drive-in screen. We'd climbed onto his roof like we'd done since we were children, sipping Cokes and laughing as loud as we pleased.

I glanced down at the page once more, over Julianne's pretty portrait. I took a deep breath and closed my notebook before tucking it in my bag.

Forty-Seven

Friday September 30, 1955

I entered the school without looking up once, though the weight of a hundred stares felt like the scorch of the sun on the back of my neck during a long day outside. It was hardly the first time I'd made my way to my locker with my head down, so each step I took came as second nature. I practically coasted on a rancid wave of whispers and pointing.

If I could just keep my head down, perhaps . . . But perhaps what? Was I supposed to do that until graduation?

No, that wasn't the answer, though I wasn't sure what was.

However, that ceased to matter as soon as I arrived at my locker. Next to it, Julianne's locker door had been transformed into a small shrine, adorned with layers of handmade cards. White roses were tucked into the vents and heaped on the floor in front of it.

It was beautiful and heartbreaking and well deserved and

terrible all at once. It made the corners of my vision go dark, so all I could see was this arrangement of flowers and notes to this lovely person I had cared about so much who was no longer here.

We'll miss you, Julianne. Gone but not forgotten. North Phoenix's shining light, Julianne Callihan. In loving memory.

The murky, nightmarish nature of her absence struck me. I had seen it happen. I had been muddling through my grief and guilt every second of every day since she had been killed.

And yet . . . it still didn't seem possible.

Would their deaths ever make sense? How could they?

Without thinking, I reached up to one of the roses stuffed above the door hinge, just barely hanging over onto mine. I wanted to feel the waxy petals with my own hands. Wanted something to ground me, to remind me that this was not some horrible dream. That this was real.

But a voice stopped me before my fingertips could touch it.

"You've got some nerve."

Peter Duke's voice was lower than it had been at the press conference but somehow much more alarming. It was wild, rough. A growl.

I flinched instantly, drawing my hand back as I spun to face him. In doing so, I dislodged the entire rose. It came apart in a swirl of white petals as it fell to the ground.

Peter's bloodshot eyes bore down on me, though he was the only one looking directly at me. The three girls who stood by his side—girls I knew had been in Latin Club with Julianne—exchanged furtive glances as they whispered behind cupped hands. A cluster of people gathered behind him, pretending to be preoccupied by an open geography textbook, but it was clear they were watching us over each other's shoulders.

I opened my mouth, but for once, it didn't matter that I didn't know what to say.

Because before I could summon even a single word, Peter had launched something in my direction. I didn't see what it was until it crashed against my closed locker door. Until it exploded, splashing all over me—in my eyes and hair and along the front of my blouse.

Milk. A carton of sour milk.

"There," Peter barked, his voice clear and sharp amid a bubbling sea of shocked giggles and gasps. "Since you want to be white so badly." He issued me one last withering glare as the first bell rang and he led his flock down the hall.

Forty-Eight

Saturday October 1, 1955

I stared at the two dresses Mamá had washed and ironed for me, draped across my bed. A gray broadcloth with white buttons down the front and an embroidered collar, a hand-me-down from Blanca. Next to it, a dark plaid dress Señora Montoya had helped Mamá sew for me last fall, a Gibson girl style with full sleeves and little pleats.

Neither seemed right.

Would anything?

What does a person wear to the funerals of their two closest friends?

There was a soft knock on my bedroom door behind me. I didn't take my eyes off the two dresses as I mumbled, "Come in."

I knew it was Blanca before she even said anything. I knew it by the sad little breath she drew when she opened the door to find me in my robe, hands on my hips, empty soup cans still rolled in my hair like we used to do when we were younger.

"I brought this," she said gently, sidling up next to me and laying a two-piece dress along the end of the bed. A charcoal tweed number with a short-sleeve jacket. The buttons looked like little pearls.

I glanced up at her with a frown.

She shrugged. "I borrowed it from Pablo's sister."

"Oh." I still wasn't sure it was right, but at least it wasn't one of my own dresses. I wouldn't see it in my closet every morning and think, *Oh yes, that's what I wore when they buried my best friends.* "Thank you, Blanca."

She squeezed my arm. "Get dressed. I'll help you brush out your hair."

I pulled on my girdle and my stockings and, even though these were things I wore most days, they felt cumbersome and bulky. Like the metal armor of a knight. Each layer of clothing I draped over myself made it harder to breathe.

The dress was a little big; the extra fabric felt thick and heavy. Blanca searched for a spare safety pin from Guillermo's diapers to tighten the cinched waist the way it was supposed to fit, but I waved her away.

"It doesn't matter," I said quietly.

For once, she didn't argue. She pursed her lips and began unclipping the cans fastened to my dark hair. I found myself studying the contrasts in our reflections as her fingers moved methodically around the crown of my head. My skin had always been lighter than hers—lighter than anyone's in our family—but now, my complexion was ashen. Sickly pale compared to the honeyed glow of her face. Blanca's face still held some of the fullness from her pregnancy. But my cheeks were now hollow, sunken. There were blue-gray circles underneath my eyes.

"I'll put some spoons in the icebox," she said, reading my mind. "They'll help you look more awake."

I dropped my gaze. A cool spoon to my cheeks wouldn't fix much about how I looked or felt. I pretended to be focused on the dress I was wearing, running my hands down the stiff fabric.

I thought of the other dress I borrowed last weekend. Julianne's red party dress. The scalloped neckline. The tight bodice that had burst open as I dashed across the Callihan lawn in panic. The chiffon skirt had hung in tatters by the end of the night. My entire body tensed as I remembered Marco's hands on my bare back when we embraced in his doorway.

What had happened to that dress? I hadn't thought of it until now.

Mamá had helped me peel it off late that night, washing the dried blood off my hands and arms with a damp cloth, but I wasn't sure what she'd done with it after. She'd probably thrown it away. Though it seemed so sad to think of something so lovely destroyed, I guess there wouldn't be much sense in keeping it.

It really had been such a pretty dress, though.

Forty-Nine

Saturday, October 1, 1955

"Hija, sit still," Mamá whispered to me from behind the handkerchief she held clutched to her face.

I flinched, the wood pew beneath me giving another loud groan as Papi tsked in disapproval. I took an unsteady breath. The air in the church felt humid from all the tears being shed. It made it hard to breathe.

It was hard to do anything, really.

It was certainly hard to listen to Father Al talk about Ramón in the past tense. About his love for his mother, about his beautiful singing voice, about his soul going to our Father in heaven.

Three rows ahead of me, Señora Montoya's shoulders trembled as she cried in the front row. One of her cousins, a gray-haired woman who lived a few blocks from us, patted her on the back. Señora Montoya was surrounded by friends and distant family members, but I couldn't help but notice that Marco was nowhere to be found. Neither of the Montoya boys had ever been terribly consistent about going to Mass with their mother, but I felt a pinch in my ribs as I wondered where he could possibly be today. I hadn't seen him since that night. Where *was* he?

I pressed my fingertips along the waistband of my dress, as if trying to dull the pain.

I couldn't stop myself from fidgeting despite Mamá's scolding.

Because I couldn't bring myself to look straight ahead.

At the casket.

I shifted and squirmed all through communion. I was the last one to my feet in our row; Papi had to nudge me down the aisle to accept the bread and wine that I nearly dropped in my desperate attempts to keep my eyes down.

This was the last time I'd ever be in the same room as Ramón. And I couldn't bear it. The casket was closed, but it didn't matter. I knew he was in there, and that knowledge was excruciating. That casket was a physical reminder that I'd never see my best friend ever again.

I knelt in prayer, hoping God would forgive me because my mind was anywhere but on the words I was reciting.

I thought of splitting fresh oranges with Ramón in the spring, our fingers sticky as we passed slices between us.

I thought of him humming, "Rosita, Rosita, una chica astutita."

I thought of him always saving a dance for me at neighborhood weddings and quinceañeras despite all the girls eagerly waiting for a spin in his arms. The way he'd tease me about stepping on his toes.

I thought of him standing at my school after the pep rally. The flush of apprehension I'd felt to see him holding out my notebook under the streetlights that bordered campus.

Father Al invited us to sing the final hymn, and as I rose, I braced myself on the pew in front of me. As our collective chorus of Psalm 23 began, I heard the sound of Guillermo chirping. Instinctively, my eyes sought him out where he was held in the back by my sister, near a small cluster of young mothers, most of them girls we'd gone to school with.

Just beyond the group of mothers, who were swaying to their own rhythms as they rocked their babies to sleep, my eyes caught on something. Someone.

"*Rosa,*" Mamá hissed, elbowing me.

I ignored her, craning my neck to see.

The pinch in my ribs intensified, a lancing pain that nearly knocked the breath out of me.

Leaning against the back wall of the church was a rumpled, haggard Marco Montoya.

"Thank you to everyone," Father Al concluded, "for being here to support the Montoya family and to celebrate the short time we had with Ramón. Please join us at the Montoya house following this service to share your condolences with the family."

As everyone began to rise around me in a flurry of sad murmurings and sniffles, I turned to seek out another glimpse of Marco.

Perhaps I'd imagined it, because he was gone.

I wondered what he was thinking, what he was feeling, how he was doing.

Most of all, as I followed the procession from the church to the Montoya house with stinging tears clouding my vision, I wondered if he blamed me too.

Fifty

Saturday, October 1, 1955

Though most people went straight to the backyard, a small group of women headed into the Montoyas' kitchen to organize the food they'd brought. The same group that had stationed themselves in this kitchen most nights, taking lids off pots and stirring bowls. I was ushered in with Mamá and Blanca even though I hadn't brought anything. I stood in the center of the hubbub, holding plates and napkins and being in the way, but I wasn't sure what else I was supposed to do.

I felt like a little girl clinging to their skirts because I was too shy to play with the other kids. Which, I supposed, was probably how I would've spent my childhood if it hadn't been for Ramón convincing me to climb trees or skip stones in the canal or come up with rhyming words for all the little melodies he dreamed up.

"*Psst.*"

I turned toward the noise, surprised. I didn't know how I even heard it with the harried chatter of women and clanging of pans, but my entire body alerted to the whisper, suddenly sure it was meant for me.

It was almost too crowded in the stuffy kitchen to turn at all, but just as I began to gracelessly sidestep Señora Ramirez and the tower of tortillas she held in front of her, I felt a warm hand on my wrist. I was tugged out the side door in one swift, stealthy motion that somehow avoided the notice of any of the preoccupied women around me.

For the second time, my eyes settled on the unexpected sight of Marco Montoya.

He appeared every bit as worn out as I felt, with the same sickly pallor and weary eyes I'd noted in myself this morning. His hair wasn't greased back. Or at least it wasn't anymore. It looked like it may have been—days ago—but was now mussed from running his fingers through it. His shirt and pants were wrinkled, his boots unpolished and dusty. And his normal sunshine and citrus smell was replaced by the sour odor of beer.

We didn't speak for a moment, and I saw his lips twitch before he inhaled, sweeping his hair out of his eyes with a skittish gesture that did nothing to actually put his curls in place.

"Verón's here," he rasped in a voice that sounded like it hadn't been used in a while.

"Excuse me?"

"We want to speak with you about something."

I frowned. With me? Though I'd seen Verón more over the

past few weeks than I had in my entire life, I'd still never spoken directly to him. "About what?"

Marco shook his head with an impatient grimace. "He wants to talk about it with both of us. Together."

"Here? Now?"

Marco scoffed, a bitter noise that rippled through him. "Why not?"

However, when he saw me draw back at this, stepping away from him and toward the brick wall of his house, his expression softened. He cleared his throat and looked down, away from me. "It's important, Rosa. Urgent."

That didn't do much to ease my apprehension. But I couldn't ignore the pain in Marco's glowing eyes. They were glassy with either drink or exhaustion, but they cut through me all the same.

How could I possibly deny him anything, after everything that had happened?

So I nodded.

"He's out front," he said without missing a beat. Like he'd known all along that I'd agree. He tipped his head for me to follow, walking around the side of the house without looking back.

Fifty-One

Saturday, October 1, 1955

"I can't do that," I heard myself repeating over and over again as Victor Verón spoke, standing in front of Marco's Chevy with his hands in his pockets.

He was almost businesslike, which only reaffirmed my certainty that we shouldn't be having this conversation at a funeral. At Ramón's funeral.

"It's asking a lot, I know," Verón conceded, a certain gentleness to his voice that I appreciated, even if I didn't trust it fully. "You don't have to decide right now, but please, Rosa, just think about it."

"I—I *can't*." Involuntarily, I glanced at Marco, hoping he'd jump in and validate the concerns that were rising up inside of me like the sour urge to vomit. Although logically I knew Marco must've agreed with him. Why else would he have brought me out here?

Marco stood, shoulders slightly stooped, with his hand cupped around his cigarette as he flicked his lighter impatiently. His movements seemed distracted, like he wasn't paying us any attention, but I could tell by the tenseness in his jaw that he was listening closely.

"I know you're new to the work we're doing, but this is a crucial moment for us. I was hoping to see you at the meeting last night so we could discuss it, but of course, I understand how painful this is for you, Rosa," Verón continued.

I got the sense that the way he kept repeating my name was deliberate. He was a skilled speaker, after all. Persuasive and compelling. He was doing his best to draw me in, and I could feel it yanking at my insides whether I liked it or not.

"We can either back down to the sheriff, or we can stand up for what we know is right. We know what the sheriff did is *wrong*, Rosa. There's no doubt about it. He isn't the first to try to cover up his crimes, and he isn't the first to think he can get away with it. And if we don't speak up, don't organize and do our part, then he *will* get away with it. Make no mistake about it."

I was shaking my head without realizing it, though I wasn't entirely sure which part I was disagreeing with.

"Right now, the sheriff's story is the one people will believe because he's in a position of power and because he's a white man, Rosa," Verón continued, patient and undeterred. "It's easier to believe what he's got to say. That he was just a father protecting his home from a dangerous brown man. But we know what really happened. *You* know, better than anyone. We have to tell everyone what *really* happened."

"I don't know," I whispered, more to myself than anything. I was suddenly thankful Marco seemed to be transfixed by the glowing ember of his cigarette butt, that he couldn't see the shame and doubt written all over my face.

"We have a platform and an audience on my radio show. We have people who will support us, Rosa. We just need a voice. *Your* voice."

All at once, I thought of Mamá begging me to withdraw from school before things got worse. Of Peter, pointing at me in front of a mob of people. Of sitting in front of the typewriter at school, my fingers hovering above the keys, the paper blank in front of me.

My pulse drowned out my feeble voice. "I can't."

"It has to be you," Marco said finally, somehow cutting through my panic. I jolted, my eyes raking over him as he took a long draw of his cigarette. He watched a thin ribbon of smoke escape the corner of his mouth. "You were there, Rosa. You knew him. You knew them both. Your name is already out there because of that cabrón, Duke."

I gaped at Marco for an instant. I hadn't considered that he would've known about what Peter said. Had he been there too? How could I have missed him? I felt like I had been seeking him out for days.

But perhaps Verón had mentioned it to him. Peter's family was well known in Phoenix, after all. The idea of the two of them talking about me and Peter and everything. Plotting and planning. It made my insides feel topsy-turvy all over again.

"You know I'm right. It has to be you," Marco repeated once more, and for the first time since we'd stepped outside, he met my gaze. Locked eyes with me in a look that was full of pleading and desperation and . . . something far too heartbreaking for words.

"You just want me to talk on your radio show?" I asked thinly, my eyes darting back to Verón, who nodded vigorously.

"What would I even say?" I hated the way the question sounded, that I had to ask, that I didn't know.

"You'd share your side of the story. You'd tell people about who Ramón was. He's not the delinquent kidnapper the sheriff wants the world to believe he is. We know that. We need everyone else to know that. You'll tell about him and Julianne, that he wasn't attacking her, that they cared about each other. You'll tell them about what happened that night. You'll offer another narrative for the world to consider, you'll challenge the version of events the sheriff is shoving down the community's throats!"

His voice escalated as he spoke, as if he couldn't help it, the passion and urgency bursting from his words. A few clusters of people in the front yard were peering at us, clicking their tongues in disapproval.

"Jeez, is that all?" I tried to chuckle, but it sounded every bit as hollow and forced as it felt.

Verón didn't even crack a smile. "It's a lot, I know. But this is important. I know you see that."

I did. I really did. And I even saw why it should be me.

Why it should be me who shared what happened that night so it didn't get swept away as a tragedy of our own making rather than the hateful crime it truly was.

But it still didn't mean I felt that I could do it or that I had what it took to go head-to-head with the sheriff, a beloved and respected public figure, a man who had shown how ruthless he was when it came to protecting what he valued.

I felt the world start to tilt and sway around me as I considered Verón's proposition. For a terrifying moment, I felt like I might faint. But suddenly, Marco took my hand, and the lurching and swirling ground to an abrupt halt. His fingers, rough and calloused, held onto mine with a loose, tentative grip.

Verón cleared his throat and shot Marco a look that he ignored. "Listen, I'm going to go. I think my presence here . . . Well, it's complicated, you know. But, Rosa, please think it over. Marco knows how to get a hold of me once you've made up your mind." He nodded his head in goodbye before he ambled down the driveway, issuing a few cordial waves at the guests who watched curiously as he left.

I expected Marco to disappear again now that Verón had made his point, but he didn't move. His warm fingers were still wrapped around mine.

"Rosa," he said so softly that I shouldn't have been able to hear it, given how many others were gathered outside. "I know it seems dangerous—"

"It *is* dangerous," I interjected. I moved to pull my hand away, but his grip tightened as if he anticipated this. He stepped closer to me, and just like that, we were close enough to be dancing if we were under any other circumstances. I watched the sharp line of his jaw tense as he grimaced.

"You're right. It's dangerous," he admitted. "What I mean is, it's not *reckless*. Verón, he's careful. He has a plan, resources. He's not rash. Like me." He chewed on his lip like he was already missing the cigarette he had just tossed aside. "Can I tell you something? A secret?" Underneath his dark lashes, his eyes traveled up my face, lingering on my mouth before locking on my eyes. "I wanted to go to her funeral tonight, start there. Cause a scene, a protest. I don't know. But that's how I wanted to be heard."

"Julianne's funeral?" I gasped. "But she didn't do anything wrong, Marco. She's just as innocent in this as Ramón is. Her memory deserves to be mourned just as much as his does."

Marco sighed and nodded with a weary disappointed shrug of his shoulders. "I know. That's what Verón said too when I approached him about it. I just wanted to do something to hurt *him*, you know?" Gently, he began stroking my fingers in his hand, and the movement was so slow and meandering I wondered if he even realized he was doing it. "Verón says we can't go about this with vengeance in mind. We do it for justice. Accountability. Speaking truth to power. I wouldn't ask this of you unless I really believed in it. You do know that, right?"

"I—" My voice caught in my throat.

"I'm not taking this lightly," he murmured. "I couldn't bear to lose someone else I care about."

Was he just saying these things—touching me like this—to manipulate me into doing what he wanted, or did he really feel this way? We were so near to one another, I was positive we'd attracted the curiosity of our neighbors. I could feel their sad surprise, their shock at whatever seemed to be transpiring at this funeral.

I was a good girl, after all. And here I was, in the thick of all this turmoil with the Montoyas.

First Ramón. And now Marco?

But despite this—and despite the fact that what Marco and Verón said *terrified* me—it felt reassuring to stand so near to him. To look him right in the eyes and to see something mournful but earnest and open. To feel him breathing. To touch his skin, rough and warm. It didn't make me feel hopeful, exactly, but it was something close to it.

"Rosa, hija, come inside and get something to eat before we have to go." Mamá's strident voice landed squarely in the negligible space between Marco and me. I didn't know who moved away first, but our hands were no longer touching as we both turned to see my mother standing at the side door, holding a large plate heaped with tortillas, rice, and carnitas.

I stepped toward her, past Marco, and mumbled without looking at him, "We are leaving for Julianne's funeral soon. I've got to go."

Though I couldn't be certain, as I walked away, I was pretty sure I heard Marco whisper one last plea for me to think about what he'd said.

Fifty-Two

Saturday, October 1, 1955

Mamá and Papi flanked me on either side as we stood on the corner opposite the looming Spanish silhouette of St. Mary's Basilica and gazed at the long queue of mourners winding their way down Third Street. Women in hats with delicate little veils and men in suits with bulky, leafy flower arrangements in their arms. Reporters holding unwieldy microphones, tinkering with cameras.

My parents hadn't wanted me to come to Julianne's funeral. They didn't say it, but I knew it. Even more, they didn't want me coming alone—not when I seemed to stumble headfirst into disaster every time I ventured outside our barrio.

So here we were.

"Mijita," Papi said in a stunned voice, "I don't think we are going to be able to get in."

I shook my head, looking down at the thin, limp collection

of flowers Mamá let me collect from her garden. "No, I guess not."

I couldn't help but wonder what Julianne would make of all this spectacle. Perhaps she'd be touched that her life had affected so many, but I thought it was more likely she'd be embarrassed or maybe even frustrated.

After all, while she and Ramón had suffered nearly identical fates, his service hadn't had news coverage or the high society elite lining up to pay their condolences. I didn't think these types of things would've really mattered to either of them, but they still struck me as significant. Worth noting.

Under the sweeping archway of the church entrance, I spotted a pile of floral arrangements, likely left by others who knew they wouldn't be able to withstand the crowd of people jockeying for prime grieving spots. A heap of waxy lilies and fluffy carnations and big looping ribbons. My modest assortment of pink roses would be lost among these more impressive bouquets, but I wanted to deliver them all the same.

"I'll just leave these by the door, and then we can go, okay?" I told my parents, and Mamá patted my arm with a thin smile. She hadn't said anything to me about Marco yet, but she kept giving me this look. It was an expression I recognized from Blanca's pregnancy mostly, when she'd comfort my sister about her swollen feet or raging heartburn, but it was never one I'd seen her direct at me.

I wasn't sure what to make of it.

I crossed the street, passing between cars cruising for a streetside parking space, passengers' necks craning to get a good look at the commotion. As I approached the church, I slid between a news van and a Cadillac, and the sound of organ music began to fill the air, low and somber, soaking up the snippets of quiet conversation from the waiting mourners.

There was a reporter standing near the mound of flowers, describing the scene around us to a video camera aimed in his direction. "Hundreds have gathered . . ." he was saying into the long microphone he held in front of him. "The service is expected to start any moment, though many will have to participate outdoors due to the number of mourners. The Callihans arrived moments ago, accompanied by close family members and a handful of sheriff's deputies. This after receiving word via a joint statement from Phoenix PD and the Maricopa County Sheriff's Department that the formal investigation into Sheriff Callihan has come to a close with no evidence indicating wrongdoing. A small consolation for the family at this difficult time, I'm sure. The Callihans did not stop for questions or comments on their way inside."

I paused, crouching down with my flowers still clutched in my fingers, the petals barely brushing the cement steps below.

Formal investigation had come to a close. No evidence of wrongdoing.

How could that be?

I peered up at the reporter, but he had already segued into describing the chic black dress and matching hat Mrs. Callihan had donned for the service.

Barely a week had passed since their deaths. Julianne's body wasn't even in the ground yet. How could the investigation already have come to a close so quickly? So neatly? Surely everyone could see how complex what had happened was.

I was frozen where I knelt, even as other people impatiently stepped around me to place their own flowers. What kind of ramshackle inquiry was wrapped up so hastily? How thoroughly could they have looked into the truth in that short amount of time?

The shades of meaning and implication tangled up in this revelation made my stomach tighten into a sour coil.

Facts and justice hadn't even been considerations. That much was clear. This was all a farce. A performance. Nothing more.

Meaningless.

In a distant universe, the organ music stopped, and I heard the muffled voice of a man greeting the attendees.

But me, I was still crouched by the flowers, my head spinning.

Fifty-Three

Saturday, October 1, 1955

I'd never snuck out of my house before.

Late-night dalliances had been Ramón's thing, not mine. I never would have dared.

But now? Well, everything was different now.

It was past midnight when I nudged the door to the sleeping porch open—slowly, so it didn't creak—and disappeared into the backyard like a shadow melting into the darkness.

I ran on nimble, quiet feet over the grass and the dirt, through our gate and down the street—practically invisible except for the narrowest sliver of moonlight.

I raced along a path I'd trodden so many times. My legs knew where they were going, but the rest of me seemed to be experiencing this route for the first time, seeing it with fresh eyes. Awake to sights and smells and sounds that had been concealed by the ordinariness of the everyday.

Everything was different. Tonight and forever.

I slid to a stop in the dusty patch of grass in front of the Montoya house and went along the dark side of the house where Marco and I had stood just hours earlier. I paused to catch my breath, though I knew it wasn't the exertion of my run that had my heart hammering the way it was.

In my plan, I'd expected to wake him, to knock softly at his window and stir him. I didn't know why this made a difference, but a jolt of electricity surged through me when I saw Marco sitting on his back step, glowing eyes already fixed on me.

I took in an uneasy breath as I forced myself to continue walking toward him.

As I drew nearer, I noticed an open pamphlet in his hands. In the darkness, I could make out the profile of a bearded man and thick block letters that read CHE GUEVARA AND COMMUNISM. I was so focused on the title that it was several seconds before I registered that Marco was in his pajamas, even though this should've been the first detail I took in since it was so unanticipated and unfamiliar. He was shirtless, in a pair of loose cotton pants. A slight sheen from the moonlight and lamplight fell on his bare skin, the drawn muscles in his shoulders, his lean arms.

My cheeks, already warm in the chilled air, burned hotter, and I prayed he couldn't see it. Couldn't sense this crack in my bravado.

He didn't say a word, but I swore I saw the corner of his mouth tug upward.

"I'll do it," I finally choked out, still walking toward him. The porch light pooled at my feet, on the saddle shoes I had slipped on with my nightgown and robe.

Wordlessly, he sprung to his feet, the pamphlet sliding from his hands and landing facedown in the dirt. In a heartbeat, he was right in front of me, even closer than we were earlier at the funeral. His closeness made my pulse accelerate, reverberating throughout my entire body.

His bare skin, my thin nightgown, the cool breeze of an autumn night.

I braced myself for the stench of beer that had clung to him at the funeral, but I was relieved to detect nothing but Ivory soap.

"I'll do it. Tell Verón I'll do it," I murmured, though I knew my words weren't needed. I knew he understood. I knew he felt what I was feeling—the first glimmer of hopefulness in the bleak aftermath we were wading through.

His expression shifted into something that wasn't quite a smile but perhaps a pit stop along the way to one. It lasted barely a second, though.

Because suddenly, Marco's arms were around me, and in a beautiful, dizzying blur of heartbreak and desperation and hope and warmth, we were kissing.

It wasn't until his lips met mine that I realized how much I'd longed for this—longed for more of him. More than traded jokes or sidelong glances. How long had I been searching—*yearning*—for this connection?

His hands settled on the small of my back, drawing me

flush against him. As his mouth moved against mine, I understood that he needed me in the same way I needed him. Now more than ever.

His kiss was an all-consuming feeling of relief I didn't deserve—a gulp of cold water or a slice of shade on a scorching afternoon.

It was . . . salvation.

Fifty-Four

Tuesday, October 4, 1955

Victor Verón's radio station was on the west side of town in an area I didn't typically visit. A small white two-story building, rather nondescript except for the metal antenna stretching up from its roof and the bold black letters above the front door that read KOY STUDIOS.

Marco and I had ridden in silence the whole way to the station, an electric wordlessness crackling between us as our pinkie fingers brushed in the center of the bench seat. We'd spent the last three nights shrouded in late-night darkness, writing out my answers and stealing kisses. The thought of the hopeful words we'd exchanged and the tender embraces we'd shared made a flicker of warmth ignite in my chest, and I tried to cling to that as nerves roiled through my stomach.

Despite the modest coziness of the studio, which was dimly lit in the last few minutes before sunrise, I found myself a little awestruck to be there. It was the place where the most popular Spanish language radio show was broadcast each morning. The source of all the familiar sounds of my family's kitchen and daily routine. A crucial part of South Phoenix's history, where so many of our most important community members had shared their opinions and stories and work with us.

I'd heard interviews from educators who offered free English immersion classes at the Friendly House, from the first Mexican American state legislator elected in Arizona, from the founders of American Legion Post 41 who organized against segregated housing alongside Señor Montoya. This show was a place where our community's history was written. And somehow, I was about to add to that narrative.

At least I hoped so.

This wasn't about me, I reminded myself, fighting off the surge of noise rising in my imagination. I tightened my grip on Marco's hand as I thought of Ramón promising Julianne he wouldn't let anything bad happen. The police sirens. The look on Marco's face when I showed up on his doorstep that night. The whispers at school. Peter's voice at the press conference. The sound of milk splattering on my locker. The reporter's voice over and over again: *No evidence of wrongdoing.*

I took a deep breath, fumbling for what I'd felt the night of the funerals when I'd run to Marco—confidence, determination, resilience.

We entered the lobby of the station, watching through the glass wall as Verón wrapped up the segment that would precede ours.

"¿Estás bien?" Marco whispered.

"Hmm?"

He bumped his shoulder into mine, forcing me to look at him. "Princesa."

I gave him a quick eye roll before meeting his gaze. I tried to nod, tried to tell him I was okay, but it just dissolved into an awkward shrug. "I—I'm nervous, I suppose. I don't feel like I can do this," I said.

He took a deep breath, like what I'd said physically hurt him.

"Maybe it should be you, Marco," I added quickly. "You know more about this kind of stuff than I do."

He shook his head, his expression hard and tight. "Rosa, you can do this." He ran his hand along the sharp edge of his jaw, looking simultaneously resolute and raw before he managed to school his expression into something more neutral. Something gentler. "Listen, I know you're scared. But it has to be you. You won't be alone, you know that. You aren't alone. I'm right here, with you. But this?" His golden eyes, wide with nerves, flitted over to Verón's recording studio. "It has to be you."

I dropped my gaze to my notebook, held in my right hand, hanging limply by my side. "I'm . . ." *Scared my words won't matter? Terrified that I could pour my heart out and have it mean absolutely nothing?*

I couldn't even finish the sentence.

I didn't have to. Marco could read it written plainly on my face.

He stiffened, and for a moment it looked like he was going to walk away. Like he was going to abandon me here with all my fears and unfulfilled promises and guilt. But instead, he stepped close to me. Lifted my chin toward him with a single finger.

"Rosa. You can do this," he said, firm and matter-of-fact. No fear or frustration on his face but clarity. Purpose.

My lip quivered, and I wanted desperately to turn away from him. To hide that I wasn't this person he thought I was. Wasn't this person he so desperately wanted me to be.

But something in his eyes held me there.

"At some point, Rosa, you're going to have to use your own voice," he said, slow and soft. His eyes flitted down to my notebook briefly. "You can't spend your whole life collecting other people's words. You've got to use your own."

The sound of a door opening behind me made us both jump. Marco's hand dropped to his side. I felt my notebook slip from my fingers, falling to the floor.

I was crouched down to pick it up when Verón leaned out through the doorway. "You ready?"

Fifty-Five

Tuesday, October 4, 1955

"You'll speak into this here," Verón said, nudging the wide base of the gleaming silver microphone toward me. It was much bigger and bulkier than the ones I'd seen television reporters hold. Tentatively, I touched my fingers to the cool metal. "You read through the questions I gave you? You practiced your responses?"

I nodded and snuck a glimpse of Marco. He leaned against the back wall, arms folded across his chest.

"Rosa?" Verón prompted.

"I practiced," I said finally. Which was true. I just wasn't sure how much it mattered. I could've rehearsed for a decade, and I would probably still feel how I did now.

I glanced down at the open notebook pages before me—the pages of scrawled notes Marco and I had compiled. Lines and lines of words in both of our handwriting. Some pieces crossed out, some with arrows pointing to notes crammed in the margins. The first real writing in this notebook. The letters jumped and danced around on the pages, and I blinked my eyes furiously, trying to steady them.

I hoped they were enough. Hoped I was enough.

Verón gave me a swift nod from across the little table where we sat, the microphone right between us. A light above the doorway illuminated with the words ON AIR.

"Good morning, everyone, and as always, thank you for joining us as you start your day," Verón said in the melodic Spanish I'd heard every morning for just about as long as I could remember. "I am su amigo en este momento, Victor, and with me today is a very brave young woman who is here to speak out about a tragic event that has recently impacted our community. Thank you for being here, Miss Rosa Capistrano."

A pinch of panic shot through me as I heard my name come out of Verón's mouth. I pictured radios all over the city—maybe even the state—echoing his words into kitchens and living rooms and cars. I pictured my own parents, who were probably puzzling over the brief note I'd left on the refrigerator at this very moment.

Verón tapped his fingers lightly on the tabletop to get my attention.

"Um," I said clumsily. "Thank you for having me." I blushed instantly, thankful our audience could not see me. I sounded like a party guest, like someone thanking their host for inviting them to dinner.

I didn't sound like someone with something important to say.

I couldn't do this.

Verón locked eyes with me over the microphone, no doubt sensing the rising terror in me. He gave me a gentle smile as he tipped his head toward me. "It's a very courageous thing you're doing today, Rosa. Many of you have likely heard about what the sheriff's department is referring to as 'an unfortunate tragedy,' the murder of South Phoenix community member Ramón Montoya, a seventeen-year-old boy. A senior at Phoenix South Mountain High School. Younger brother to Marco Montoya. Son to Olga Montoya and the late Manuel Montoya, a veteran of the Second Great War." Marco's breathing hitched behind me, and I somehow resisted the urge to look back at him. "And, of course, the key detail that the sheriff doesn't want us to know about, the detail we are hoping Rosa can speak about today: boyfriend to Julianne Callihan, the daughter of Sheriff Callihan and the other victim of the egregious violence that took place on September twenty-fourth." He paused, and I wondered how he knew so intuitively when to give our distant listeners the time to react and reflect. I could practically hear them gasping and whispering amongst themselves, exchanging bewildered looks over cups of coffee. Could see Mamá's blanched face. Papi's solemn shaking of his head. "Rosa, to get us started, will you please share with us how you knew both Ramón and Julianne?"

I leaned forward, drawing in an anxious breath, placing my finger on the first line of text in my notebook. I could feel the grooves the pencil had made in the paper under my fingertip. "Julianne is—*was*—my classmate and friend at North

Phoenix High School," I read aloud, my voice trembling as if I'd never seen these words before. As if I hadn't recited them dozens of times. As if I hadn't lived them.

The words started to swirl on the page again. I blinked, my blood pounding in my ears. "And I've known Ramón all my life. Our fathers served together in the war, and our families are close friends." This part I mostly remembered, had memorized, but the rest of the page had melted into a blur of indecipherable gray markings.

Dios mío. I really couldn't do this.

I glanced up to meet Verón's eyes, which brimmed with concern. "Breathe," he mouthed to me, gesturing for me to take a deep breath.

Feebly, I nodded, following his instructions. "Ramón was . . ." I tried again. "He was . . ."

Defeat began to wash over me. It was all for nothing. All those nights Marco and I spent talking about these people we loved, about what we hoped to achieve, about the violence and injustice that wound its way through our community—it was all a waste.

I was failing.

Ramón and Julianne's legacy—what they had been trying to prove, what they had inadvertently given their lives for . . . it was for nothing.

Because of me.

I was failing Ramón and Julianne. I was failing Marco. I was failing my own sense of what was right.

My pulse was thundering so loudly in my ears that I didn't

even hear Marco move toward me. I only noticed him when he reached across me and flipped my notebook shut.

I flinched, peering up at him. He pressed one finger to my chest, to my heart. The nearness, the spark of movement, the unexpected, intimate contact—all of it made my mouth fall open. What was he doing?

"Speak from here, princesa," he whispered as quietly as he could, his lips brushing my ear. He swiped my notebook off the table, taking it with him as he retreated to the back of the room.

"Ramón was . . ." Verón echoed, gentle and encouraging.

Ramón. I didn't need my notes to talk about Ramón.

Right?

Speak from my heart, Marco had said. "He was my oldest friend, my best friend," I began again, my eyes closed as images of Ramón illuminated in my memory. Free-spirited and laughing, singing and dancing, smiling and . . . I opened my eyes. "He was *wonderful*. Optimistic and funny and full of love. He was incredible. They both were."

"Yes, of course," Verón said, his face brightening with relief and perhaps a smidge of pride. "You said Julianne was your classmate, correct? You go to North Phoenix High School?" There was a tone of affected curiosity to his voice that told me this was all part of the performance, the storytelling.

"Yes. I transferred there last year."

"Do you live in north Phoenix?"

"No, I live in Golden Gate," I said. "My family and I decided that I should switch schools for better academic opportunities than I was finding at the high school in our barrio. As many of you know, our schools are often underfunded and not really designed to prepare us for college, which is my goal. We thought at North, I would have access to more rigorous academic material and a better chance of higher education." These were similar to the words Marco and I had written, but somehow felt different—easier—falling from my mouth now.

"Very good," he said. "I think that is an opinion many of us can relate to, unfortunately. What has your experience been like at this school? Has it met your expectations?"

When Verón had initially shown me the talking points he wanted to cover a few days ago, I'd pushed back against all these questions about me and school. This was about Ramón and Julianne, so why did he want to discuss the minutiae of my day-to-day life at school? It seemed trivial and unnecessary but also like an intrusion. It was way more of myself than I wanted to put out there.

But Verón had been insistent that my story was a key component to all of this. That people needed to understand me and my circumstances in order to rally around this moment.

So I told him—and everyone listening—about what it was like to be Rosa Capistrano. I told him that even though school segregation was no longer legal, I had taken painstaking measures to make sure no one there realized that I was Mexican. Until now, of course. I told him about my alias, Rosie. I told him about the neutral colors I wore and the hair clips I used to wrangle my thick, dark hair—all strategies to avoid drawing any attention whatsoever.

And, of course, I told him about meeting Julianne Callihan.

About our neighboring lockers, about joining newspaper club together, about her quiet bravery.

"So it sounds like you've been living a double life for the past two years," Verón said. "That must be very challenging."

My lip trembled as I nodded, nearly forgetting that only Verón could see me respond to him. "It has been, yes." My voice cracked, and I took another hearty gulp of air to steady myself. "I've always thought it would be worth it, though. The hardships would be worth it to go to college."

"Mm. Do you still think it's worth it?"

I knew he was going to ask me this. I had discussed it with him and then with Marco every single night leading up to this moment, but the question still knocked the wind out of me. "Now that my friends' lives have been lost in their pursuit of equal treatment? No."

"Can you please elaborate on that point?"

It took me a moment to find what I wanted to say. The first couple times I opened my mouth, I felt like my thumping heart was about to burst right out of my throat. "Ramón and Julianne were in love," I finally started. "I—I didn't know what to make of it at first, to be perfectly honest. They fell for one another very quickly. I knew there were going to be a lot of people who didn't like the idea of a Mexican boy dating a white girl, especially this particular white girl. But all that aside, they cared for each other. In the brief time they had together, it was quite clear. It may not make sense to some people, but they were in love. And they felt that their love could be a message to the world."

"What kind of message?"

"A message for equality," I said simply. "They wanted to be an example for integration and acceptance and respect. That's what they hoped to demonstrate that night at the dance. The night they were killed."

"Mm," Verón said softly, allowing the time and space for my final statement to sink into the hearts of anyone listening. "Can you tell us a little more about that night from your perspective?"

I swallowed, wishing desperately I'd thought to ask for a glass of water before all this began.

"I know it must be terribly difficult for you to recount these events. Please, take all the time you need." He leaned back slightly, as if turning the microphone over to me entirely.

I nodded to myself, thinking I'd need to take another moment to sort through the memories and anguish, but the words came rushing forth before I even realized I was speaking. Our plan. Our dresses. Ramón and Tim. Mrs. Callihan. Sheriff Callihan's unexpected arrival. His outrage—quiet at first before erupting along Julianne's cheek. The light in Julianne's window. The sheriff's resounding footsteps. The gun. Five shots. The ambulance and police cruisers. How I disappeared into the night unnoticed.

I even recounted my meetings at the sheriff's department. About their lack of interest in what I saw. It terrified me to share these details—into the invisible abyss of the airwaves where anyone might hear it—but I did it anyway. I told them how I suspected I was being deliberately silenced rather than utilized, my knowledge and perspective being shoved down somewhere to ignore rather than to help bring truth to the situation.

And that was why I was here. That was why I was telling my story on *En este momento*.

Marco's breathing had turned arduous behind me, deep breaths punctuated by sniffing, but I knew I couldn't look at him. I wouldn't be able to keep going.

I was surprised to see that Verón seemed to have lost his train of thought. He consulted his notes in front of him for the first time as he seemed to transition back from listener to radio show host.

"That is . . . that's very hard to hear," he finally admitted with a rawness to his voice that I'd never heard before. This wasn't Verón the community organizer or "su amigo Victor" speaking to me right now. This was just a man who had listened to me, who had been moved by what I had to say. "As I'm sure it's been hard to experience," he continued, regaining his composure with each syllable.

Silence took hold of the two of us, but unlike earlier pauses, I was not sure it was an intentional one. We stared at each other in a mutual loss for words. His face had a look of mournfulness and exhaustion that I felt inside myself, warm and murky like a caldo.

He cleared his throat finally. "There are many questions that remain unanswered, of course. But I just have one last one for you, Rosa. If that's all right."

I gave a slight nod then caught myself and added, "Of course."

"Where do we go from here, in your opinion?"

I'd been working my way through this question for the past few days; in some ways, I'd been seeking its answer my entire life. But still, the perfect answer eluded me.

I tried to think of what Marco and I had written. I remembered discussing it, trading ideas, writing and rewriting notes. But for the life of me, I couldn't recall a single thing we'd come up with.

Where *did* we go from here?

"I—I don't know if anyone has the answer to that question," I said quietly. "But I know personally, I want to make sure we honor the memories of both Ramón and Julianne, who paid the ultimate price for their beliefs and aspirations."

Verón's expression was soft and compassionate, his eyebrows arched in encouragement. "And what does that look like to you?"

I let my gaze fall to the metallic gridwork of the microphone. "Speaking truthfully about what happened, as a start." I felt my jaw tense as I tried to summon the next words. "Sheriff Callihan was in the wrong that night. He let his anger and his prejudice take over, and that led to the deaths of two innocent teenagers. He is misleading the public by falsely claiming he thought Ramón was a kidnapper when he very well knew who he was to his daughter. He just didn't like it. This man is unworthy of the public's trust and should not only be removed from his position but should be charged with the crimes he so clearly committed." My fingers grazed the metal stand of the microphone idly. "If we don't hold Sheriff Callihan accountable for what he's done, he will continue to abuse his power. He'll go on pretending to care about integration and justice and progress while perpetrating violence and oppression when it serves him. And that, I'm certain, is something neither Julianne nor Ramón would want."

When I finally looked up again, I was met with Verón's wide eyes, his mouth slightly ajar. He rubbed his chin thoughtfully, and for the first time, I glanced over my shoulder at Marco. He was standing straight, arms folded across his chest. And though his eyes were glassy with tears, a wry, appreciative smile—just a flicker of one—rested on the corner of his mouth.

Fifty-Six

Tuesday, October 4, 1955

Verón switched over to a slow song by Los Tres Caballeros as soon as he ended our segment. His lips were pressed into a thoughtful line, eyes gleaming, as he shook our hands.

"I'll see you at the meeting, yes?" he said with an excited edge to his voice. "Excellent work, Rosa. You should be very proud of yourself. This . . . this is big, señorita."

"Thank you," I told Verón before Marco and I began making our way toward the exit. We navigated the hallway in silence, but I could sense he was watching me. I blinked dazedly at the brilliance of the morning sun as we stepped outside. It felt like I was in that station talking all day, when in reality it was only about thirty minutes. It was still a bit early to go to school, but I also wasn't sure what I was supposed to do now.

We had talked with Verón about our plan for the coming days—El Foro meetings, pamphlets, even a march—but I'd failed to consider the moments immediately following his show. I'd just done either the bravest or the most foolish thing in my entire life, and now I was supposed to do what? Make a souffle in home ec? Dodge dirty glances from freshmen at the drinking fountain?

I glanced at Marco finally. His copper eyes were locked on me, scrutinizing and completely unabashed. Though I knew Marco's response to what I'd shared would likely be different than the rest of our community's—after all, Marco was nothing if not contrarian—I still felt an intense curiosity about what was going on in his mind. A curiosity that was somehow stronger than all the other fears and anxieties that were coiled up inside of me.

The expression on his face, however, remained unreadable.

"Let's go grab a cafecito before I take you to school," Marco said at last.

He took me to a diner in a part of town called the Deuce, a nickname made popular by the cops who frequented the area. I'd heard it was short for "produce" since it was in the heart of the grocery warehouses, which is perhaps how Marco knew his way around so well.

It was only a few streets over from the gleaming bustle of downtown. I could see the steeple of St. Mary's, where Julianne's funeral had been held just last week, peeking over the squat ramshackle buildings that lined Washington Street. It wasn't particularly far from Golden Gate or from school either, but it was an area where I didn't spend much time. Where I wasn't supposed to spend much time.

Still buzzing with a jittery, unfocused energy and eager for a distraction, I considered the dilapidated scene around us. The darkened windows of passing cocktail lounges and bars. The sun-worn paint of dowdy little hotels with faded awnings advertising single-room vacancies. The lone lingering Chinese restaurant, the last remnant of the Chinatown that had withered away ten years ago when construction of the railroad that divided the city came to a close. A peeling billboard bearing the graffitied face of the incumbent candidate for governor.

Marco found a parking spot near a filthy alley that made my eyes bulge, though I caught myself before I voiced my hesitation. He tossed a few coins at a panhandler slumped against the wall of a liquor store then guided me inside a diner that boasted breakfast all day, though the restaurant's sign had been broken and vandalized beyond the point of legibility.

The waitress gruffly instructed us to seat ourselves, so we claimed a table by the window. We sat right across from each other in the narrow booth.

"¿Tienes hambre?" Marco asked, gesturing to the two large menus tucked behind the napkin dispenser.

I shook my head, and Marco ordered us two cups of coffee before I could tell him that I didn't like coffee. I could feel his eyes on me as I continued to watch the world outside the window. A truck pulled up with crates of soda and beer bottles to unload next door, and the rhythm with which the driver unpacked the wooden boxes was oddly soothing. The dull thud along the sidewalk. The subdued chime of glass bottles rattling against one another.

"I used to come here a lot when my dad was still alive." Though his voice was gentle and soft, almost quiet enough to not be heard above the din of the nearby kitchen, it caused me to jerk toward him nonetheless. It was the revelation, more than his tone, that surprised me.

"*This* diner?" I asked.

The waitress reappeared, setting two steaming mugs between us. He gave her a thin smile and waited for her to depart before answering me. "Sometimes this diner. But this part of town, mostly. See that bar?" He tilted his head toward a building across the street, one shop down from where the delivery man was unloading boxes.

I craned my head to look at the brick-faced tavern he was talking about, wedged right between a supermarket and a Mexican movie theater. I nodded.

"That was my dad's favorite bar." He turned the coffee mug in a circle on the table in front of him, running his fingers along the handle. "His, er, favorite place to get drunk."

I thought of Señor Montoya clapping along to music or teaching me and Ramón the steps to a cumbia. In my memory, he was always singing or laughing. Perhaps Ramón and I had been too young to know if those good spirits were fueled by alcohol. Ramón had never once mentioned his father drinking. It made me sad, suddenly, that Marco's memories of his father were colored by this secret.

The smell of my coffee wafted in front of me, but I made no move to drink it.

"Your father would bring me down here with him," he said, his eyes peering into his coffee wistfully.

"My papi?"

Marco nodded, dragging his hand along his jaw. "Ma, she'd get worried when my dad wouldn't make it home. I just remember her crying at the sink. She'd try to hide it—she didn't want us to know—but *I* heard her. Saw her. Sometimes she'd get so desperate, she'd ask your dad to go pick him up and bring him home." He sighed. "I'd run over to your house because it was faster than her going, and I'd tell your father. I'd beg and *beg* for him to let me go with him. Sometimes he would say no, maybe when he knew my dad had a bad day or something. I'm not really sure. But most of the time he'd let me come. He'd tell me I had to wait in the back seat no matter what, but he'd take me." His mouth twisted with a little uncertainty. "I just . . . I remember staring out the back window at these loud and dirty and bright places with music and shouting and fighting, you know. Waiting for him. Wondering what shape he'd be in when your old man finally dragged him out." He looked like he had other things to say, maybe other memories that had surfaced, but he paused and took a long, slow drink of his coffee instead.

"I never knew any of that," I admitted. "Ramón never said anything. I don't even remember you ever coming over alone, let alone going anywhere with Papi."

Marco nodded knowingly, looking up to meet me with a heavy stare. "You and Blanca were usually asleep," he said. "Do you remember how he died? My dad?"

I shook my head, a flush of embarrassment and anxiousness rushing to my cheeks. "I'm sorry," I added hastily, but he brushed it off. Blanca had been right; I knew so very little.

"Don't be. You and Ramón were young."

"So were you," I said feebly, and that made him smile a little, though it was a sad smile. Like he'd never thought of himself as a child before. "Twelve isn't exactly an adult, Marco."

"Ma tried to keep it under wraps, all the details. It was complicated." His eyes caught on my coffee cup, and he cocked his head. "You're not drinking your coffee."

"Oh," I said, surprised by this interruption. Hurriedly, I brought it to my lips and took a big, hearty gulp. My tongue instantly scalded with the burning acidic liquid, and I could do nothing to conceal my grimace as I set it back on the table.

Marco didn't laugh at me, but there was an unmistakable flash of amusement in his eyes as he took a small silver pitcher of cream sitting between us and poured a generous dollop into my cup. He gave it a quick stir, his spoon clinking melodically against the cup, and then nodded at me. "Try that."

I complied, this time in less of a rush, and I was relieved to find it much less bitter and a little cooler. Not just tolerable but comforting. "Thank you." I took another sip for good measure, hoping he'd continue talking now that the issue of my coffee had been settled.

It took him a few moments. Not because he'd forgotten what we were talking about, I suspected, but because he was working himself up to it. I got the impression this wasn't a story he'd told before.

"One night," he began a little unsteadily. "One night, it was the same as the others, really. Ma was upset. She was getting ready to have me go down to your dad when the police arrived instead. We were standing in the kitchen together, and suddenly there were all these red and blue lights flashing through our house." Even as he was saying it, I knew both of our minds were immediately leaping back to the night of Ramón's murder. To the police pulling up to destroy their lives yet again. To the brutal, unsettling symmetry of his brother's and his father's deaths. "He'd gotten in a fight at that stupid bar." His eyes flicked upward at the tavern with a furious glare that he was unable to sustain. Like he was staring at the sun, he could only hold his gaze for a moment before returning it to the tabletop. "We never found out the exact details, but it wasn't the first time something like that had happened. But this time, he hit his head on the corner of the bar top. He was knocked unconscious, and he just never woke up. That was it."

"I'm so sorry, Marco. I never knew." How was it possible that I had lived my life so close to this family and I'd never known any of this? I hated my own ignorance, hated that I'd failed to understand so much of the story.

He nodded, blinking quickly. He downed the last drops of his coffee, smacking his lips as he set the cup along the edge of the table for a refill. "It was hard on him, you know? Being back from the war. He never knew how to put it into words, I don't think, but after everything that happened there, he just wanted his life to be different. And he didn't know how to handle it when the life he wanted remained out of his reach."

I hummed in agreement, thinking of all those nights our fathers spent talking about opening a dance hall. "Papi never talks much about the war either," I said. I didn't remember what he was like before he left, but I had to think some of his seriousness—the way he viewed the world in such stark extremes—was due to what he endured overseas.

"Ramón reminds—*reminded*—me a lot of him," Marco said, barreling through his mistake though pain flickered across his face as he corrected himself. "What I remember about him, anyway."

And though I knew what he meant about these two dreamers, I also couldn't help but think about how neither of them ever attained what they wanted. That both of their aspirations were ultimately crushed by this cruel world. And though I felt a prickle as the tears crept up inside me, I was able to wash them down with a quick sip of the coffee, which really was kind of soothing now.

The heaviness in Marco's eyes said he was thinking the same thing. He reached across the Formica table and set his hand on top of mine. Rough and warm and surprisingly tender. "But, Rosa, I know they both would've been really proud of what you said today."

Fifty-Seven

Monday, October 10, 1955

The ripples of aftermath following my interview began immediately. First at home, and then everywhere else.

My parents were the first to bring it up with me. The evening after my interview, we sat at the dinner table as we did every single night.

"We wish you would've told us about it before," Mamá said, her voice slow and purposeful. It was clear she was fighting to contain the warble in her voice. "But we are proud of you."

Stone-faced, Papi nodded. "We just want you to be careful. Your safety is what matters most to us, hija."

Their reactions surprised me. I'd anticipated some outrage. Some nervousness about speaking out in this way—so publicly. They'd spent my entire life making the most of what we had, focused on not stirring up any trouble. I knew it was scary to see me going against what they'd always tried to instill in us. I was unspeakably heartened to see that they not only understood why I had to do this, but that they seemed to feel the same flicker of hope I was nurturing. A hope for justice, not just for Ramón, but for all the wrongdoings my family had endured just because of our race—the deportations, the segregation, the discrimination, *everything*.

It was complicated, I knew that. What wasn't? Everything was a mix of good and bad, of easy and hard, of beautiful and ugly, of right and wrong. Things were not just black and white—or brown, for that matter.

Some days it was hard to sustain hope; some days it felt impossible. But as I hugged my parents that night, long after Verón's voice had signed off, my hope felt bigger than my fear for the first time since the murders.

Then, the next day, Verón announced a formal vigil for both Ramón and Julianne, a time for unified grief, an organized call for action. A community demonstration. A march.

Finally taking a stand, as Marco had put it in begrudging appreciation. "No more endless talking. Some action at last," he'd said.

Verón shared it on his show and talked about it endlessly, both on the radio and at El Foro. He began making flyers, collecting candles, and recruiting supporters from other community groups, from LULAC to *El Sol* newspaper.

"This is our moment for justice," he said to us so many times that I caught myself murmuring it under my breath often. Walking to school or lying in bed or watching Marco's brown eyes gleam in the moonlight.

Our moment for justice.

Though I doubted anyone at North listened to Verón's show, word got around anyway. Ripples. That's how it went with these kinds of things. I had been able to badger Tim enough to get the general consensus of the student body out of him, although I probably could've pieced it together without interrogating my only friend until he was fidgeting and tripping over his own words.

"You know I don't feel the same way as the rest of our classmates, don't you?" he'd said, his palm pressed to the striped center of his sport shirt. "I think it's brave, of course. I sure as heck couldn't do what you're doing, out in the spotlight like that. I'm worried about you, but it took a lot of courage to speak up about what happened."

"Thank you, Tim."

"But, well, I think folks are saying that you're a bit of a troublemaker." He grimaced, the tops of his cheeks and ears pink. "An agitator, you know? With everything everyone is already dealing with, it seems some people are mad that you're . . ."

I steeled myself. "Sharing the truth?"

He bit the corner of his thumbnail. "I think what I heard Peter's buddies say at practice was that you're making this into something it's not."

"Like this is *my* fault," I grumbled, rolling my eyes, which earned a scornful gasp from a group of girls watching me from their lockers. I was tired of schooling my facial expressions into something palatable. I was tired of blending in to make things easier for others. I was just *tired*.

"You know how people are," Tim said tepidly. "And you know how Peter is. I just want you to be careful."

Sullenly, I nodded.

As if on cue, Connie and a few other girls from our homeroom walked past me, glaring. Connie threw her shoulder into mine, snickering, "Go back to Mexico!" to the delighted squeals of the girls whose arms were linked in hers.

Tim locked eyes with me.

Peter was vocal about his prejudice, sure; he always had been. But it was clear he was far from alone.

Fifty-Eight

Tuesday, October 11, 1955

I'd managed to avoid Peter Duke since my interview aired, enduring nothing more than distant glimpses of him across the courtyard or regurgitated insults from his buddies—but on Tuesday, my luck ran out.

He was waiting outside the library as the lunch bell rang. And the second our eyes met, my wariness bloomed into deep-seated dread. He didn't wear the same distracted impatience he'd had that day I'd found him looking for Julianne outside the newspaper room. No, today his expression was firm and settled. He was no longer searching for anyone or anything.

Over the past couple weeks, Peter had become like a dripping faucet, his fury a *ping, ping* of water droplets in a pot at the edge of my consciousness. I knew that sooner or later, it was bound to overflow.

He was grieving. You didn't have to study his uncharacteristically mussed hair, the wild glimmer in his red-streaked eyes, and the puckered, pinched set to his scowl to understand that he was struggling to cope with Julianne's death. After all, he did care for her in his own misguided way. He had to miss her.

However, it was clear that his anger was far larger than his grief.

He didn't just want to mourn Julianne. He wanted to avenge her, and as soon as our eyes met through the library doorway, I realized he had set his crosshairs on me.

Tim shot me a look of alarm as he held the door open for me, but he didn't say anything. So many of our lunches together lately, holed up in the library, were wordless. By now I could read his face as well as any of the books in there.

Let's go back inside, he was thinking. *Let's run.*

But no, I couldn't hide from Peter any more than I could hide from anything else that had happened since Ramón and Julianne met.

"I can't believe you still hang out in here with *her*," Peter spat at Tim, thrusting an angry hand in my direction. "I mean, I knew you were a real loser, but this is low, even for you, Buckles."

Tim stepped through the doorway in front of me, and I caught the briefest flash of indignation on his face before it was blocked from my view. People were usually hustling to class at this time, but Peter's shrill tone had commanded the attention of a small crowd of students who peered at us from their lockers. It seemed guys like Peter always had an audience at their disposal.

I could barely see Peter from where I stood since his face was partially obscured by Tim's body, but I saw his lip curl—in anger or disgust or both—as he began pacing, fists clenching and unclenching at his sides.

"You know who she is, don't you?" Peter snarled, eyes wide with accusation. "You know *what* she is."

"Take it easy, Duke," Tim said, his voice quiet but firm. Protective. Cautious.

"Not only is she a fucking liar," Peter went on, his voice growing louder as the halls simmered to a hungry hush. "She's a goddamned spic too."

In a flash, Tim barreled toward Peter. He didn't throw any punches or grab Peter in any way, but his size and swiftness in closing the space between the two of them was enough to make Peter flinch. I could barely hear Tim telling him to watch his mouth, his voice low and steady, as everyone around us broke into shrieks and gasps.

Peter's composure returned a little unevenly as he realized that Tim hadn't hit him, and his cheeks flushed as he straightened, tugging at his shirt irritably. He ran a hasty hand over his hair, glowering. "What? You don't care? You don't care that because of people like *her*, people like Julianne die?"

Tim stood his ground, looming over Peter. "You don't know what you're talking about."

Peter snorted. "I've always known there was something off about you. Something weird." He turned to the boys clustered behind him—his usual posse of football players—and they nodded in vigorous agreement. When he turned back to Tim, his eyes were wild with double meaning. "But I figured it was no concern of mine. You were a halfway decent lineman. So what if you were a total square? So what if you never kissed any girls? Who cared if there was something that you seemed to be hiding? But now . . . now it's an issue. Now I can't keep my mouth shut anymore. Now you've made it all into one hell of a mess I can't ignore." He leaned toward Tim, craning his head up to meet his eyes, and growled between gritted teeth. "You, Tim Buckles, are a race traitor and a homo."

Fifty-Nine

Tuesday, October 11, 1955

Tim's whole body shook as he sat in the driver's seat, his head buried in his hands. I could see the faintest outline of the burgeoning bruise on his temple peeking out between his thick fingers and disheveled golden locks.

We'd fled the scene after the fight. Left school completely.

Tim had pummeled Peter straight to the ground in a move that I was sure was second nature to him after a lifetime on the football field. Though Peter had gotten in a couple good swings before someone shouted that teachers were coming, he didn't stand a chance against someone as big and strong as Tim Buckles.

His cheeks were tear streaked when I finally got hold of his arm, tugging on his shoulder and repeating his name until his clumsy punches slowed. Horror-struck at all the blood that was pouring out of Peter's nose, he scrambled off him and followed me down the hall.

"Run!" I urged him over my shoulder, and we raced out the side door to his car.

He seemed surprised but appreciative when I hopped in the passenger seat, and he sniffled something about how I didn't have to come.

"Please, we outsiders have to stick together, right?" I said wryly. "Now step on it!"

He nodded shakily as his car roared to life, and we peeled out of the parking lot. The tears really set in when the school disappeared from the rearview mirror and our adrenaline began to subside. He pulled over in an alley behind a flower shop when it got too difficult for him to drive.

"Do you want to talk about it?" I asked, leaning toward him, trying to catch his eye, but he kept his gaze fixed on his steering wheel. On his white-knuckled fingers wrapped around it.

He opened his mouth slightly but closed it before he said anything. He did this one more time before he shook his head.

As I watched him, at war with himself over how to explain what had just happened, I thought of Tim calling us outsiders. I thought of his relief when I'd asked him about the dance.

All along, we'd been linked together by otherness without ever having to say it out loud. It both warmed my heart and broke it at the same time.

I patted his shoulder. "Would you like to go somewhere?"

He shook his head again, his breathing ragged. "There's nowhere to go. I just want to drive around for a bit."

So that's what we did. We cruised the grid-like streets of Phoenix with no radio, no words, just the occasional whimper from Tim as he swiped at his eyes with the back of his hand, pulling into neighborhoods and restaurant parking lots whenever he needed a moment to catch his breath. The hours passed by this way, just as fleeting as the palm trees and streetlamps that coasted past our windows.

Around three thirty, I realized he'd begun to drive in the direction of my house. With a trembling lip, he muttered, "My dad is gonna kill me."

At first, it seemed like a figure of speech. But as his words settled into my brain—where memories of Julianne actually being killed by her father thrived—my heart lurched. "Oh, *Tim.*" Sure, I knew what it was like to be an outsider, but I'd always had a home where I belonged, despite my differences. I couldn't even imagine what it was like to be an outsider in your own family too. "Tim, I'm so sorry."

He came to a stop three doors down from my house, just like he did the day of the press conference, and covered his face again. A heartbroken howl escaped him as his shoulders slumped forward.

I reached for him, placing my hand on his arm, and pulled him toward me. I wasn't strong enough to draw him into a hug without his cooperation, and at first, he resisted, shaking his head. But finally, he melted into me, burying his wet face in the nape of my neck, and I held him until his crying subsided once more.

When he pulled back, his eyes were red and swollen, and

his cheeks were splotchy. I noticed, for the first time, a cut on his lower lip where Peter must've hit him. "Thank you," he mumbled with a sniffle, leaning back into his seat.

"I'm so sorry that happened," I told him. "I'm sorry any of this has happened." I wanted to tell him how unfair it was that the burden of standing up for the downtrodden so often fell on other people who were oppressed, but the words tangled in my throat.

He gave me a meaningful look, though, and somehow, I thought he understood what I meant without having said it. He had a knack for that, for reading between the lines.

I gave him a kiss on the cheek before I exited the car, and the uninjured corner of his mouth turned upward into a sad half smile.

I waved to him as he drove away, and I watched his baby-blue Bel Air turn around in the dirt road, its tires grinding in the dust.

For the first time in a week, I didn't meet with Marco that night.

I lay in my bed, clenching my eyes shut as I heard the rustle of leaves in the breeze, the distant sounds of neighbors' low evening voices, the occasional roar of a car sputtering by.

The web of interconnectedness of everything grated at me. Made me feel raw and laid bare. My world was a knot, and I was the one who was unraveling. My sense of pride after the radio show was frayed by the plummeting despair I felt for Tim.

The thought of facing Marco like this . . .

I wouldn't know how to explain what occurred today. Tim's secret wasn't mine to tell, after all. And even if it was, I didn't know how I could possibly burden Marco with this additional level of hardship. To ask him to consider the unintended implications of our actions on other people on top of his own grief.

Because these two events—Ramón and Julianne's murders and my new notoriety—were connected. Byproducts of the same rotten system. Both dangerous and hurtful—though in different ways. Perhaps what happened to Tim today was just a warning, a precursor of the kind of challenges that were wrapped up within big changes.

Every time I rounded a corner and thought my fear was finally behind me, that I'd faced the biggest hurdle, some new threat emerged.

How was it possible to be hopeful and brave and strong when the world took every opportunity to beat down those you cared about?

Would it ever get easier?

Was it foolish to hope so?

Would I ever be prepared for the dangers that awaited me, or was I doomed to constantly throw those I cared about in the line of fire by the very nature of who I was and what I wanted?

It wasn't fair. And perhaps that was the point.

Sixty

Wednesday, October 12, 1955

Though many people joined us for the meeting to listen to the logistics of the vigil—where we would gather that night, what to bring, what to expect—the atmosphere at El Foro remained tenuous at best.

It wasn't just me who was having a bout of nerves, it seemed.

I was new to the meetings, sure, but even I could tell this was unusual. There were no lively discussions. No disagreements. No chatter.

I'd helped hand out flyers for the vigil at the beginning of the meeting, urging stone-faced attendees to spread the word. Now I twisted my own flyer into a ropy crumple of paper in my lap as I listened to Verón try to elicit input from the crowd of uneasy attendees. But he was met with nothing but silence when he asked if there were any questions, and the meeting dispersed fifteen minutes early in a frenzied hush.

"What's going on?" Marco asked with a scowl as the three of us collected discarded flyers and rearranged makeshift furniture that had drifted in the shuffle.

Verón shook his head, sighing. "People are scared. It's to be expected, unfortunately."

"Scared?" Marco barked, accidentally kicking a wooden crate. He hissed in pain but kept his eyes trained on Verón. I was thankful he didn't see my own eyes widen at this. "We finally do something other than sit around and talk, and now they're scared?"

"Sí," Verón responded wistfully. "There've been more cops around here ever since Rosa's interview. Some of the farmers have warned their workers not to get involved in any of this. They've threatened their jobs. Change always brings its share of fear, and this is what it looks like. On both sides."

Despite Verón's calm tone and his clear expression of acceptance, Marco was visibly alarmed. "Well, what are we going to do? This isn't the time to back down!" I could feel his eyes cutting over to me even as I avoided them. "How do we convince people to overcome their fear?"

"We've done all we can do. Now we must let people decide for themselves. We can't drag them there, kicking and screaming." He tucked his hands in the pockets of his slacks, giving us a sympathetic look.

What do we do if no one shows up but us? I wondered, my hands beginning to tremble as the thought occurred to me. I nearly dropped my bookbag, and as I scrambled to secure it on my shoulder, I looked up to find Marco watching me intently.

His brows furrowed, almost as if I'd asked that question out loud.

"We can't let ourselves dwell on what could go wrong," Verón continued with a sigh. "We must have faith that people will do what's right."

Marco's eyes, still on me, flared up with dismay. He let out a frustrated groan through gritted teeth.

"You two get home safely, eh? Get some rest," Verón told us gently, ambling toward the exit. "I'll see you at the vigil."

We watched him leave, but I continued to stare at the doorway long after Verón had disappeared from view.

"I'll drive you home. You ready?" Marco said after a moment.

"I think I'll walk," I told him. "Fresh air."

"Okay, I'll walk you home." He tried to sound casual despite the seriousness in his expression.

I shook my head. "No, no. It's not that far. I'd like to clear my thoughts a bit." Even as I said it, I knew it was the wrong thing.

"I missed you last night," he said softly. It wasn't a question, though there was something asking in his amber eyes. Something searching.

"I missed you too," I told him, hoping that would be answer enough for him, that he would be able to see that I meant it, even if I didn't want to explain it.

He took a step closer to me, squaring himself between me and the doorway. Head bowed, he asked, "Are you all right, princesa? You've been awfully quiet all evening."

I huffed a quiet, humorless chuckle. "I *am* quiet, remember?"

He didn't laugh at this. Not even the faintest hint of a smile. Instead, he brought his index finger to my temple. "What's going on in there, hmm?" He lingered there for a moment before trailing his fingertip down my jaw, to my chin.

"Nothing," I murmured. "Everything. It's a lot."

He hummed in agreement, lifting my chin with his finger and placing a soft kiss on my lips. "Sí. But you don't have to bear it on your own. We're in this together. If something's bothering you, you can always talk to me."

My lips still tingled from his kiss as I pressed them together. I hadn't told him about Peter or the fight or anything that was happening at school. I wasn't sure I knew how to unravel it all—or how to make sense of the all-consuming terror that was winding its way through me, even without Tim's secret mixed up in it. I knew this was a moment to stand out. To speak out. To be bold. Just like the radio show, the vigil was another pivotal moment.

And yet, just like the radio show, I could feel myself shrinking away from the task at hand, my belief in my ability to stand strong crumbling.

I wished I'd grown since then—that I'd become a braver person since my voice took flight over the airwaves—but here I was, quiet and quivering like always.

"I know," I finally managed to say in response. "I know that."

He pressed his forehead to mine, his skin warm. The dark tendril of hair that swept across his brow tickled my forehead.

I hated that he was worrying about me. That I was one more burden for him to bear. He'd been through as much as I had, after all, and now here I was, laying my inadequacies at his feet.

"I'm okay, really," I told him. "I'll be fine." I straightened, pulling away. I hoped he didn't notice how different those two statements were as I tried to settle my expression into something less morose. "I'll see you tomorrow, Marco. At the vigil?"

He shoved his hands in pockets, nodding. I could tell there was more he wanted to say, but uncharacteristically, he kept it to himself. He issued me one last inquiring look that set my heart ablaze with something dangerously close to heartbreak. "Hasta mañana, princesa."

Sixty-One

Thursday, October 13, 1955

Almost as soon as I arrived at school the next day, I caught wind of rumors that both Tim and Peter were in the principal's office with their parents. My heart ached for the tearstained image I held of my friend from the day before, but I tried not to listen to any further speculation as people hissed comments about Tim being kicked out or losing his spot on the football team.

I knew I should heed Verón's advice, that I shouldn't lose myself worrying about everything that could go wrong. The way Marco had regarded me last night—with concern and care and something deeper that I just couldn't put my finger on—stuck with me like the haze of a dream I couldn't shake. I tried desperately to cling to some notion of hope, which was what I felt certain Ramón or Julianne would do.

However, any feeble attempts at positive thinking evaporated when I was called to the principal's office too, my name ringing out across the loudspeaker in last period. It was the first time that had ever happened. I'd spent over a year going almost unnoticed, and now my name—or at least the name I used here—reverberated around the halls where I lived my second life.

I paused for a moment, my eyes locking on Miss Shaw's. I was surprised to find her face every bit as alarmed as I felt. She gave me a quick, subtle nod of silent encouragement as she tried to recapture the class's discussion on iambic pentameter.

I scrambled to collect my books, distinctly aware that despite Miss Shaw's best efforts, everyone was watching me. My hands were trembling when I finally made it to the hallway. I paused to listen to the muffled sound of her voice directing the class to open their readers before I continued down the hall.

The school secretary greeted me somewhat impatiently and escorted me to the back of the office where Mr. Williams's door, with his name emblazoned on it with a shiny plaque, was shut. I peered around the unfamiliar office space as I followed her, searching for any sign of Tim or his family, but the nearby chairs and desks were unoccupied, save for the registrar, who huffed at me disapprovingly over the top of her typewriter.

The secretary knocked softly on Mr. Williams's door and opened it without waiting for a response, motioning me inside.

Mr. Williams was seated at his desk in a dark brown suit, thin hair combed across a wide forehead. He adjusted his wire-rimmed glasses and sighed heavily as I entered. Without a word, I sat down in the cushioned chair across from him as if being forced down by some invisible weight.

On his desk, next to his chipped coffee cup and a stack of worn manila folders, was a crisp piece of paper with my name typed on it. Immediately, my heart quickened.

"Miss Capistrano," he said, drawing my attention before I could try to read the rest of the paper. His eyes narrowed when I looked up at him, as if he was trying to place me. As if he hadn't been the one to call me here.

"Y-yes, sir?" I shifted in the chair.

"How are you?" he said wearily, and I got the impression this wasn't so much a question as a habit.

"Um, I suppose there's quite a bit going on lately, sir."

"Hmm, indeed." His bony fingers were interlaced on top of the papers on his desk, and he glanced down at them briefly. "Terrible tragedy. You and Miss Callihan, you were friends."

My throat tightened, squeezing the air out of my body, at the casual mention of her name. At our past tense friendship. At the murky purpose of this meeting. I nodded.

"And you were friends with this Montoya boy as well."

I froze, no longer made of flesh and blood but struck into stone. I wasn't sure I'd ever get accustomed to the way my worlds were mixing these days.

"And it seems you and Mr. Buckles are acquaintances too?" His mouth pressed into a thin line of displeasure.

I couldn't bring myself to confirm any of this. I wasn't sure it mattered anyway.

"Hmm," he said again, interpreting my silence as the only response he required. "You may know, then, that I am a close friend of the Callihan family."

What I knew from Julianne was that Mr. Williams was a tolerated guest at the Callihan dinner table on occasion, part of the sheriff's whole "man of the people" routine. The sheriff often invited community members over for backyard barbecues or the like. Their mailman, local business owners, and even our principal. Julianne had told me she'd caught her father drinking twice as many gin and tonics one evening just to make it through Mr. Williams's never-ending monologue on how far over budget the drama department went on the spring musical last year.

As if somehow sensing my doubt at the use of the term "close friend," he cleared his throat and said, "The thing is, Miss Capistrano, I realized I didn't know much about *you*. Or your family. Your name seems to be everywhere these days, and yet I don't believe I've met you or your parents. So I had my secretary pull your file." He paused, staring at me placidly, and it occurred to me that, even though this wasn't a question, I was expected to respond.

"Oh" was all I could muster.

He swept aside the neat stack of papers bearing my name. And then I saw it. Something I recognized instantly—but not here. No, not on Mr. Williams's desk. *No.*

The flyer. For tonight's vigil.

"Oh," I said again, but this time, it sounded like I'd been punched in the gut.

"You appear to be a fairly smart girl, even given your *upbringing*," he said. "But I do want to make sure I'm making myself perfectly clear, given the sensitive circumstances." His lips twitched, and I wondered if this was a speech he'd practiced before I arrived. If he was recalling his lines. Playing a part more than anything else. "It's come to my attention that you don't actually live in the school zone to attend our campus. It appears you should be attending a school that can offer you courses that are more tailored to your learning needs. Considering the way you are acting out due to recent events, it is clear that this is not the best environment for you." The twitching began to spread across his face, causing nervous blinking and eyebrows that rose and dipped seemingly of their own accord. He slid the papers on his desk toward me. "With that in mind, I must require that you transfer to the appropriate school for you."

That's what they were.

Transfer papers.

For Rosa Capistrano.

Everything else was a blur, but I saw Phoenix South Mountain High School somewhere within the fuzzy sea of letters swirling around before me.

Mr. Williams was saying something about it being best for everyone, that if I didn't transfer voluntarily, they'd have to take disciplinary action and perhaps even legal action against my parents for falsifying official documents, that hopefully I'd learned my lesson, that it was in my best interest. These unfeeling phrases, so hateful in their lack of specificity, in their inability to truly understand what was happening, flew around me, buzzing and stinging like mosquitos after a monsoon.

Sixty-Two

Thursday, October 13, 1955

I flung open the front door of my house, bolting straight to my bedroom and dropping my bookbag on the floor like it weighed a thousand pounds and I couldn't possibly shoulder the weight a moment longer. I jerked the top drawer of my dresser open and crammed the transfer papers—now crinkled and damp with sweat from being clenched in my fists the entire bus ride home—inside. I swept my stockings and slips over the papers to hide them.

I couldn't think about this mess now.

I couldn't be deterred by something so self-centered. Not today. Today was about more. More than me. More than just Ramón and Julianne, even. It was about change. It was about injustice. It was about the big picture.

I spun around, beginning to gather the things Verón told us we'd need. I swapped out my loafers for my saddle shoes, more worn and better for walking. I filled my canteen and tucked some extra change in my pocket for a pay phone in case I got separated from the group.

I turned toward the mirror, avoiding my flushed complexion and the wild look in my eyes and focusing instead on my hair. I untied the ribbon that held it in place and fished around for the bobby pins that were barely restraining my mass of dark waves. I began the process of coaxing my hair into something more secure. It was still warm out, and we had a long walk ahead of us. I'd want it off my neck, away from my face. I was running my fingers through my curls, working out the tangles, when I suddenly heard the soft creak of the back door. Brush in hand, I paused.

I assumed it was too early for either of my parents to be home from work, but perhaps I hadn't been as quick as I'd thought. "Mamá?" I called out anyway, peering out my open bedroom door toward the kitchen.

The only sound that answered me was a tentative footstep on tile, a shuffle far too cautious to be either of my parents. I opened my mouth to utter my sister's name next, but the words caught in my throat as Marco appeared in my bedroom doorway.

For a moment, I was more surprised by how he looked than by his presence here. It was hard to explain, but he suddenly seemed so *different*. His dark hair was still slicked back in the same way. He wore the white T-shirt and jeans he always wore when he wasn't at work. But still, somehow, there was something calm, settled, *stable* about him. He stepped closer—into my bedroom—and I noticed his cheeks were smooth and glowing with a clean shave. His luminous eyes were clear and steady, without the gloss of tears or alcohol or sleepless exhaustion that I'd grown so accustomed to seeing over the past three weeks.

But his composure quickly fell away as our eyes met, and I saw a rosy tint creep up his neck and to his cheeks, a pinkish tinge to his brown skin. It was so inconceivable to me—Marco Montoya *blushing*.

What was he doing here? The words died on my tongue as he reached forward and ran the ends of my hair between his fingertips.

"I've never seen your hair like this," he breathed, his dark brows rising.

Heat filled me, my own bashfulness meeting his, and I shook my head, though I wasn't sure why. "I have a lot of hair. It's easier to keep it pinned up."

He returned his hand to his side, but his gaze lingered on me. "I like it."

I waited a moment—for what, I wasn't sure—before I continued what I'd been doing. I swept my hair up and tied it into a ponytail. I kept my eyes fixed on the mirror, sneaking glances at Marco's reflection over my shoulder.

He chewed his lower lip as he looked around my bedroom. The stacks of books arranged on my dresser and on the floor, the narrow twin bed against the window with its threadbare quilt. "I wanted to see you," he said, answering the question I hadn't asked out loud.

My chest tightened at this, but for some reason, I fought to conceal how touched I was. "You couldn't wait fifteen minutes?" I teased instead.

"No," he said simply. Tenderly.

We were quiet a moment, my back still toward him, before I took a deep breath and turned around. He was closer than I expected, and his eyes brightened as we came face-to-face. Slowly he reached toward me again, letting his fingers brush the one strand of dark hair that had already worked its way free. A lone curl by my ear.

"I'm scared, Marco." I said it on an exhale, not trusting my true voice to get the words out.

He nodded instantly, like he'd been expecting it. "I know. Me too."

"You are?" The idea of fiery and defiant Marco Montoya, scared? I couldn't register it. His face was inscrutable as ever, not a trace of fear in his gold-flecked eyes or the firm set of his jaw.

"Claro," he said anyway, as if it were obvious. "Rosa, you've been through a lot, and I know none of this is what you wanted."

And then I understood it, as his thumb brushed against my cheek. He was scared—for *me*.

I snorted in irritation, more at myself than him. "*You've* been through a lot. You haven't gotten what you wanted either."

"I know that," he said solemnly. "We'll face this together, all right? I'm right here with you. Don't forget that."

"Marco . . ." I breathed, not sure why. I didn't know what else to say, but I knew I had to get something out. I couldn't let my silence swallow us both. Not now. Not when we both needed to focus on the task at hand rather than get tangled up in concerns about me, of all things.

He tugged me closer, into the warm cotton of his shirt, and placed a kiss on my temple. "We'll face it together," he murmured against the top of my head. "All of us."

He wasn't going to tell me it was going to be okay. Of course he wasn't. How could he after everything that had happened? These weren't the kind of assurances we were foolish enough to make at this point.

It would have to be enough.

I nodded, savoring the feel of him against me for a moment longer before I took a step back. I gave my hair a quick pat, sweeping the stray lock back behind my ear. My pulse hammered wildly inside me, and my ankles felt a bit unsteady, but I clenched my jaw and tried to arrange my expression into something firm and resolute anyway. "Vámonos, hmm?" I said, and led him out of the house without meeting his gaze again.

Sixty-Three

Thursday, October 13, 1955

Gauzy orange clouds gathered around the surrounding South Mountain peaks as Marco and I walked to the church. It wasn't quite dusk yet, but the threat of an incoming monsoon gave the late afternoon sky a hint of darkness. He commented once about the prospect of rain, and we both agreed that these types of storms usually pass quickly, but aside from that, we were quiet for most of the walk. Tangled up in our own thoughts.

Verón stood in the center of the dirt parking lot, talking to the handful of people who arrived before us, people I recognized from meetings. A few picket signs rested on the ground, their wood handles propped up against Verón's legs as he spoke.

Marco greeted them as we walked up, but I barely heard the words exchanged.

What if we are the only people who show up today? I couldn't fight off this question. We'd been banking on the community coming together and rallying around circumstances that affected us all. But what if that was too idealistic? Too naive? What impact could it possibly have if it was just a few of us calling out the injustice to a world that was content to ignore it all?

Verón's stare drew me out of my worries, and I realized by the inquisitive expression on his face that he must've said something to me. And then, because the three other men and Marco were also looking at me, I suspected he needed an answer.

"I'm sorry?" I said weakly.

A flash of concern crossed Verón's typically impassive face, but he was quick to clear it. "I was just checking that you are okay to be at the front of the march. You and Marco."

I tried not to think about the empty parking lot. I tried not to worry that "march" might just be too grandiose of a term, though there was still time for others to join.

"I'll be right there behind you," he went on in that warm, persuasive tone of his. "It could get messy, of course, but I think it's very important *symbolically* that you two lead us downtown."

Marco reached for my hand, hooking his pinkie in mine for a fleeting moment. Just a squeeze. The quickest reminder that he was here with me.

I nodded at Verón. "All right. Yes. Th-that's fine." I cut a quick sideways glance at Marco.

"Mm, together," Marco agreed, his voice rough and unwavering, like the jagged edge of a cliff.

And no one said anything more. We just stood there in a

half circle beside the church, in the shadow of looming dust clouds.

We were set to begin our march at six o'clock. The sun wouldn't set until just past six thirty, but it'd be low enough along the mountains that we could light our candles. We'd make our way up Jefferson Street, toward downtown, and arrive at the capitol building around seven.

Verón reminded us all along it would be quiet, it would be tranquil. Despite Marco's urging, Verón was clear this was not a protest. This was a vigil. Even though we hoped it would also draw attention to the lack of justice for Ramón, it was first and foremost about honoring the lives lost that night—together, for the first time.

We would march in silence with our candles lighting the way.

"Peaceful," Verón said. "Reverent. Let our actions speak for themselves."

Was I imagining the way Verón's eyes lingered on Marco?

Nods rippled around the twelve of us.

Twelve.

I tried not to be disheartened. I had hoped to see Señora Montoya. My family. Tim perhaps. I had held out hope that they'd stand with us despite everything.

In *spite* of everything.

It hurt that their fear could get in the way, but I tried to remind myself I probably wouldn't have had the courage to be here three weeks ago. If I hadn't seen it all firsthand, I would've seen this as reckless and foolhardy too. *Rosie* certainly would have.

Marco held his candle out toward mine, the soft glow of firelight playing on his sharp features in the fading sunlight. It struck me as strangely familiar—how many times had I seen his cheekbones aglow as he lit a cigarette? But of course, this was different in every way imaginable.

The wicks of our candles met, and after a few seconds, mine was burning too.

He remained in front of me, and we both watched the fire grow from a thin spark to a flame, flickering and wavering just a tiny bit at first.

"Gracias," I murmured, and as Marco's long lashes lifted, he looked as if he was about to say something more than "de nada." Something that had clearly been on his mind. But he paused, his mouth slightly ajar. The only part of him that moved were his eyebrows; they shot up, his attention caught on something behind me.

And he wasn't the only one. Verón turned too, a bright, confident smile spreading across his face.

Slowly, I followed their gaze.

Coming around the corner of the church at the very edge of the lot, beneath the motionless branches of juniper trees, was a steady line of figures drawing nearer to us. It was a crowd of people I knew and people I didn't know. Neighbors from the barrio and strangers who wanted to join us. And there were my parents! Blanca. Señora Montoya and some of the girls Ramón and I grew up with. Pilar from the law firm even. And towering above most of them, a head of fair hair that belonged to Tim Buckles.

My confusion melted into surprise and then *gratitude* as tears welled up in my eyes.

"Bienvenidos," Verón called, immediately busying himself with distributing candles, dispatching a few others to light them with a quick nod of his head.

A tear slipped down my cheek as my parents and my sister embraced me. Over Blanca's shoulder, I saw Tim give me a shy smile that reached his eyes, if not fully across his broad, bruised face.

Together, Marco had said. *Together*.

It echoed in my mind over and over again as I hugged each of them, clasping hands and readying ourselves for our march.

Sixty-Four

Thursday, October 13, 1955

I stared at the candle in my hands as I walked.

    I willed myself to concentrate solely on the light I was carrying, to not let myself get swept up in my own nerves and fear. I just focused on the flame in front of me as my feet carried me toward the looming shapes of the downtown Phoenix skyline, my head bowed. I told myself all that mattered was keeping this fire going. As I stared into the orange flame in my hands—as it flickered with every step I took—images drifted and blended across the blue center, across the licks of yellow at the edges.

    In this tiny blaze, I saw Ramón racing down the edge of the canal to go swimming on warm afternoons, dark curls flouncing as the green-blue surface of the water shimmered in invitation. I thought of the first summer, when we were twelve or thirteen, that girls suddenly took notice of his warm eyes and bright smile and never stopped noticing him. I thought of the gentle movements of his fingers along his guitar strings, the husky thrum of his voice, the way he'd sing, "Rosita, Rosita, Rosita, una chica astutita." I thought of his crinkle-eyed laugh as he'd peer at me across a pile of books at school in the days before I transferred. His swaying, joyful dance moves at every occasion from his cousin's baptism to Blanca's wedding. The dreamy, dopey way he'd looked at Julianne those few ludicrous weeks they'd had together.

And Julianne. My first friend in that other half of my life, my only friend at North for a long while. Someone I should've never had anything in common with, and yet someone I shared so much with. It felt truly inconceivable that I only knew her for a year, that so much could be packed into what, in the grand scheme of things, was such a small scrap of time.

Julianne, with her angelic blond curls and deep blue eyes that never missed anything. The subtle way her lips could switch between a smile and a defiant scowl without any notice. Sharing ideas in newspaper club, standing under the lights at a football game, sweeping her charcoal pencil across her drawing pad right in the middle of class, walking down the hallways at school with her head held high. My quiet, kind, brave friend.

These two people who were gone now. They hadn't gotten to live beyond their childhood because of something spectacularly ordinary. Something that happened all the time.

Love.

They'd fallen in love. It was fast, sure. Maybe it was just a crush, but did that really make a difference now? They did something almost everyone did at some point in their lives, that most teenagers did, even. They fell in love.

My grip tightened around the waxy base of the candle.

Marco was a half step behind me, head cast downward as he walked, careful to let me lead but still deliberately close. I stole a glance at him out of the corner of my eye; I could feel his presence with every bit of me without looking at him. His warmth, his resilience. Our togetherness. When his eyes did meet mine, there was a glisten to them, the trace of tears brimming along the lower rim.

Love. Surprising and wild and reckless and powerful.

I shifted my candle into my right hand, freeing my left to reach out to him and loop my arm through his. I pulled him into step with me. Our shoulders brushed up against one another, and I let my fingertips rest along the smooth, warm skin of his upper arm, just below the soft fabric of his shirt.

Love. It may not have been what any of us expected it to be, but it still mattered.

Just like city hall had been the ideal backdrop for the sheriff's conference, the capitol felt like the perfect destination for us tonight. I imagined it in a newspaper, in a black-and-white photo. The domed peak of the capitol building, the bronze angel statue on top. A group of people bearing signs and candles as they plowed forward. Faces indistinguishable, just the contrast of the capitol and the grainy figures surrounding it.

It made sense. So much of history was about appearance, I was beginning to realize.

Marco had argued for a demonstration at the courthouse,

or even the Callihan house. "It needs to be impossible to ignore," he'd demanded at El Foro, his anger slicing right through the discussion. "It should feel *personal*," he'd added, and Verón had been unable to summon a response to that other than a clear look of pity.

"What if we held it here?" I'd chimed in. "At the church?" I gestured around us, hoping to shift some of the attention away from Marco's outburst.

"What we are doing needs to be bold but neutral," Verón had said, eyes still resting on Marco. "Not on anyone's home turf. We must transcend our traditional boundaries. From the south side, downtown. Together. Not an act of vengeance but a recognition that what happened impacted two communities and needs to be addressed accordingly."

Without realizing it, my gait slowed, and I stumbled slightly as Marco and I fell out of rhythm with one another. My hold around his arm tightened, and he shot me a concerned look.

"It's okay," he murmured, just loud enough to be heard above the steady crunching of feet on asphalt all around us, but soft enough that I was sure I was the only one who'd heard him.

Together, we rounded the bend toward the capitol lawn, past the wavering palm trees caught in the wind, past the historic Victorian homes that were older than the state itself—when, suddenly, we saw them.

The flashing lights. Red, blue, red, blue.

Instantly, I was back at the night of the murders. The pulsing brilliance. The contrast against the monochromatic darkness.

Everything in me tensed. Braced for what, I wasn't sure yet, but somehow, I kept moving. Kept walking forward. Kept leading the crowd of people behind me.

Kept going.

In the dim background—in front of the buildings, in between the freshly illuminated streetlamps, along the sidewalks—onlookers began to materialize. People not necessarily supporting but watching. The probing glimmer of their eyes and the audience-like silence poked at me. Drawn like moths to a flame, though it seemed it was the police lights, not our candles, that had summoned them.

I heard the crisp pop of a car door swinging open, and from one of the dozen cruisers blocking the road leading up to the capitol, out stepped a commanding figure I'd recognize absolutely anywhere.

Of course he was here. He wouldn't let our voices be heard without a challenge. He had come to impose on us—on our grief—with his presence and power and the intimidation that came with it.

Had that been the point? I wasn't sure anymore. We wanted to draw attention, but somehow I'd failed to consider what it would look like and feel like to share this space with Sheriff Callihan.

An infinity passed, my thundering heartbeat the only marker of time, the sole grounding force as memories and fear charged at me like a hot, stinging dust cloud. *Ramón and Julianne, kissing, smiling at one another in that heartbreakingly oblivious way, reaching out for each other even in those final moments.* The sheriff, boots on the gravel. *The radiant look in Marco's eyes the day he took me to my first meeting and every night we've held each other on his porch.* The sheriff, stance squared off, facing us with grim resolution. *My parents, scared but hoping for more. More for Blanca, more for me. More than this. More, more, more.* The sheriff, shielded by his car door. *The kids at school, everyone at the press conference, all the people here now. Watching. Gawking. Silent witnesses.* The sheriff, his eyes finally on me. His gaze firm, so unyielding it was almost tangible.

"Halt," he said, bringing to his mouth a megaphone that squeaked and only projected the last half of his command. The sharp crack of a *t*, like a whip. *Or a gunshot.* "Do not proceed any further."

Murmuring began to bubble up behind me, and out of the muddled mix of whispers, I heard Verón tell me, "You can stop, Rosa. Remember, we are doing nothing wrong. We'll hear him out peacefully. *Safely.*"

Mouth dry, I tightened my hold on Marco and stopped walking, much more suddenly than I'd intended. I felt Marco stop beside me and heard the sound of many footsteps behind me slow and cease. All except one.

Verón's body moved past us to the front of our crowd. "Good evening," he called out. His voice was so steady, so restrained, there was almost an edge to it. Like we could all feel the white-knuckled control he was exerting in this moment. That kind of caution and effort was almost more alarming than if he were to burst forth shouting and thrashing.

Another screech of the sheriff's megaphone. "This is an unlawful gathering. You do not have the required permits—"

"This is a peaceful vigil." Even without the megaphone, Verón's voice was loud enough to cut him off. "For the victims of unspeakable violence. Including your daughter."

The sheriff held the megaphone in front of his face for several beats before he spoke again. "We have reason to believe this gathering is intended to escalate recent events. Looting and rioting will not be tolerated. We are here to maintain the peace."

Verón nodded and held up his hands in the air like they were clear evidence of his intentions. "I can assure you, we are not here to cause any damage or destruction. We aim only to draw attention to the injustice that has occurred. Surely, as officers of the law, you can understand that peace without justice is a falsehood."

The officers flanking the sheriff began to shift and squirm. Though most stood behind their open driver's doors like the sheriff, I could see their hands moving in a way that made me wonder if they were reaching for their guns or just touching them instinctively, perhaps for reassurance or preparation.

The sheriff, however, did not move at all. Did not return the megaphone to his mouth. Did not address the officers around him. Just stared. It looked like he was fixed on Verón. We were standing fairly close together; Verón was maybe two steps in front of me, just to the right. In the relative darkness, that might have been who he was looking at.

But an unshakeable feeling deep inside me told me that the sheriff's gaze was locked on me instead. On the girl who didn't belong. Not at school, not in his daughter's life, and certainly not at the scene of his crime.

Finally, the sheriff's voice rang out once more. "You all need to turn around, do you hear me? Go back to where you came from, and no one will get hurt. This is your final warning." Gone was the careful, cautionary tone of a trained officer. Of a political figure. This was hostile. A threat.

Whispers erupted around me. Urgent, frightened, unsettled. The shuffle of feet. I couldn't tell if they were actually leaving or just preparing to, but I didn't turn around to see. I kept my eyes on the sheriff, returning his unfaltering stare.

"We have every right to be here, Sheriff." Verón's hands were still up as he spoke, but now they were extended out from his sides, gesturing toward all of us.

"Whether you like it or not," someone added in a clear, determined voice that quelled any rustling uncertainty around us. Those six words ground our moment to a stop, like water tossed on burning embers.

Even though Verón had been speaking for us since we arrived, it was clear that this time, the words didn't belong to him.

For the first time since I spotted him, I dragged my eyes away from the sheriff and glanced around me, seeking out the source of the voice.

Instantly, I noticed everyone was now looking at me. Tim, my parents, Marco—even Verón was now staring over his shoulder at me. The same wide-eyed expression.

And that's when I realized that it was me. I was the one who spoke those words. It was my voice that hung in the air.

It was *me*.

Sixty-Five

Thursday, October 13, 1955

"We are here." I was still talking. It was still my voice. *Me.* I couldn't believe it, and yet I kept going. "You can't keep us separate forever. You can't keep us from taking up space and making our voices heard. We all belong here. All of us—even Ramón. Even me."

From behind me, a warm breeze kicked up, fluttering the fabric of my skirt against my legs as it swept all around us. Even from a distance, I could see the sheriff's tuft of straw-colored hair wave in the wind. The rest of him remained stoic and unmoving. Too still to be effortless.

"Haven't you already caused enough trouble with all your lies and deception? What more do you want?" His voice had a distressed hitch to it. He took a deep breath, letting his eyelids droop, as if to steady himself. But when his eyes popped back open, his anger appeared untouched. "This is why you and your kind have no place here! Look at what's happened! Julianne was a *good girl*." His voice caught, but he forged on. "She never would've done something like this if it hadn't been for the likes of you and that hoodlum!"

Suddenly, Verón's face, still looking over his shoulder toward me, shifted from one of intrigue to one of distinct alarm. He reached out. Not toward me, though.

Toward Marco.

Marco, who was propelling himself forward—past me, past Verón, toward the row of squad cars. His pace was urgent and uneven. A half run, half stumble, his arms gesticulating wildly as he moved.

My body seized in horror when I realized what was about to happen.

"Say that again, you *pig*!" he shouted, the words barely reaching me above the wind, which was now coursing around us with much more force. "How *dare* you speak to her! How dare you talk about my brother like that! You're a *monster*! After everything you've done! How *dare* you! You pig, you coward. You're a goddamn murderer!"

"*Marco!*" He didn't hear me. Whether it was the raging winds or the storm building up inside him, he was lost to me in this moment. Lost to us all.

"Listen here," the sheriff cut in, pivoting to exchange glances with the officers to his right. "I don't want anyone to get hurt." Behind him, a flash of lightning ripped down the sky, illuminating his features into an almost skeletal image of agony and apprehension. "We've had enough bloodshed."

"Because of *you*!" The look in Marco's eyes was terrifying. Unhinged. Wild.

I felt like something split open inside of me.

"Now, now," Sheriff Callihan said, and with that, I was sure of it. There *was* a trembling uneasiness to him. In both his voice and his body. Something inside of him—his fear, his grief, whatever it was—was threatening to break through. To destroy him. To bring him to his knees.

Abruptly, Marco paused, nearly skidding to a stop. Something had caught his eye, it seemed. His back was still to me, and I had no idea what it could be. The way the wind was tugging the light fabric of his shirt gave him a slightly puffed-out, ghostly quality where he stood in the center of the street. He turned his head, affording me a fleeting glimpse of his stark profile. A determined grimace. Those fire-like eyes glowing with something unstoppable.

And then I saw what Marco had spotted. My heart plummeted.

A beer bottle, clattering quietly against the curb, rolling against the cement in the building wind.

He stalked toward it, scooping it off the asphalt and clutching it in his hand.

Like a grenade.

The wind was growing stronger and stronger with each warm gust that swept around us. It kicked up a good deal of dust, trapping us in an increasingly murky haze of orange. Some of the candles were now extinguished, but the police lights still burned bright in the dimness, even if their colors were slightly muted.

"Marco!" I shouted once more, but in that same instant, a crack of lightning ripped across the sky, followed by a deafening rumble of thunder.

Though there was no way he actually heard me, he glanced at me over his shoulder. There was something apologetic in his expression, wiped clean when he turned back to the sheriff a moment later. He raised his arm back and hurled the beer bottle across the street, where it shattered in a loud burst of glass on Sheriff Callihan's windshield.

For an instant, the entire world was silent and still.

The shards of glass exploding in front of the sheriff froze in midair.

The raindrops about to fall from the rolling storm clouds held themselves in for a moment longer.

The tear gas that was about to erupt and ensnare us all hovered around the canisters, not yet spread.

For an instant, we were caught in the almost rather than the after.

But of course, that couldn't last forever. Moments like this, as spectacular and monumental and life-altering as they were, had to end.

And we had to contend with what came next.

Sixty-Six

Thursday, October 13, 1955

I wasn't sure which spilled forth first: the rain or the tear gas.

But at some point, they were both unleashed—and the chaos that ensued was all-consuming.

There was screaming and wailing, thunder and pounding footsteps—but mercifully, no gunshots. Amid my terror and burning pain, I found the faintest glimmer of gratitude for that. Tears and vomit and sweat and widespread panic unlike anything I'd ever seen, but no more bloodshed. At least in that respect, Sheriff Callihan was a man of his word.

My parents found me, and we held each other in a soaking, trembling huddle, Blanca and me tucked in between them like when we were little girls.

Before my vision was overcome by the piercing torment of the tear gas, before I buried my face in Papi's shirt, before the thick sheet of summer rain turned our world into muddy meaninglessness, I caught one last glimpse of Marco.

Taken down by two police officers.

Wriggling and roaring, soaking clumps of black hair in his eyes.

Forced onto the hot, wet asphalt of the street.

Struck by billy clubs and wrestled into handcuffs.

Blanca held on to my hands—both of them—as I cried out his name over and over again.

Sixty-Seven

Thursday, October 13, 1955

Papi held my transfer papers out in front of him later that night. It seemed like such an inconsequential thing, really, after everything that had happened. But all the same, it was also impossible to ignore.

"Ay, niña," Mamá sniffled, her face still red and splotchy even though the effects of the gas dissipated after we splashed water on our faces. "What are we going to do?"

I knew she didn't expect me to answer, but I still shrugged, the weight of circumstances outside our control heavy on my shoulders.

What was there to do at this point?

Was there anything I could do that mattered?

I wasn't sure what the right choice for me was, but I was certain I did not want to—could not bring myself to—walk into that school ever again. And it wasn't just because Mr. Williams had been clear that they'd expel me.

My parents were disappointed in me. And maybe, a month ago, I would've been disappointed too in my inability to keep my head down and stay focused on what I was there to do. This was, after all, how I'd felt when Ramón and Julianne first revealed their relationship to me.

But things had changed in ways that I couldn't explain. In ways that hadn't fully revealed themselves. In ways that were still sprouting deep down inside of me.

My disappointment was boundless and immense. It was tangled up in everything around us.

I once thought I'd understood this world we lived in. I thought I could manipulate its shortcomings and pitfalls to my benefit. I thought I could succeed in it, but it was clear that it would not only let me down but keep knocking me down, time and time again.

"Everything you worked for, Rosita . . ." Mamá continued, her heartbreak written all over her face.

My heart was beyond breaking, though. After all, how many pieces could a heart truly be broken into? Could shards forever continue to be shattered?

After everything that had happened, wasn't mine just dust by now?

HAILEY ALCARAZ

Phoenix South Mountain High School to Welcome Four Hundred Students in the Fall

The Arizona Republic
July 25, 1953

The new Phoenix South Mountain High School will open its doors for the first time next month. All high school students who live south of Salt River are required to attend this new campus.

Phoenix South Mountain and Camelback High School are two new high schools opening this year largely in response to the recent integration case in Arizona.

Sixty-Eight

Monday, October 17, 1955

There was a moment when I opened my eyes on Monday morning that I felt like time had turned back. Like someone had flipped my calendar pages back to the before. Before I transferred schools, before I took on this double life, before *any* of this happened.

There was a moment that was just streams of sunlight on my bedspread, birds chirping outside my window, the cool October breeze in my curtains.

But the heaviness of it all couldn't be avoided. It came crashing down on me in a blink.

There was a soft knock at my door, though it didn't open. "Rosa, levántate," Mamá murmured, her voice lacking its normal morning immediacy. "Time for school."

Nothing would ever be the same. I would never be the same. I was no longer the girl who believed hope and hard work and following the rules would help me succeed.

I didn't know what I believed anymore.

Since I didn't have to make the hour-long commute to the north side, Mamá and Papi were walking out the door when I finally emerged from my bedroom. Mamá paused in the doorway and strode back toward me. She kissed my forehead. "Have a good first day of school," she said somberly.

Papi nodded without looking at me, and they left without another word. The house was so still and quiet, I could hear their footsteps in the yard, the squeaky gate they swung open, the indistinct, worried tones of their conversation as they walked away.

There was a lone plate waiting for me on the kitchen table, huevos y papas, with a dishcloth draped over it. The eggs were cold, a little rubbery by now. I took one bite so as not to feel too guilty about wasting food, but I wasn't hungry.

As I was washing my dish in the sink, I heard the sound of a car pulling up in front of our house. The nearby crunch of tires on the dirt road and the idling sound of an engine. I paused, holding the damp plate just above the sink, but I didn't hear anything more.

With a frown, I dried my dish and set it back in the cupboard before collecting my bookbag and making my way to the front door.

Once again, I stopped. Because, through the front window, I could now see the car I heard.

Parked just in front of our house was a tan sheriff's department cruiser.

And in the driver's seat was Sheriff Callihan.

Sixty-Nine

Monday, October 17, 1955

The chilling dread hit me in two waves.

First, when I saw him.

Second, when he saw me.

My fear was a silent spectator looming over me as I took a careful, detached tally of my circumstances, each detail twisting my stomach into a knot.

I was alone.

A powerful, armed man was outside waiting for me.

I was the sole witness to a crime that had destroyed both of our lives.

But there was no running. No hiding. Though we were separated by a pane of glass, he knew precisely where I was.

I took a deep breath and stepped outside. Even as I turned my back toward him to lock the door behind me, I knew he was still staring. I could feel it, like a breath on the back of my neck.

"I just want to speak to you," he called out, clambering to exit his car. He held up his hands, not unlike how Verón had stood before him four days ago. *The universal sign of coming in peace*, I supposed, though I could still see the sheriff's gun clipped to his side. "Don't be scared. Please. I just want to talk. Could I . . . could I offer you a ride to school?"

Frozen on my front steps, I frowned.

"Right, right," he said hastily. He started to shake his head then nodded—more to himself than anything. "Of course. I understand. Listen, I'm going to put my gun in the car, and we can talk out here. Would that make you feel better?"

Would that make me feel better?

What would make me feel better at this point?

It was almost laughable, that question—that is, if laughter were even something I was capable of anymore.

Without waiting for a response, he unholstered his gun and placed it in the car, tossing it through the open window with slow, exaggerated movements. He waved his empty hands at me, seeking my approval.

"I just want to talk, Rosie."

"It's Rosa," I said emphatically, and took a seat on my front steps, smoothing my skirt around my knees as I placed my bookbag beside me on the cement. "You know that."

Sheriff Callihan's eyebrows shot upward. "Right. Okay, *Rosa*." He bobbed his head in tentative agreement as he moved toward the fence, placing his hands on top. "May I come in?"

I shook my head. "No."

"Okay," he said again, his weary face struggling to conceal

how put off he was by my directness. He was not a man who was told no often. "I suppose that's fair." He began to pace idly on the uneven roadside, his hands resting on his hips. He was looking down at his feet when he said, "I'm sorry about . . ." But then he stopped. He stopped walking and talking and just looked at me. His expression was unmistakably pained, like he'd been punched in the gut, like the wind had been knocked straight out of his body. He shook his head a little bit, as if trying to brush off the feeling that had seized hold of him, but it didn't work. His eyes were glistening when he finally spoke again. "Everything, really," he choked out. "I'm sorry about everything. All of it."

I felt my jaw fall open. An apology was certainly not what I'd expected—especially not a tearful one. But I forced my mouth shut with what I hoped was a passive, stern expression.

"You may not believe me," he said. "And I guess I can't blame you for that, but I didn't mean for any of this to happen." His voice was steadier now. Not quite as creaky but still audibly distressed. Each word sounded like a struggle to get out.

"I believe you." I cut in, my own flat tone standing in direct contrast to his quivering words.

His eyes widened. "You do?"

I gave him a slow nod, just one.

I *did* believe him. At least mostly. He was a father, albeit a flawed one. But just because he was deeply troubled didn't mean he hadn't cared for Julianne. If Señor Montoya's story had taught me anything, it was that it was possible—and likely, very common—to both love your children and cause them immense harm with your imperfections. It was a disastrous combination, of course, but the two qualities were not mutually exclusive.

I didn't believe the sheriff had set out to hurt Julianne that night. I knew he hadn't meant to kill her. What had happened was the result of a misguided attempt to protect her.

And Ramón? Well, I didn't know. I couldn't excuse what happened, of course. But did I think the sheriff had entered the situation planning to murder Ramón? No. Hate and fear and a gun led to his irrevocable mistake.

That didn't absolve him—could never absolve him—though it did explain it a little bit.

But just because I understood it didn't mean I'd forgive it.

"What I came here to talk to you about, specifically, though," he said, "is school."

I didn't respond.

"I didn't ask Mr. Williams to expel you." He sighed. "I want you to know that—not that it matters, I guess. But I am sorry. About school too. I wanted to make you an offer. I won't call it a favor because, well, it's not that. But I wanted to do something for you."

The morning sun was starting to get a little warmer, but I suspected the sweat building up along my neck and on my palms was not due to the heat.

"I'd like to write a letter of recommendation to Arizona State College for you," he said.

I scoffed, disdain thick in my throat.

He held up his hand. "I think it would go a long way, might even make up for some of the recent turmoil, to have someone like me on your side. Especially given our roles in recent events." He grimaced, taking a deep breath. "I want to use my position as sheriff, as a public figure, as a . . . Let me help you, Rosa. *Please.*"

I rubbed my temples, the plaid pattern of my navy skirt swimming in front of me as my heart hammered, not out of nerves or fear but out of anger. Frustration. "No," I spit out without looking up at him.

"Don't be rash. Think for a minute about what this could mean. For your future."

Tension gripped my spine, my neck, my shoulders as I registered the change in his tone. Now, this was the man from his office. The man from the press conference. This was tactical.

This wasn't about me.

This was about his own guilt and his image.

Bile rose in the back of my throat at the audacity of this man.

Slowly, I got to my feet, dusting off my skirt like I had all the time in the world. I could feel him watching me. "Sheriff, let me be clear," I said as evenly as I could manage. "Nothing can ever undo what you've already done."

I watched his face blanch then flush bright red. "I—I know that—"

"*Do you?*"

His mouth twisted into an expression of pure discomfort. He ran a hand over his face, nodding. "What am I supposed to do, then?" he asked quietly, his voice painfully rough and ragged. The way he was watching me—the clear agitation in his eyes—told me this wasn't rhetorical.

"You need to figure that out," I hissed. "You killed *two* good people that night. And what happened on Thursday?" My voice broke at this, and I paused, inhaling slowly until my tone was clear and cutting. Until my message was blunt enough that he couldn't brush it off. "I know Marco isn't blameless in what happened at the vigil, but neither are you. You need to own what happened—what *you* did. All of it. Only you can figure out how you go on with your life. You have to make the choice. You have to be the one to decide if you're going to hide from this or learn from it."

"I'm trying—"

"Try harder," I cut in. My fingertips tingled with fury, blood coursing through me as I collected my things. I focused on slow, deliberate movements so I wouldn't fall or falter. I shouldered my bag and marched straight to the gate, maintaining eye contact with him the entire way. "This?" I gestured between the two of us. "It's not enough. This is bigger than me and you. You see that, don't you?" I waited for him to nod begrudgingly, his jaw iron tight, then I swung the gate open and stepped out. "What you do moving forward has to be bigger than us too."

He was gaping when I turned on my heel and walked away.

Seventy

Monday, October 17, 1955

My anger had subsided during the walk to school, but my heart still raced as I entered the front office. Nerves. Exhilaration. Some dizzying combination of it all, no doubt.

I'd never actually been inside Phoenix South Mountain High School, since it had opened the year I'd transferred. It had been the whole impetus behind our plan. Papi had said if I had to switch schools anyway, from the Mexican classes they were running in the back buildings of Phoenix Union High, why not make a change that could benefit us for once?

It was a new building, sure. But it was smaller, more industrial. Much simpler than North's pretty campus.

The guidance counselor was sympathetic but not exactly warm when he gave me my schedule. "Most of the better electives are already full at this point in the year. But if you come see me at the end of the semester, we'll see what we can do," he told me as my eyes drifted numbly down the neatly typed script in my hands. *Homeroom. Typing. English Composition. Gym. Home Economics.* I hadn't even made it to the bottom of the paper before he stood, motioning me toward the door. "Your first period is just this way." I followed him into the hall.

"Right, thank you," I mumbled as he ducked back inside his office.

"That's her. I told you she'd be here," I heard someone whisper. I resisted the instinctive urge to look up, even as someone else responded, "I always thought she was in love with Ramón. Who wouldn't have been? Qué terrible to have him choose her best friend over her and then to lose them both."

The paper in my hand crinkled in my tightening grip. The bell rang, drowning out further commentary—at least for me—but I was certain it continued.

Heads turned toward me as I walked, but I kept my gaze trained forward. I desperately wished their grief didn't feel so much like an intrusion, but I also knew that's what it was. It was their confusion and sorrow and resentment. They had lost Ramón too, after all.

It wasn't about me. Just like I'd told the sheriff, it was about *more* than me.

It always had been.

Seventy-One

Monday, October 17, 1955

I went to Blanca's house after school.

    I knocked softly on the front door before easing it open, not waiting for a response. My sister leaned out of her bedroom doorway, her body only half visible to me, and placed a finger to her lips. In her other arm, I could see a bundle of blankets that must have been my sleeping nephew. She ducked back in as I entered her living room, gently shutting the door behind me.

    A few minutes later, she joined me, collecting a few stray burp rags and smoothing her hair in a flurry of quick, quiet motion. "¿Qué haces aquí, hermanita?" she asked. She paused, finally ceasing her busy tidying long enough to look at me, and her harried expression melted into a tender smile. "Guillermo has another tooth coming in, and it's just . . . I'm sorry. How are you feeling? It was your first day back, no?" For a moment, her eyes shone with deep concern, but she pushed it aside. Instead, she brightened her smile, an action that appeared to take conscious effort on her part, and took a seat at her kitchen table, waving at me to do the same.

I shrugged and sank into the chair across from her. "I feel as good as can be expected." I fidgeted, trying to get comfortable. "Have . . . have you heard anything about Marco?"

She winced sympathetically. She was much more in tune with the neighborhood chatter now that she was firmly in the fold of wives and mothers. "I know they've still got him in the jailhouse downtown. Señora Montoya visited him yesterday after Mass. But I heard he's refused to see anyone else. Verón's been turned away twice."

"I didn't know you could visit," I whispered, almost to myself. I wondered why he wouldn't see Verón. And then I wondered if he'd see me.

"Mm," Blanca said, and I knew she could read those exact questions on my face.

"How are you?" I asked before she could inquire about whether I planned to visit him. I let my eyes rove over her face, searching for any hint of the pain—physical and emotional—we'd endured at the vigil. I thought of her holding my hands that night as we cried.

She dropped her gaze. "I'm okay," she said quietly, running her fingers along the edge of her kitchen table idly. I got the impression she was thinking of Guillermo, thinking of the tiny figure she'd held in her arms moments ago.

We sat in silence for a moment before I forced myself to say what had been weighing on me all day. "The sheriff came to see me this morning."

Blanca snapped her head up, dark eyes wide. *"Why?"* It was barely more than a gasp.

"To write me a letter of recommendation for college," I said dryly, as if it were some mundane piece of gossip. "To help undo some of the damage of . . . everything, I suppose. To ensure I could move forward. Or maybe that *he* could."

"Rosa." She was shaking her head slowly. Back and forth.

"I told him no, of course."

"Rosa!" She jolted, seeming to surprise herself with her volume. She leaned forward, dropping her voice. "You didn't!"

I made a face. "I did. And a few other choice words."

Her eyebrows rose as she considered this, seeming more impressed than alarmed. "A letter from that man . . ." She tsked.

I waited.

"Well, it would be absurd, wouldn't it?" A humorless bark of laughter tumbled out of her mouth as she shuddered.

"Absurd?" I repeated, uncomprehending.

She nodded, as if it were obvious. "Meaningless, you know?"

I eyed her dubiously. "People do listen to him. A recommendation from him is like a golden ticket to most places."

She rolled her eyes. "Yes, I know that," she said. "But you and I know what he says or does—it doesn't really matter."

I frowned, still not understanding.

"You don't need him to accomplish the things you want to," she said soberly. "Him or any of the other white folks who don't know two things about you, for that matter. I know we thought you needed them, but we were wrong." She sighed. "Look at you. Look at everything you've endured. You are strong and smart and brave—and you can do this on your own."

I gave her a small smile, feeling tears prickling at the back of my throat. "Well, not *all* on my own."

"No, not all your own." Her face softened. "We'll always be here for you, hermanita."

Seventy-Two

Tuesday, October 18, 1955

Gingerly, I took a seat in the cool metal chair before me. On either side of me, people were having low conversations, holding black telephone receivers to their ears, leaning forward to the counter.

I stared straight ahead at the vacant space on the other side of the glass, trying to work out what I wanted to say.

Maybe when I saw him, I would know.

But what if he refused to see me too? What then?

My chest felt tight just considering it.

I glanced down at the ruffled edge of my bobby socks as I waited. They looked so silly here in the county jail, but I'd come straight from school. And really, I wasn't sure what type of socks were appropriate for a place like this.

The sound of a buzzer caught my attention, and my head

jerked upward in time to see a door on the other side of the glass swing open. It remained empty except for a dour-faced guard holding it ajar, and I felt a knot of defeat beginning to settle in my stomach.

But then, suddenly, someone stepped forth.

Clad in black-and-white stripes, head bowed so all I could see was a tangle of black hair, he made his way to me.

He sat heavily in the chair across from me, separated by a thick pane of glass.

I gaped. I couldn't help it. I wasn't sure how long I stayed that way, too stunned to move.

But then he looked up.

His golden eyes met mine, and even with the required distance, it was enough to make my eyes well up instantly.

His entire face was a war zone. Black and blue around his temples. Cuts left untreated. One eye swollen shut. His lip split in two.

He was almost unrecognizable.

"Marco," I choked out, though he couldn't hear me. A shadow of pain passed over his face as I said his name, though I had no idea how he could possibly hurt more than he already did.

He tipped his chin toward the telephone receiver on my side before grabbing his own. He held it loosely in his hands, not quite up to his ear, as he waited for me.

Nervously, I scrambled for mine, though when I finally brought it to my mouth, I still didn't have the words I needed.

"Don't cry," he finally growled, and by the sound of his voice, even talking hurt him.

"I'm not," I lied, tasting the salt of my tears as I said it.

He winced, looking away. "What are you doing here?"

I scooted forward to the edge of my seat, desperate to close some of this miserable distance between us. "I had to see you." I wasn't sure I'd said it loud enough to be heard. Marco's hardened expression certainly gave nothing away.

He moved the telephone receiver from his face, just an inch or so, and took a deep breath. But he said nothing.

"We're raising money at church for your bail," I continued. "And we've all been checking on your mother. Pilar—you remember Pilar from El Foro—she's talking to the lawyers she works with about getting you better representation. Verón says—"

"Don't." Suddenly, his eyes cut upward to me, searing and intense.

"We want to help. We're worried about you, Marco," I pleaded, my voice hoarse with concern. "I'm worried—"

"Just give it a rest," he said through clenched teeth, hunching forward slightly and lowering his gaze. "I can't deal with all the pity and pleasantries, all right?"

"It's not pity." I lunged forward, pressing my hand to the glass, desperate for him to look at me. If he wouldn't listen to me, I just wanted him to *look at me*. "Together, remember? We're in this together."

His battered profile, just beyond the outline of my fingertips, knifed through me as the word "together" spilled out of my mouth. Together—but he looked so alone in there.

He shifted almost imperceptibly in his chair. He must've sensed my nearness, even if he didn't acknowledge it.

"I love you, Marco," I said, one desperate, last-ditch effort to get him to look at me. To come back to me. To recognize that, even if we were apart now, we *were* in this together. That I wouldn't leave him. That I needed him—and maybe he needed me too.

His eyes flashed upward at last, still simmering with hurt and anger but also shock and something else I couldn't make out. He stayed silent, though I could see how hard he was working to keep his gaze steady. I could see the war of emotions going on just beneath that deeply marred surface of his. The shame. The fear. The pain.

"Marco—"

A muscle ticked in his jaw. "No, don't." In one fluid, furious movement, he got to his feet. "I can't . . . not to you." He held the phone too far away for me to hear him clearly—but even so, I wasn't sure I understood anyway. "I've done enough." He swallowed as he brought the receiver to his mouth abruptly. "For your own sake, Rosa, just leave me the hell alone," he hissed into the phone before letting it fall out of his hand, dangling uselessly on the cord.

As the guards led him away, he didn't look back.

Seventy-Three

Tuesday, October 18, 1955

I managed to fight back my tears until I was outside, but as soon as the late afternoon sun hit me, they poured out, warm and incessant as they coursed down my cheeks. I took a deep breath, swiping at my face as I leaned against the brick wall of the building, trying unsuccessfully to catch my breath. All I could see was sunlight, my own tears, and the bruised face of Marco Montoya glaring back at me.

I can't. Not to you. I've done enough.

I didn't hear Verón walk up, but I still wasn't surprised when his voice greeted me. "I wondered when I'd see you here."

I took another deep breath, peeking up at him through my fingers. "He's . . . It's . . ."

Verón nodded understandingly. He knew Marco, after all. He offered me a sympathetic half smile. "He's angry," he said simply.

Leave me the hell alone, he'd said. Just thinking about it made me shudder.

"He's always been angry, but this . . . this is so much worse."

"Yes, that is also true." Verón looked up at the clear blue sky peeking between the skyscrapers of downtown, garishly beautiful on a day as hard as this. "He's been angry at the world. Now I think he's angry at himself too."

I considered this, brows furrowed. "Why do you say that?"

"When bad things happen to people we care about, we are often quick to blame ourselves, no?" He paused, as if he knew I was thinking about Ramón and Julianne. How much of the burden of their deaths I had assigned to myself over the past few weeks.

"But," I said, my voice reedy and hoarse, "he was the one who was hurt."

"Physically, yes," he conceded. "But I suspect he feels like he let us down with what happened at the vigil. With the way the sheriff spoke to you and the way Marco . . . reacted. The turn of events." He spoke softly and slowly, as if anticipating the way this sentiment would sting.

I turned to look back at the doors to the jailhouse, as if I could see him from here.

"Protecting Ramón was so important to him after his father died," Verón continued.

He didn't have to say the rest.

That this need to protect was Marco's truest expression of love. That he not only saw his brother's death as his own personal failure, but he bore the continued violence of the vigil as his own trial too.

Still, the way he'd looked at me when I'd said I'd loved him . . . I didn't know what to make of it.

"He's strong, Rosa," Verón assured me, and I knew he was right. I just wished Marco didn't have to be *that* strong.

I nodded, sniffling.

"How are *you*?" he asked. He bowed his head toward me, affording me a glimpse of his temple, where a yellow-green bruise sprawled from the neat locks of his hair down to the area under his eyes. Flashes of him running toward Marco in the chaos of it all and being driven away by billy clubs raced toward me without warning.

I met his question with a question instead. "How was the meeting last week?"

"Quiet," he admitted. "Understandably. I think what happened scared a lot of people. Which makes sense. It's exactly what they wanted, to provoke us and then intimidate us. But it's unfortunate nevertheless." Verón's gaze drifted as he nodded at an old woman entering the jailhouse before returning his focus to me. "You and Marco, you were missed. People asked after you."

I gave him a disbelieving look at this attempt to comfort me. It was hard to believe my presence was of any consequence at this point. Aside from my blip of notoriety on his show, I'd hardly done more through all of this than be a bystander.

"There were only a few of us there, but we did have one new person," he said. "He was hoping to speak with you."

"Me?"

Verón nodded, clearly amused by my skepticism. "A professor. At Arizona State College."

"At El Foro?"

There were academics at the meetings, sure. Students and professors and writers. But why someone new would come the night following the ill-fated vigil and why they'd be seeking me out, of all people—that I couldn't understand.

Verón nodded once more, ever patient. Behind him, a red Thunderbird honked as the car in front of it tarried at a green light. "They're starting a new program at the college. It's called Broadcast Journalism."

"Broadcast Journalism?" I hated the way I was just repeating chunks and bits of what he was saying. Like I had to seize hold of these words, feeling them on my lips, or else they'd slip out of my reach forever.

"Radio and television," he added, though that wasn't the part that perplexed me. "They've got a print journalism program, and from what I understand, it's a good one. But they say the future of reporting isn't in newspapers anymore." He smirked, and I wondered if we were both thinking of his show and the tremendous impact it had on the people in our community. "You are planning on going to Arizona State College next year, ¿verdad?"

"Yes," I told him, wishing it were that simple. That it was just about my plan and not about the countless things that had happened over the last few weeks that might render that plan implausible. I tried to push my encounter with the sheriff—my quick refusal of his offer—out of my mind. "But how did this man even know who I am? Why did he want to speak to me?"

"Rosa." He said my name as if that were an answer in and of itself. When no signs of comprehension appeared on my face, he continued. "He heard you on my show. He came to the vigil because of you. He was impressed by what you said there too."

"He was?"

"You have a powerful voice. You realize that, don't you?"

"I . . ." I pressed my lips together. Nothing about me felt powerful right now. "You'd better get in there if you're hoping to see Marco before visiting hours end."

Verón nodded sagely. "I always have hope."

Seventy-Four

Friday, October 21, 1955

I survived my first week at South Mountain, and at some point, the relentless storm of whispers and staring and gossip devolved into a mild sprinkle, a curious droplet here or there. Collective memory was fleeting, and after a few days, I was far less interesting. To my peers, I was once again the quiet, studious girl with light skin and a tangle of dark hair. Blanca's little sister. Ramón's friend. Except, without these people around, I was even less intriguing than before.

Time was murky with loneliness and anticipation, but at some point, Marco was released from jail. Blanca had whispered the news to me as we helped Mamá clear the dinner table one night.

"Where did Señora Montoya get the money for bail?" I'd asked. "It was a fortune."

But my sister had shaken her head knowingly. "She didn't. The charges were dropped. They just let him go."

"They?" I paused there by the sink, holding our five plates in my hands. "Do you think the sheriff did it?"

Blanca's eyes widened in response as Mamá interrupted us, asking me to pass her a dishrag.

Would the sheriff have done that?

Had he really listened to what I'd said to him that day in our yard?

I wondered about it constantly—so much so that when the news of his resignation broke a day later, I almost felt like I'd been expecting it.

The news was *everywhere*. Bold headlines shouted it from the glass-paned boxes that sold newspapers for five cents outside grocery stores and diners. All the radio hosts, including Verón, chatted about it relentlessly. There was an air of speculation, maybe a trace of scandal about his motives, but nothing substantive. Nothing that stuck to him.

First Marco, and now this. Was Callihan truly seeking to make amends for what he'd done? The investigation hadn't found any evidence of wrongdoing, of course, but perhaps he was holding himself accountable. Perhaps he had listened to me. Perhaps he would change.

Was it ridiculous to hope so?

But then the next piece of news broke.

Former sheriff John Callihan was running for governor, hot on the heels of a heartbreaking personal tragedy.

He'd been on this path since he joined the force, people were saying. It was only a matter of time. Though no one would ever have predicted or desired the recent circumstances, it was a season of transition nonetheless. It made sense in its own strange way.

But it was still surreal.

I hoped he wouldn't forget what we'd talked about—but even so, I wasn't naive enough to bank on it. I couldn't look at his billboards without thinking of all the versions of this man I had come to know. My earliest impressions of him had been similar to the man on these signs, a uniformed officer with a faint, dignified smile and a stern, no-nonsense gaze. But now, I saw him as the angry, violent father, unmoored by what he considered the worst kind of disobedience. I saw him as a killer. I saw all the ways his grief had molded him—his scramble for control, his desperation for forgiveness, his stark uncertainty about his place in the world for what was probably the first time in his life.

I saw both his power and his pain, and I would never be able to forget it.

I walked into the church for the weekly El Foro meeting a few minutes before five o'clock. It was the first time I'd come here alone.

I spotted the professor with no trouble at all, and not because he was the only gringo. It turned out Verón hadn't been exaggerating the diminished meeting attendance when we spoke the week before; there were only eight of us. A far, distant cry from the packed, standing-room-only meeting Marco had lured me into all those weeks ago.

Verón pointed me out to him as I entered, but he didn't introduce us until after the meeting, after he'd spent the majority of the time fielding concerns and questions about the sheriff's recent announcement and trying, rather fruitlessly, to convince us we shouldn't be disheartened. That we should focus on what we could do next: voter registration, community events, and supporting Mexican American candidates for other offices. There was a man running for the Arizona State House, he said.

"Rosa, this is Professor Michael Curtis," Verón told me after the rest of the attendees had cleared out and it was the three of us in the roofless space. "Professor, this is Rosa Capistrano."

The bespectacled man extended his right hand to me, the left clutching a pamphlet to his torso. "Miss Capistrano, it's a real pleasure."

Perhaps a few weeks ago I would've felt heartened by this warm greeting. Perhaps even more than that. But now a wan smile was all I could muster.

"I understand you're applying to ASC," he said.

I nodded, thinking about the unmailed application on my dresser. Every time I looked at it, I was reminded of what I said to the sheriff, and every time, it stirred up a mix of pride and trepidation.

"Have you considered what you'd like to study?" he asked.

"I—I used to think I wanted to be a writer," I admitted. "Now I'm not so sure."

"Mm," Professor Curtis said. "You've certainly been through quite a bit, haven't you?"

I nodded, though that felt like far too simple of a gesture for everything that had happened.

"Well, I hope it wasn't too forward of me, but I brought you ASC's course catalog," he said. "I've taken the liberty of flagging the courses on Broadcast Journalism. Granted, you'd be taking some general education courses for most of your first year, but I'd be happy to give you an override into some of the more advanced courses, perhaps in your second semester, if you'd like. Given your experience with Mr. Verón's show and community work, I think you'd be a very strong candidate." He held out the pamphlet, a stack of pages featuring the college's name and a decorative cactus on the cover. When I hesitated to take it, he kept talking. "We're just a division of the English department for now. But we're growing. I think we'll have our own department in the next few years, maybe even before you graduate. But I just thought you might like to take a look and consider what your next steps might be."

"You . . . you really think I'd get into a program like this?" My voice sounded thin and feeble compared to what I'd said to the sheriff, but I couldn't conceal my anxiety as I gingerly accepted the catalog from him, unable to resist the urge to thumb through a few pages right away.

"Certainly," he said without missing a beat. "We'd be lucky to have you. I believe you have real promise, Miss Capistrano. The perspectives and insight you've been able to offer here and on Mr. Verón's show? Remarkable, especially for someone so young. You could be the voice of a generation with the right platform and technical skills. Truly. I've written my telephone number on the back cover should you have any questions. Please, Miss Capistrano, I'd be happy to help in any way I can," he said, and I was thankful to have the booklet to focus my attention on as my eyes welled with tears.

"Thank you, Professor," I told him.

Seventy-Five

Saturday, October 22, 1955

I awoke before sunrise the following day. The air was crisp and cool, biting on my cheeks as I stepped out my front door into the quiet of predawn. The mountains glowed with their first hints of sunrays, but the rest of the sky remained a hazy purple.

I wrapped my arms around myself, an envelope in one hand, as I made my way down our walkway.

I'd stayed up late the night before, poring over the course catalog Professor Curtis had given me. I'd set it on my bed, right beside my leather notebook, and flipped through all the classes he'd flagged. And on my second read-through, I'd gotten a pencil out of my bookbag, and I'd begun leaving my own notes on the crisp white paper. Circling classes whose descriptions I was excited about. Underlining words I wasn't familiar with. Jotting notes and reactions and thoughts in the narrow margins.

I'd only fallen asleep an hour or two ago. Somewhere, distantly, I knew I should be tired, but for the first time in so long, I didn't feel bogged down with my own fatigue.

I felt the faintest glimmer of hope—of possibility—as I slipped my application to Arizona State College into our mailbox and raised the tiny red flag.

Seventy-Six

Friday, March 9, 1956

I woke up on my eighteenth birthday like I did on any other day. I lay in bed for a moment to savor the familiar hum and bustle of the neighboring farms, the smells from Mamá cooking breakfast in the next room, and the cool morning breeze on my face.

And then I got up.

It was a symbolic day. Eighteen was the age I'd graduate high school and hopefully go to college. It was also the first birthday in a decade I'd celebrate without Ramón crooning "cumpleaños feliz" to me every chance he got.

But it was also just another day in most ways.

The thing is, at first it horrified me, the way life went on. And then it didn't—at least not all the time. I realized that was the point. That life went on, no matter what happened. It was beautiful and excruciating. And perhaps, most important of all, it just *was*.

It didn't matter how I felt about it. Life gave us no choice but to move forward.

And so that's what I did.

It wasn't easy, but some days it was easier. The days I went to El Foro, for example, gave me peace and clarity, among other things. Verón was tireless as ever in his efforts to organize our community in a fight for civil rights, bringing in speakers from all over. In November, a man from California named Cesar Chavez joined us, and listening to him, I felt something similar to what I'd felt when I first enrolled at North. The sensation that what lay ahead would undoubtedly be filled with challenges—but that I was where I was meant to be.

I'd felt that same way at my first El Foro meeting too.

Afternoons spent with Tim were also good. We had plans to get ice cream and peruse a record store this weekend in honor of my birthday.

Once or twice a week, he'd pick me up after school in that baby-blue Bel Air of his. When we first started meeting up, I couldn't help but think of all the times we'd fled from disaster in this car. The night of the murders. The press conference. His fight with Peter. And though I still thought of those events often—I was certain I'd remember them for the rest of my life—most days, I thought of them less.

Slowly, we were building new memories together. Some days we'd go to the public library and sit across from each other, just like we had when we first met. One time, we drove past a restaurant on Seventh Street that he'd heard turned into a secret gay bar at night. We hadn't gone in; we'd just peered at it from the car with stifled wonder. Other days, we'd split a Coke float and exchange stories about our final weeks of senior year. Stories that seemed mundane in light of everything else but ones we were grateful to share together as friends.

Tim told me about the colleges in California he'd applied to, about how he thought maybe it would be good to get a fresh start somewhere. He was particularly interested in San Francisco. He also told me how Peter had gotten injured at the end of the football season and torn a muscle and now spent most of his time at doctors' offices or talking about what a drag college football was anyway.

And I told him about El Foro, about the mice and snakes that would sometimes get into the back buildings at South, about how some days it hurt less to think of Ramón and Julianne.

"I still miss them," I'd told him as we each slid a dime across the soda counter for our float, now drained except for a dollop of ice cream at the bottom. "So much. I still catch myself thinking about how I wish I could undo it all. If I could go back and not switch schools or talk them out of their whole plan, I'd do it. In a heartbeat, you know?"

Tim nodded, thoughtful and somber. How many times had we had this conversation? "But you can't," he'd said gently.

"But I can't," I agreed.

Death was one of the few things in this mutable world that was permanent, after all. And in the same way I was certain the grief of this past year would stick with me forever, I knew I'd be working out the lessons of this tragedy for the rest of my life too. Because even though Ramón and Julianne's deaths were unnecessary and senseless, I also knew it would be a disservice to their memories not to learn from them.

Tim and I visited their graves sometimes; we'd bring flowers from the Japanese gardens near my house, and we'd sit with them and the complicated feelings of it all. It was both painful and healing. I couldn't undo what had happened, but I'd never forget it. I'd carry their sacrifice with me forever—in everything I did. I was certain of it.

One day in December, when school was out for Christmas break, Tim and I decided to go to Arizona State College. Though Tim's parents took him every fall for the homecoming football game, it had come up that I'd never been.

"It's not even fifteen minutes from here!" he'd said. "We have to go. You have to go. You must! I won't take no for an answer, Rosa."

Part of me thought I should wait until the fall, until I was a student there. And part of me agreed with Tim. What was the sense in waiting anyway?

And so that's what we did. The students had already gone home for the semester, so the campus was quiet, serene. We were the only ones there as I stood on the steps of the Old Main building, peering up at its brick facade and arched windows.

Acceptance letters wouldn't go out for a few more weeks, so I still didn't truly know if I belonged, but I was here anyway. Hoping.

After everything that had happened, I still had hope left in me—and that was something.

No matter how bad things were, there was always good to be found. There was showing my parents the top marks I'd earned on tests and watching Guillermo take his first steps and hearing Verón's voice on the radio and the scent of orange blossoms in the air when I walked home. There was good, and there was hope—even if you had to fight for it.

Yes, there was still hardship. There was the sadness in Señora Montoya's eyes when I'd see her at Mass. There was the sheriff's campaign, his commanding face on every billboard across this damn desert. There were recurring nightmares of Ramón and Julianne falling, falling, endlessly falling. There was grief and exhaustion and pain—all of it. Of course there was.

Because that was life. There was good and bad. Nothing was simple or straightforward. Nothing was black and white. Everything was a mix. Everything had its own story.

That's what I'd remind myself as often as I could. I thought of it that day at ASC back in December. I thought of it as I'd sit in my backyard, alone, watching the laundry on the line billow in the breeze as I thumbed through my leather notebook yet again. And I thought of it practically any time Marco Montoya crossed my mind.

He'd stopped coming to El Foro meetings. I hadn't seen him since I visited him in jail. It was hard to completely disappear in a neighborhood like ours, but he'd come pretty darn close. He was scarcely more than a rumor, a shadow in my life. Sometimes I'd see a dark-haired figure carrying a book across the street or catch a whiff of sunshine and citrus when I entered a store, and I'd wonder if he'd been there. If we'd just missed each other.

If he missed me the way I missed him.

My last image of him was bruised and battered, telling me to leave him alone. And it broke my heart every single time I thought about it.

He had never been my boyfriend, of that I was pretty sure. He was my best friend's brother. And maybe some other things, things that were harder to label, harder to give voice to, harder to define. But that just made it even more difficult to understand the way he'd uprooted himself from my life.

Nothing was simple.

"Give him time," Verón would tell me. "He's on his own journey. We all are, hmm?"

Seventy-Seven

Friday, March 9, 1956

Days were getting longer, slowly but surely, and dusk was just starting to color the sky when I arrived home after that evening's meeting. It had been a lively discussion about a variety of political candidates for various offices. The governor's race, of course, but also local campaigns. Verón was encouraging us to not only support Mexican American candidates but to broaden our horizons to advocate for black candidates too.

"We are all in this together," he'd said. "Inequality might look different across different groups, but the fact remains that inequality is inequality. Maybe someday in the future, we'll have Navajo names on the ballot. Or Chinese American. Who knows? We must strive to eliminate racism in all its forms. For all of us."

I was still mulling it over, smiling to myself as I swung our creaking gate open. The lights were on inside the house, and I could hear the soft thrum of voices from within. Mamá was making pozole to celebrate my birthday, and I knew Blanca had wanted to come over early to help. She'd complained that her broth never turned out quite right and was eager to learn Mamá's secret.

I wandered over to the mailbox. Recently, I had caught myself checking it every time I walked past, even if I knew the mailman hadn't come yet or that my parents had likely already collected the mail.

Idly, I flipped the little door open, casting a distracted glance inside.

I had to do a double take; my eyes nearly missed it the first time.

But there it was. One letter resting just inside.

The sunlight was disappearing by the moment, but I recognized it immediately. The ASC logo on the crisp white envelope.

I withdrew the letter like it was made of smoke, like it could dissolve at any moment. I held it flat in my palms, savoring not just the weight of it but the possibility of it. The hope of it.

"What do you have there?"

I nearly dropped it at the sound of the unexpected voice, clutching it to my chest clumsily. Heart racing, I dragged my gaze up to find Marco watching me from the other side of the fence, the barest hint of a smirk on his face.

Marco.

My jaw dropped as I took in the sight of him. Despite the thousands of questions I had, no words came out. My grip tightened on the envelope, the paper crinkling quietly in my hands.

He looked . . . like Marco, honestly. After months and months apart, he still looked like himself. Dark curls, stark brow. Maybe a bit thinner. There was a small white scar across his forehead, no doubt from the vigil. But he was still Marco. All this time, he'd continued to be . . . *Marco*.

I couldn't understand it.

"Rosa—"

"Where have you been?" I demanded, my voice tight. "What are you doing here?"

"Those are two different questions," he quipped, cocking his head. "Can't a fella stop by to wish you a happy birthday?"

"Don't do that," I said with a scowl. "Don't act like nothing's changed. You . . . you *vanished*. After everything we'd been through—everything we'd lost—you left me." *You'd said we'd face this together*, I thought with heart-surging urgency, but I couldn't bring myself to say it out loud.

I could see his throat bob as he swallowed, nodding slowly at this. "I didn't *leave*, Rosa. I was here the whole time."

I blew out a puff of exasperated air. "You know what I mean."

And again he nodded, quickly this time. "I do. I—I'm sorry."

I pressed my lips together; I could feel the weight of his apology sinking into me like a needle or a cactus spindle to my flesh. Sharp and piercing, his words were almost a physical pain. "I didn't know you knew when my birthday was," I murmured.

"Of course I do," he said without missing a beat. "Just because I was too big of a fool in the past to say anything doesn't mean I didn't notice."

A long stretch of silence settled between us, but his eyes didn't leave my face. Bright and incisive as ever.

"It's a letter from ASC," I said abruptly, unable to quietly languish under his stare any longer. I tipped the envelope toward him with one hand and tucked my hair behind my ear with the other, fidgeting. "Your turn."

His eyes widened, dropping to the small rectangle in my hands before darting back up. "You got in?"

I leveled him with a look. *"Marco."*

"You really don't want to open it first?"

I shook my head once, my hair falling over my shoulder with the motion. "Your turn," I repeated.

He took a breath, bracing himself, and tucked his hands into the pockets of his jeans. He looked up at the periwinkle sky and then down at the tufts of weeds growing along the roadside. He looked anywhere but at me. "Okay. *Okay.* Can we . . . ?" He gestured behind me, toward my front steps.

"Sure," I said, holding the gate open for him. "Sure, let's sit."

The sounds from inside grew louder as we settled next to each other. I heard Guillermo let out a wail, heard the thump of cabinet doors closing—and I heard Marco's palms rub together as he sat beside me, wringing his fingers together. We weren't touching—a half inch rested between our arms—but I could feel the heat of him, the warmth of his skin, on this temperate spring evening.

"When you came to see me in jail," he began slowly, "I was

in a bad place, Rosa. I guess you know that. You saw me, and even more than that, you *know* me, but I still think I need to say it. It was . . . a very bad place." His eyes were downcast, on his hands or his shoes or the grass at the base of my porch, but I watched him as he spoke—dark lashes and quavering lips and all. "The sheriff got the charges dropped. I'm guessing you know that too, and sure, that was a good thing. Looking back, I see that. My ma couldn't have afforded bail or legal fees or anything. Christ, how could she have made ends meet on her own if I was locked up for good?" He chewed his lip, shaking his head at himself. "But still, I was so mad at that man for everything when I was in there, and after I got released, I was even more mad that I'd needed his help. That I had no choice but to accept it. I was *ashamed*."

I felt the urge to reach out to him at that, to link my arm in his or take his hands in mine. To tell him that it was okay to need help, that we couldn't possibly face things like that on our own. But I quelled it all for now, as much as it hurt to do so.

"And then I lost my job." He said it like it was a surprise to him too, to hear it. "Did Pablo tell you that?" He glanced at me fleetingly.

"No, but he stopped mentioning you. I thought it was just because he knew we weren't speaking to each other, that he knew it would hurt to hear about you," I said.

He hummed thoughtfully. "They said I'd missed too many days when I was in jail," he ground out, his note of disbelief audible. "I thought losing Ramón was rock bottom. And then I just kept falling." He brought his hands to his face suddenly, rubbing at his temples. "And I was still mad, of course, but even more than that, I was *lost*. Everything I touched turned to shit, and I . . . I didn't know what to do. And that made me even angrier, which then made it even harder to do anything else. Does that make any sense?" He dropped one hand slightly—just enough to look at me.

I nodded. "Of course. I was mad too, Marco. I'm *still* mad. I wanted to be there for you, to be together. I tried—"

"I know," he cut in. "I don't blame you, Rosa. It's my own fault."

"Well," I said on an exhale, "I don't think it's quite that simple."

He snorted softly. "Maybe. But at least part of the blame is mine." He ran a hand along his jaw, considering his next words. "I thought a lot about my old man, actually. I think that this must've been how he felt. Betrayed and hurt and just out of his mind with anger, you know? And I thought, I don't want that to be the end of me. I don't want those feelings to destroy me." He frowned as he said, "You don't get to choose when or how you die, you know? That much is clear after everything. Death is random and unfair, but you do get to choose how you live. And that made me think of Ramón." His voice cracked as he said his brother's name. "Believing in something better. Standing up for what he cared about. That's . . . that's how I want to be. Not angry and drunk and alone. I want to be like my little brother."

His profile grew watery as tears formed in my eyes. "I miss him," I murmured, and he nodded instantly.

"It took me a long time to figure out how to do that, though," Marco continued.

"To miss him?"

He let out a breath that seemed strained. "Well, yes, I suppose that too. To let myself miss him—to not just feel angry but to feel other things. To be sad but also to feel hopeful. That it won't be like this forever." He laughed sadly as he added, "Ramón made it look easy, huh?"

"He did."

"And it took me a while to ask for help," he confessed with an edge of remorse. "I'd always thought I had all the answers, and to finally admit that I didn't know anything—that was *hard*."

My chest tightened as I thought of all the times I'd felt the same way over the past year. I thought I had it all figured out, going to school at North. Papi and I both did. We'd assumed that if I kept my head down, if I worked hard, if I did just as the white kids did, then I'd be just as successful as the white kids were. If I played by their rules, how could I not?

Now, of course, I knew it wasn't that simple, but what a hard lesson that had been to learn.

Together, Marco had said. The memory of him saying it at the vigil resounded through my entire body. Again, my fingers tingled with the urge to reach out to him, to take his hand in mine, but instead I just turned the envelope over in my palms, fidgeting.

"Thank God for Verón," Marco continued, sincerity in every word. "He helped me get back on my feet in every way that mattered. He got me a job at an auto shop. It's hard work, but it's better than the Bashas' warehouse. The fellow who owns it is Mexican. He's from Cuatro Milpas, you know, just down the road. It's a lot of grunt work, but I'm learning a skill, not just heaving boxes of fruit around. And either way, I needed a job. I couldn't leave all that up to my ma, you know?"

"That's great, Marco," I told him, uncomfortably aware of how inadequate that sounded. I meant it. I meant so much more, but I wasn't sure how to say it. Or if I *should* say it. I dropped my gaze to the envelope once more, tracing over the letters and lines of it with my fingertip.

"Now that I'm settled with the new job and everything," he continued slowly, chin bobbing with each word as if to emphasize the point, "I've been . . . trying to do more. I've been doing some canvassing, you know, for the elections this year? I know most people don't think we've got a shot against the sheriff, but maybe with some of the smaller elections . . . I don't know. We can elect some people who can stand up to him or at least make things difficult? I'm not sure, but that's what Verón says."

"He does," I agreed, thinking of him saying those same things earlier that evening.

"He's even been talking to me about getting a GED. It's mostly for veterans, but he said I could take a test to get my high school diploma and maybe go to college like you someday." He gestured playfully at the letter in my lap.

"You could," I told him. "You could do anything, Marco."

A soft smile played at the corner of his lips. I watched his fingers twitch slightly, and I wondered fleetingly if he was about to reach out for my hand, but he stilled himself. "He says education is at the heart of everything," he continued thoughtfully. "I'm still working out what I think about it all, but it feels good to do something—something that matters."

I nodded slowly, considering his words with a soft hum of agreement.

"You're quiet," he prompted after a beat of silence had passed between us.

"I'm thinking," I told him, just like I had way back then.

I didn't have to look at him to know he was smirking now; I could hear it in his voice. "Rosa Capistrano loves to think."

I leveled him with a glare that had precisely zero bite to it. His face brightened as our eyes caught. The way he was staring right back at me—the twist of a smile and a glimmer in his amber eyes—made me certain he was thinking of that first time he brought me to El Foro. Of sparring as we walked home together, trying to make sense of everything we'd heard and everything we thought we knew.

Despite how hurt I'd been by his rejection at the jailhouse, by his sudden withdrawal, I felt a fluttering in my heart at that memory. A fluttering that defied all logic.

I thought of how confused and frustrated I'd been by the way Ramón and Julianne had been so swept up in their feelings for one another. And yet here I was, even after everything that had happened, yearning for what Marco said next.

"I miss you, Rosa," he said, his voice low and steady.

It shot through me, tingling so much it almost hurt. I bit down on the thrill I felt hearing him say those words out loud, instead asking, "Why now?"

I braced myself for another joke about my birthday, an excuse to brush off my attempts at getting to the root of our heartbreak.

Instead, a flicker of hurt flashed over his face as he considered how to answer that question. "Again, it would have been a lot easier if I were more like Ramón. If I knew myself well enough to know how I felt earlier, faster." He paused, turning toward me and shifting his body on the step so he was looking at me straight on. Tentatively, he reached one hand toward me, tucking a strand of my dark hair behind my ear. We both stiffened at this sudden contact, but he didn't pull away. Instead, he finally moved to take my hand in his. The lightest embrace, just our fingertips linked together on top of the envelope in my lap. "I missed you even as I told you to leave me alone. I just needed to find my way out of that pain. I needed to make sure I wouldn't let my anger hurt anyone again—myself or you. I needed to find my way forward. And maybe, hopefully, even to find my way back to you, if you'll let me."

"Marco."

"Rosa," he countered. "I want to be better. For Ramón, for you, for Golden Gate. For myself."

"Marco, I'm not sure it's quite that simple—"

"Of course it isn't," he insisted. "Nothing that matters is. But I just need you to know, I thought of you while I sat in jail every single day, telling me you loved me. I didn't deserve that kind of love from someone like you then, but I want to be the kind of man that does." He took a breath. "Rosa, I love you."

My breath caught at this—it had hurt so badly that he

hadn't said it back. A small part of me had been longing to hear it ever since, and still it caught me off guard. I searched for some logical rebuttal, some way to refute the way my pulse quickened as soon as our fingers had touched. "It's easy to make promises like that. Things won't always be easy."

"When have they ever?" he joked, his voice humorless.

"There will be hard work for both of us. Obstacles. Challenges. We can't run and hide—even from each other."

"I agree," he said, his eyes tracing over my face.

"And I could be going to college in just a few months, you know." My voice grew soft and breathy under the heat of his gaze.

"You definitely are," he replied. "I'll drive you some days, if you'll let me."

I fought a smile on the corners of my mouth. "And I still probably won't agree with you most of the time."

"It would be boring if you did."

"And." I bit my lip. "I want you to come back to El Foro."

For all his quick remarks and grand proclamations, this one surprised him. He arched an eyebrow. "Oh yeah?"

I nodded, resolute. "Yes."

"Why's that?" His voice was low and gravelly, riding the line between tenderness and playfulness.

"Because I want to face whatever happens next together. We need each other," I told him, knowing that wasn't exactly true but not caring. Sure, it was possible to confront the unknown on our own. We'd both done it before. But why should we when we had each other? When we had someone who saw us and cared about us as we were? Love might not have been enough on its own to resolve all the problems in this world—but I knew now what Ramón and Julianne had known all along. That it was a key part. That we needed love to move forward.

Love.

"I couldn't agree more, princesa. Let's start with this, hmm?" His luminous eyes dropped to the letter in my hands.

I lifted it slowly, carefully, holding it out in front of us. "It doesn't really matter, does it?"

His brows dipped, disbelieving, but that was the only response he gave me.

"After everything that's happened, I mean. Everything we've endured and overcome. This is just one more thing. Either way . . ." My voice became thinner, wispier as I spoke. I couldn't control it. "Either way, I'll be okay. I'll find my way forward."

"Mm, claro."

With a sharp intake of breath, I hooked my index finger in the seam and ripped it open unceremoniously. The paper trembled in my hands as I unfolded it. The words were bouncing up and down as I took them in.

We are pleased to inform you . . .

I was on my feet before I could read the rest. With a shriek, I flung myself into Marco's arms, the paper flying out of my hands and into the dirt. His grip tightened around my waist as he pulled me close, and before I knew it, I was crying.

Not just crying. *Sobbing.*

Suddenly, the weight of it all hit me. Of this achievement. Of the cost.

"Rosa?" Marco rasped, pulling away just enough to look at my face.

I didn't answer him at first. I just stared back at him, tears pouring down my face, my arms wound around his neck. And I allowed myself to feel it all. The hope and the remorse too. It was important that I acknowledged both. That I always acknowledged both. Even my greatest accomplishments would still feel connected to the tragedy of this past year.

I managed one slight nod in response to Marco's question. *Yes.* Yes, I'm here. Yes, I'm okay. Yes—and then I closed the distance and kissed him.

If I'd surprised him, he didn't show it. He met my kiss with the same hunger and urgency and need, tightening his hold on me as his mouth moved against mine.

I didn't know what the future had in store for us. I thought about that even as my fingers tangled in his hair, as his tongue caressed mine, as our breath became one.

I didn't know if we had what it took to truly challenge the sheriff. I didn't know if I would be the kind of voice Verón and Professor Curtis hoped I'd be. I didn't know if the feelings I had for Marco would end in anything but more heartbreak.

But I knew I was going to try.

I had to try.

AUTHOR'S NOTE

I first began writing this story in the spring of 2020, when the US was erupting in Black Lives Matter protests in the aftermath of the murder of George Floyd. As friends, family, and I shared social media posts, participated in marches, and read books on anti-racism, I found myself wondering how this kind of passion and vigor for a cause is sustained beyond a singular tragic moment.

It is inspiring to watch people be moved into action. And yet I couldn't help but feel unsurprised when our collective interest and energy began to wane. We live in a complex world, and we are, unfortunately, barraged with a variety of crises every single day. It is challenging and draining to maintain such concerted energy for every single cause that demands action—no matter how worthy these causes are.

But how do we create change otherwise?

I wrote this book as an exploration of this question. Not

because I have the answers—certainly, I do not—but to encourage others to have this conversation.

What does changing the world look like beyond the big catalyzing moments? What does progress look like on a daily basis? What happens when next steps are unclear?

The path to true, meaningful change is likely rife with pain and grief. It forces us to question assumptions we've long held about ourselves and the world around us. In most cases, it is grueling and slow, filled with both learning and unlearning. Perhaps it comes with compromises and steps backward. Maybe each day brings more questions than answers.

I hope Rosa's story helps to highlight the many components of a social movement—the idealism, the justified anger, the teamwork, the resilience, and the many complicated questions, often unanswerable, we must explore as activists.

While there are certainly countless fascinating social movements I could've written about, I chose this story, set in the 1950s, for a few reasons. Initially, it was because of the way we tend to remember this time in history. There's a certain enduring nostalgia for the music, clothing, and values of this era that often forgets the immense racism and sexism that underscored virtually everything. Many works, particularly for young adults, focus on what the fifties were like in the South and in big cities. This makes sense, as Jim Crow and the subsequent Great Migration are worthy topics of study, and those stories are illuminating and powerful in understanding our current climate. But, as someone who received the vast majority of her schooling within the state of Arizona, I found myself wonder-

AUTHOR'S NOTE

ing what this time period looked like here. When you think of Arizona history, you're often told about the Indigenous tribes, the Spanish conquest, and the Wild West, but the thing is, the 1950s happened everywhere, and I was eager to dive into how the culture of that period manifested specifically in my home state.

The more I dug into my research, the more interested I became in what the Mexican American identity looked like at this time. Not Black and not quite white, Hispanic people experienced a wide variety of challenges and unique experiences as they tried to navigate a world that was filled with blatant injustice for many different groups.

The year 1955 in particular was a fascinating transition point, caught between two ideologies. In the wake of both the Mexican–American War and Operation Wetback, the once-popular ideology of assimilationism—claiming whiteness in order to enjoy the same privileges as white people—was beginning to taper out. People were starting to see that no matter how hard they tried to emulate the culture and practices of white people, they were still largely regarded as inferior and other. Additionally, an emerging cultural identity for Mexicans born in the United States was growing, and that led to a sense of pride and cultural cohesion that challenged the foundations of assimilation. This would later be called the Chicano movement, though my story takes place before that term was part of mainstream rhetoric.

Pilar Palomente, the law clerk at El Foro, serves as a mouthpiece for this "not quite white" experience as she explains the legal insights into why this was so complex, but so many of Rosa's relationships—with her parents, with Verón, with Marco—are meant to highlight the tensions of this time period as young people and activists sought to find their own place in the midst of an era defined by the struggle for civil rights.

Many of Rosa's experiences are colored by my own experience as a white Latine. She recognizes the privileges of being white-passing, but she also discovers a lot of confusion and loneliness when it comes to her sense of belonging. No matter the time period, my hope is that these feelings are something any white-passing person can identify with.

Rosa's home life is largely inspired by stories from my father and my best friend's mother, Margarita. For the rest of my research, I read other books set in the 1950s, relied heavily on my local museums (though sadly, Phoenix is the largest city in the US without its own dedicated historical museum), joined historical groups on social media, read academic articles and texts, and perused magazines and newspapers from the time period. The articles Rosa saves are based off real articles I encountered (yes, even the etiquette one; that is based on an excerpt from *Americanization through Homemaking* by Pearl Idelia Ellis).

It was often challenging to find pictures and historical records that focused solely on South Phoenix. There are some, of course, and some good ones, but largely this area was not as well preserved or documented as central and north Phoenix—which makes sense since South Phoenix was and continues to be where people of color have historically resided. I relied

AUTHOR'S NOTE

heavily on wonderful sources like the South Phoenix Oral History Project, the Rogue Columnist, and the City of Phoenix Historic Preservation Office. That being said, any inaccuracies that may have arisen as my imagination filled in the gaps for the sake of storytelling are mine and mine alone.

Rosa By Any Other Name is a work of fiction; the characters in this story, though perhaps based on real figures—and, in many cases, a composite of real figures—are of my own creation. Sheriff Callihan, Victor Verón, and El Foro in particular are fictional.

The groups represented at El Foro were real community organizations that operated in Phoenix. The Sacred Heart Church was a real church and a cornerstone of the community. Father Al, mentioned briefly, was the real leader of that church. The building itself still stands today, though it is not currently in operation; community members are fundraising for the revitalization and reopening of the church at the time of this book's publication. The radio show *En este momento* is based on *La hora mexicana*. Golden Gate, where Rosa lives, was also a real place, though it was demolished through eminent domain in the 1970s for the expansion of Phoenix's Sky Harbor Airport. Arizona State College would become Arizona State University in 1958; the new radio broadcast program to which Rosa is applying would later be part of the Walter Cronkite School of Journalism. Both high schools, North Phoenix and Phoenix South Mountain, are real schools that operate to this day, and the reality of their relationship to segregation is historically accurate. I'd like to point out that, at the time of its opening, South

AUTHOR'S NOTE

Mountain only had freshman and sophomore classes. According to the timeline in this book, Rosa was a junior when the school opened and therefore would not have been able to enroll there, even if she'd wanted to. There were many elements about the year 1955 that I wanted to include, and it was imperative that this moment occurred during Rosa's last year of high school, so for the purposes of this story, that particular detail about the first students at South Mountain has been intentionally omitted.

FURTHER READING

Nonfiction

White but Not Equal by Ignacio M. Garcia

Mexican Americans/American Mexicans: From Conquistadors to Chicanos by Matt S. Meier and Feliciano Ribera

Greasers and Gringos by Steven Bender

Chicano: The History of the Mexican American Civil Rights Movement by F. Arturo Rosales

Bad Mexicans by Kelly Lytle Hernandez

How the United States Racializes Latinos: White Hegemony and Its Consequences by José A. Cobas, Jorge Duany, and Joe R. Feagin

Fiction

Bad Girls Never Say Die by Jennifer Mathieu

Shame the Stars by Guadalupe Garcia McCall

All the Stars Denied by Guadalupe Garcia McCall

ACKNOWLEDGMENTS

Emotionally, I wrote this book somewhere between the dreaded sophomore slump and the hope of writing the book I wanted to read as a young person. People often say that your second book is so much more difficult to write than your first. I could write an entire series on the levels of imposter syndrome that came out to play while I wrote *Rosa*, but I won't. I'll just say they're right; it's very hard.

The second thing I constantly thought of was the book I was unconsciously searching for as a young reader. The questions about culture and identity and history that I had and the representation I craved.

Both sentiments were incredibly daunting, and I'm so deeply thankful for everyone who helped me navigate them to create the book you're holding in your hands today.

First and foremost is my family. Always. My husband is the definition of teamwork, and I am so lucky to have as supportive of a partner as him. It's impossible to list all the things he did to help me fulfill the dream of writing this book, so I'll just list a few highlights: watching movies from the 1950s with me for research, cooking 90 percent of our family's dinners (not just when I'm on deadline), always reading my terrible first drafts, "suggesting" I go write at a coffee shop during our baby's naps, and letting me bounce ideas off of him as I plot-hole spiral at all hours of the day. Mitch, "thank you" doesn't even cut it close.

One of the special things about this book is that my eldest daughter, who was an infant when my debut novel was being written and revised, is now old enough to participate in some of the fun. She's loved seeing the cover of my "Rosa book" and asks about it when I'm hunkered down over my laptop. Everything is better because I get to share it with both my girls, including my writing career. Helen and Marian, being your mom is the most important thing to me, but thank you for allowing me to pursue other goals as well. My greatest aim is that watching me chase after my writing goals will encourage you to follow your own dreams one day, just like my mom did.

On that note, no book would ever be much more than a handful of snippets on my phone without my parents, my sister, and my in-laws. Not only do they help provide the childcare necessary to write, but they're the most enthusiastic champions of my work as well. My mom is the best early reader and has helped me brainstorm so many different parts of this book. Additionally, it was many of my dad's childhood stories that first led me to the idea of Rosa; in so many ways, he's always

ACKNOWLEDGMENTS

inspired me to work hard and try my best at new things—an influence that extends far beyond this one story.

The team of book professionals I have at my side are truly the best of the best. My agent, Amy, is the ultimate sounding board. She never runs out of ideas—or patience—and I am so appreciative to have her on my side. She believed in this book from the first time I pitched it, and it wouldn't have gotten this far without her pep talks and early editorial vision. Thanks for always standing behind me and my complicated leading ladies.

This book also marks four years of working with my editor, Jenny, and I am so lucky she wanted to take a chance on a story that was something new for both of us. She helped hone it into the emotional, message-driven piece that I envisioned, and I can't overemphasize how much my writing has benefited from her input and expertise.

The entire team at Penguin—AZ, Danielle, Sola, Jim, Jackie, and anyone else behind the scenes—also get huge kudos for bringing my vision for this book to life. Nicole Medina gave me this gorgeous cover that continues to delight me with how vibrant and detailed it is every time I look at it.

Thank you to all early readers and author friends who have celebrated and championed this book in all its stages. Your support means the world to me.

And last but not least, thank you, readers, for spending time with me and Rosa. For years, I've wanted a young adult book that looks at this time period and setting from a Latine lens, and I am so profoundly grateful to have had the opportunity to tell this story.